D1257383

The Handsome Sailor

The Handsome Sailor

a novel by
Larry Duberstein

THE PERMANENT PRESS
Sag Harbor, New York 11963

PS
3554
U253
H36
1998

to Lee

(and to Watatic's Most Excellent Majesty)

Copyright © 1998 by Larry Duberstein

Library of Congress Cataloging-in-Publication Data

Duberstein, Larry.
    The Handsome sailor / by Larry Duberstein.
    p. cm.
  ISBN 1-57962-007-8
  1. Melville, Herman, 1819–1891—
Fiction. 2. Novelists,
American—19th century—Fiction. I. Title.
  PS3554.U253H36   1998
  813'.54—dc21
                                97-29805
                                    CIP

All rights reserved, including the right to
reproduce this book, or parts thereof, in any form,
except for the inclusion of brief quotes in a review.

Manufactured in the United States of America

THE PERMANENT PRESS
Noyac Road
Sag Harbor, NY 11963

37397946   /7141

Concerning my own forthcoming book—Don't you buy it—don't you read it, because it is by no means the sort of book for you. It is not a piece of fine feminine Spitalfields silk—but is of the horrible texture of a fabric that should be woven of ships' cables & hawsers. A Polar wind blows through it, & birds of prey hover over it. Warn all gentle fastidious people from so much as peeping into the book—on the risk of a lumbago & sciatics.

—*Herman Melville to Sarah Morewood, 1851*

Life is a long Dardanelles, My Dear Madam, the shores whereof are bright with flowers, which want to pluck, but the bank is too high; & so we float on and on. . . .

—*Herman Melville to Sophia Hawthorne, 1852*

I

Brooklyn Bridge

(1883)

It is the 24th of May, 1883, a breezy noontime at East River and lower Manhattan Bay in New York. Here today, after fourteen years of extraordinary labor—inside the caissons, on the rising block, at the drawing-board—the bridge to Brooklyn opens, as a public thoroughfare. Hung from a million strands of steel, a road across broad water!

Sunlight plays in the band, catching a red jacket sleeve, winking off the oboe, dodging among the drums. Out in the harbor, boats are gridlocked: who knows how they got there, or how they will get away? The filthy water is barely visible in the interstices of smokestack, hull, and sail. Your own feet are barely visible, for that matter, more presumed than glimpsed.

The speeches have begun, and mark how the speeches grow. Ten minutes from Mr. Hewitt, fifteen from Dr. Storrs, more than twenty from the Mayor. It is as though the disease of speeching is progressive.

No one minds too much, though. No one listens to speeches at a wild party such as this. Up and down South Street, brash sailors shove their way from keg to keg, while candy butchers cry out like crows and street arabs peck at every gentleman's pocket. A happy kennel of humanity.

Past Burling Slip, down Water Street, stands the trio we have come to see: a man, a woman, and a child. They are a safe enough distance from the hearing of any speeches, yet close enough to feel the democratic jostling (maidservants and lawyers vying for a look at President Arthur) and to admire these miraculously risen granite towers, the harplike stream of steel depending.

From a distance, we might guess the woman's age at forty. Hazel eyes, chestnut hair, and some outdoor color in her cheeks. Her gent is definitely older, past fifty, in a dark and slightly dated suit. He looks distinguished nonetheless, his rough black beard woven with gray, blue eyes narrowed and watchful. Maybe it is his posture that gives him the look of command: head high, back locked ramrod straight, a proud and almost regal stance.

The young boy resembles neither (skin as white as a cod-fish belly, pumpkin-colored hair) as he entrusts a hand to each, and tugs away with constant questions. He does appear happy and they appear, at a glance, a small happy family.

In fact they are not a family at all. The attractive woman is no one's mother and no one's wife anymore, either— though she was both, not long ago. And she is only thirty-three this month, though that was an easy error to make, given her companion and our natural tendency to average them toward a common denominator.

Still, even the carnival sharp would never have guessed that this upright athletic fellow, whose bristling presence seems electrically charged, has celebrated his sixty-third birthday—or endured it, at least. He does have a wife, not two miles from here, and one living son, who prefers to stay a few thousand miles to the west. He has the son and two daughters, the youngest of whom is twenty-eight.

So what we see is not what we appear to see; it is 1883, remember, modern times are upon us! We must come a good deal closer for a good deal longer if we are to learn even a little about this threesome, and particularly about the vigorous bearded gentleman, who happens to be one of the great men of the century—with Lincoln, Edison, Eakins, and the like—though on this afternoon in May, late in the century and late in his life, no one knows it.

No one. Far from being widely hailed, he is commonly thought to be long since dead, if he is thought of at all. Even within the confines of his family (where he is known to be extant) he is most frequently called eccentric, a delicate way of saying unstable.

Certifiable, they would readily have agreed had they seen him in this neighborhood one April evening six years ago, hurrying up the temporary gangway to the Manhattan tower of the bridge. He got near the top and stood there crowing, flushed and erumpent, on humming ale.

He did it in fun, of course, as he told the wire-winders who climbed from their trapeze seats to lead him back down to the anchorage. He had sat the crow's nest of old sailing vessels, he explained, and was always drawn to such stations, high above the rolling water. "Parterres of seaweed on the terraces of swells!" he gave assurance.

"He's just an old salt, Johnny, like you or me," said the taller of his two escorts. "Give him a few cents for another tot of grog."

II

WEDNESDAY

(1882)

"It's six." *Lizzie's voice; cock-crow. Or hen-crow.*

Six o'clock it is, and here in a rumpled bed is our sturdy undervalued sexagenarian, looking every day of his chronologic age. Shorn of the watery bright surround and of the ruddy cheek pinched by brandy, shorn of hat and cane and gay companions. It is a year before all that, a very different Wednesday—though much the same for our protagonist as five hundred Wednesdays prior.

A dim world at this hour. His is a north-facing room in a narrow brick row-house, and it will be late afternoon before a little angled sunlight leaks into the narrow window. The cretonne drapes will still be charcoal gray, the bed-posts black cast iron, and the fine old afghan (slightly frayed) predominantly midnight blue.

This theme of darkness is not unwelcome, or accidental, to judge by the cluttered mahogany desk or the dark stained mahogany book-case above it. Even the books are darksome in their leather bindings: olive, umber, raisin-black. And though the many sheets of paper were no doubt once a linen white, they look like enormous randomly settled ashes in the muting backstairs gloom.

"Ten after!" (*Hen-crow, Book the 2nd.*)

Lizzie is a blurred silhouette afloat between the door jambs, her features and the fretwork of her dress barely discernible to him. Especially indoors, his eyes are not good.

"Thank you, Lizzie," he says, and a moment later, when she has snugged the door behind her, he stands and steps to the tin basin. They have indoor plumbing, of course, but he finds the old system more soothing, at daybreak.

For a man who happens to hold public opinion in pretty low esteem, he will spend a deal of trouble on the business of wash-and-groom, so by the time he descends to the breakfast table he comes complete and polished as a stage player. Suit brushed, hair brushed, the copious beard brushed and clipped four-square.

This brindled nest is in a way his most prominent feature. It dwarfs his eyes and neat straight nose, and camouflages his mouth completely. Steering down the mahogany handrail, he is every bit of sixty-two, yet soak and shave him clean and the man might juvenesce by decades, a Channel-swimmer or Catskill-climber in the instant.

He never will shave it, though, no more than he will change his brand of shoe; certainly he is set in his ways. There is a shabby sort of elegance to him, as to his narrow house. True, he does not care much for public opinion, but he cares a great deal for his own opinion, on every subject, not least the subject of himself. He replaces the public's opinion with his own, as it were, and his is a system considerably harsher.

As she hears him near the kitchen door, blackhaired Mattie will step back from her cook-stove. She can time him by unvarying footfalls—now—and know the door will swing ajar, know that she will speak her line ("Bilin," by which she means boiling) and that he will approach the ratcheting kettle with the air of a wartime general inspecting his troops, to measure out the coffee grounds. Mattie can make the water boil, he has conceded, but to measure out the grounds has proved a more demanding task.

Mattie is valuable. She can time an egg with the very best, and never once has she served him up the dreaded "Irish toast" which her predecessor Maureen served daily. ("Bread on one side, toast on the other," as he explicated the Irish toast to John Hoadley.) But we all have our failings.

Now he takes up the morning edition, folding it always to the column he is reading (folded and refolded constantly into quadrants, almost more folded than read) as he sits alone for the moment at the large ornate table. Then comes Mattie with the coffee pot and a rack of buttered toast. She will draw the drapes and raise the window sash exactly eight inches—not seven, not nine, but there is the faint hash mark on the frame to guide her—before stealing back to her kitchen to make up a tray for Bessie, the chronically ailing adult daughter.

He glances up from the newspaper as his wife comes in to join him, and a tiny smile occurs down in the depths of his beard, like a tiny white seashell down in a cubic yard of brine. "Good morning, Lizzie," he says.

"Did you have a good sleep?" she says.

"Yes, Lizzie. And you?"

"Oh, I am fine. Just concerned for you."

"No need at all, my dear, truly."

"You never smile, you know."

He would be surprised to hear this, had he not heard it last week and the week before. Today, though, it occurs to him to wonder: would Lizzie be surprised to hear that *she* never smiles? Or is that a given?

"You are kind to be concerned," he says. "Dullheadedness is my only symptom, and that always eases off in the walking. It will dissolve into the sunny air."

"You look so weary."

"Let us take solace from that, at least."

"Oh?"

"Well, my dear, you have found me a good deal worser than weary. Agitated—distracted—morose. Wouldn't I rather loom up a weary man than a madman, in the official version?"

"Oh, Herman."

"I do enjoy it when she Oh-Hermans you, man. It has such a nice home touch about it. No one ever Oh-Everts me, you know."

"Not ever, Evert?"

"Never, Oh-Herman. Though I am occasionally Oh-Christ-Duyckincked."

"I have done that much for you."

"All too often!"

"Nonsense. You can't Oh-Christ a man too often. It is a tonic absolute, like Doctor Wellgood's celery juice. And really, my friend, I would have Oh-Everted you nonstop if I had only understood the importance of it to your emotional substructure. I'd have done it daily—with charity, clarity, claret, and Grace everlasting."

"Oh, Herman."

"Do you know, Lizzie, there are so many people I miss."

"Mackey."

"Most of all Mackey," he says, sorry to have started her, for he had been thinking only of Evert when he spoke. He hands his napkin to her now, to dam up the sudden freshet of tears. "So many others, too. Allan and dear Augusta. Duyckinck. There is no one to take Duyckinck's place—not remotely. He was my one contact of that sort any more. And do you know he is gone four years already?"

"Nor Mackey's place. No one takes anyone's place, I don't imagine."

"You are right, of course, Lizzie dear."

In the silence, sipping coffee, Herman remembers the first time he was able to smile after Mackey's death. The case of the Mad Hatters. Mr. Knox on one side of Broadway and Mr. Genin on the other, vying for the dandy's dollar. They put up a fancy footbridge for Mr. Genin's sake, then tore it down when Mr. Knox came caterwauling, and all in the name of hats-for-sale. It seemed one had to smile.

When he told the tale back home, he told it on a firm foundation of whiskey (might never have told it otherwise) but he also did believe in relief; believed in mercy; in smiling if you could smile. And Lizzie could not. Only the grieving was admissible at home. *The good man pours from his pitcher clear and only brims the poison well.*

And while he understood it, and grieved his full portion, it was likely then that he ceased to risk a smile at home. That was the least of it, in '67 and '68, as through the gloom flew arrows of guilt and blame; you caught one at many a door or portal. Blame he took, and guilt aplenty. More than once it overflowed, and engulfed her willy-nilly. Herman had not always been gentle with Lizzie, when deeply wounded by those arrows.

Meanwhile, Lizzie has turned her glance to the window and beyond, where sparrows have taken over a small linden tree. She is thinking that the birds are fatter than the spindly branches, and far more numerous than the sparse shade-side leaves. Most likely they have migrated from Union Square, where for years now the sparrow flock has proliferated grotesquely, blackening the skies. But by now their silence has stretched too far to let in this sort of conversation. Herman returns to the *Herald*, folds down a new quadrant, and feels her patting the back of his hand. When he looks up, a second later—or possibly five minutes—the door is swinging to a stop behind her.

Lizzie so sad. She never came back to life, the poor sad girl. A ghost walking, all these years; a mother's lot, no doubt.

But what is a father's lot? Why is a father less invested, or less damaged? Why is a father more blameworthy? Who do you blame, between the rock and the sea?

A man can't know the future, nor know how another man will respond. Thus I may say a quiet hello and you may claim I have tried to evade you. If I shout a hearty hello, you may call me disruptive of your peace. How does anyone predict what anyone else will think, or do?

Who could suspect that a boy fullgrown, a man—employed, responsible, outwardly sound—would ram a bullet through his ear.

And who will pretend to know why? Who knows if something said or not said, done or not done, could have changed it?

And we don't know it, even looking backward we don't. What Mackey done he might have done without reference to anything said or done, by me or by persons unknown. We know nothing. Could have been some girl involved—ain't that the likeliest? Or some fool question of illusory honor, given his military hobby-horse.

It could have been an accident, Lord knows, if Lord is. We will never know.

So what is a man to do? Every day for fifteen years I have seen her face—so gray in her dress, so grave in her cap, so sad—and have wondered what to do. There is Stannie, and in a way, therefore, Stannie is "what to do."

If it weren't such a futility. When he is off in the watery blue distance, I can put him fine lines and maybe a two-dollar bill; one or the other may have its use. But when he is here (and how little he is here) it is not possible to speak the fine lines. For the most part, it is impossible to speak a line at all.

It is not Stannie's doing, that he goes a little sullen when he feels most tender-needy, nor mine to go fishblood when I feel aflame. We all know what to be, yet cannot be it.

There are two ways to eat the mango-fruit, as my colleague Doctor Longo put the case, five lifetimes yore in the wild Tahiti outback. You quarter it up and eat outward toward the skin, or you peel it and eat inward toward the core. Just so you may proceed from argument to truth, or from truth to argument; either way the going gets hard. The seed is hard, the skin is hard, and either way your eating stops short, somewhere in the middle.

Ah the good Doctor, in all his sotted ribald wit!

Manhattan has sprawled uptown. It has raced on past the Croton Reservoir, past Central Park, until the brooks and muddy farms of Harlem are paving over. Five or six stories of residential masonry are quickly risen, block after block,

70th Street, 80th Street, points north. And Broadway is an ongoing hurly-burly whose chaotic miles of interlocking shops, of clashing broughams and omnibuses, Red Birds and Blue Birds, our protagonist sees every day, from the soles of his feet. No buses for him.

For here is a man who once climbed off a packet-boat with a month of nothing but sea legs underneath him, stepped onto British soil, and announced to his lazy astonished shipboard friends that they were setting off together for breakfast in Canterbury (Heel toe, you pilgrims!), eighteen miles of pleasant strolling to get a good ham-and-egg appetite.

The spirit ran higher then, but the legs were no stronger than they are right now. At sixty-two, Herman still covers a minimum six miles daily, his roundtrip distance between workplace and home. It saves his pennies to stroll (six cents going and six coming back, so much the more pennies for oysters and ale) but he does it more for the flavor of air, and the feel of being under sail. And then there is his profound discomfort (more than physical, less than metaphysical) at sitting inside the fetid rattling Third Avenue car. Whenever he watches it lumber past him, Herman conjures a farmyard image, of the chicken coop, with a hundred twitching heads wriggling desperately toward some slot of sky.

Lizzie does not approve of the air. In the city, particularly, it is dank and threatening. But Lizzie has always been suspicious of air, where Herman has always loved it, more simply than anything else. When living well, by his lights, he has lived directly in it—inside the heart of half a gale, whether blue-devil days or better. It might be a cool salt wind massaging your scalp, or a hillborne breeze tickling your brainpan; even these filthy Manhattan gusts will bring you alive like smelling salts.

These days he must walk north, straight up the island. He preferred the worn old westerly footpath to the matronymic Gansevoort Pier, preferred the look of the older buildings.

Everything on this new route, after all, is *new,* with nothing
organic about or behind it. It did not happen so much as it
was foisted on us by those who plumb for dollars. Thus it
is fresh-built, under-built, and over-dressed, all according to
how the dollars are best extracted.

Also true that younger legs were bearing him along the
crosstown route, younger eyes were measuring up the passing circus. Still he feels strong, undeniably so, and the legs
in particular almost freakishly so, more strengthened over
time than depleted. Could he get up and go the eighteen
miles for breakfast today? Easily.

"Good morning, you old salt, and ain't it a lovely
spring day."

"Transcendent, would be fair to say, young James."

James McBride is not one year younger than our man, and
given his snow-white mane (and a bulby nose that maps its
own blood supply precisely) he could pass for Herman's
daddy. But there is something in Herman of the inborn sachem, that makes him not older, yet *senior* to men of all ages.

"I see the *Coast of Maine* has docked. With potatoes?"

"No, Herman, no more than the *Isle of Dogs* brought us
in a load of dogs. She has some books, as it haps—right in
your sights there—plus a roomful of wine and another with
a stack of Turkey carpets. Chin high. Barclay has called for
the ratter."

"Even *sans* potatoes! No rush, if we have to wait for Eli
Carnes. Let's give it half an hour."

Left alone for the moment, Herman is smiling—that tiny
shell again, in a barrel of brine—at the recollection of a raw
November morning on Gansevoort Street. While the ratter
was down in some squalid hold, Herman had snatched a
private hour by the coal-stove, to block out a comic lecture

on the topic of Mister Rat. A talk designed to edify the ladies of the lyceum circuit.

In another life (between *other* lives) he had invested some years in travelling about and lecturing the public: in drafty town halls, church basements, museum parlors; in cities as farflung as Buffalo, Cincinnati, Milwaukee. To remark the fine points of marble Greeks, or the charms of a South Seas sojourn. A would-be canny move, delivering tropic palms into the landlocked hemlocked north, but Milwaukee is a long way to go for such a purpose, however canny.

The experience left Herman baffled as to why those Buffalonians ventured out to hear him (if and when they did) on those arbitrary, stultifying nights. Well, they were there to hear him whysomedever, but Herman knew why he was there, and it surely was never to hear himself. He was there for dollars. How easily the picturesque will yield to the pocketesque, when dollars damn you.

And yet, he reasoned—that morning by the Gansevoort coalstove, with half a flask of brandy to tussle the chill and little inclination for the wet sleet flying against the bare clapboards—if a man could write without pay (and that much he had done, both before and since) then surely a man could as easily lecture without pay. To that noble end, he set about the subject of Mister Rat, with all the while a clear image before him of five wide rows of Cincinnati matrons, intensely furrowed under their fur hats. Talk about a "secret absurdity" attaching to one's literary enterprises!

He had even rendered the rat lecture, to an audience of one at the Penny Restaurant. Oyster stew a penny, lambpot pie a penny, a penny for the apple dumpling, and *gratis* the lecture. Duyckinck sat through "The Rat in America" and applauded it enthusiastically, but then alas, pronounced our young nation a little unready for such edification, unless those tribes of midwest ladies could first be plied to the eyes with a lethal schnapps.

The rat is by far our most prominent immigrant. For as much as he likes to sail the seven seas, rarely will he neglect to disembark here in the land of the free.

Many a sailor's pantaloon has been grated at the cuff while he slept, and many have started up the rat-lines of the shroud, only to find the honoree a stride or two behind them. Nevertheless, a ship without rats is always accounted unlucky or accursed. And a rat going over the side is a sailor's coalshaft canary, a safety inspection worth more than the chief petty officer's ten cold pages.

Of late, the rat has taken possession of the port of New York. He outnumbers his counterpart, the human, two to one, and he is now nearly as large. In Maiden Lane last week, I watched Mister Rat at luncheon, sitting on a crate in broad daylight, chewing a Bermuda onion. And crying as he chewed. He sat there and ignored me, because he knew he owned the town.

But the rat is not always adorable. At Reisling's Poultry Market in Gansevoort Street, one rat tore out the throats of forty live chickens, for fun. He ate only one of them. The rat is not always benign. Another rat in that fine neighborhood sliced through the bottoms of burlap sacks and then shook them in his sizable incisors until he had flooded a warehouse with a thousand pounds of rice and corn meal, just for the fun of it.

The most disturbing supper I never et owed all to Mister Rat. It took place in the forecastle of a merchant ship where a comrade and I had hidden a luxurious tin of molasses—borrowed, shall we say, from the cookshack for our private use. Aye, we had pilfered it, and with it each evening would decorate our otherwise dusty and tasteless seabiscuit.

That stash was the spice of our dreary lives, until the precious tin ran low. One night, near the Coral Islands, we had to upside-down it in the dark to fetch a trickle and, as we did so, something besides the molasses slipped out. . . .

"With the Captain's compliments," says William Barclay, a wonderfully half-corrupted officer of the District. The corrupted half is naturally the half which benefits himself (or what would be the point?), but where the typical weigher might both take and give, take a dollar for giving a soft count or take a fiver to blind-stamp your manifest, Barclay will cheerfully take your dollar, or your crate of Madeira wine and then just as cheerfully weigh your cargo to the nearest half gram. Thus he remains true to both self and country, and untrue only to some *fully* corrupted scalawag who is out to rob our nation in the name of getting rich.

Besides which, morally speaking, he considers this wine a portion of his pay—surely four dollars a day cannot be all of it? Why, such a salary as that would open a saint to temptation, not to say a humble half-corrupted civil servant in the bustling port of New York.

"You keep them, young William. Or cut Bridey in, if you like. He is generally for Madeira."

"I hate to see him miss out, but alas he's tucked up at O'Reilly's just now."

"What about Carnes?"

"At O'Reilly's? Never. The man's a teetotaler."

"He'll be along," says Herman, mostly to himself, then steps outside. The gangways creak and clatter pleasantly, and there is a strong whiff of tar in the air. He sees the *Maine's* captain pacing his boards, whistling a fitful tune.

Herman lights his pipe and takes a deep breath of the sweet strong tobacco, and waits contentedly enough. In truth, he has always preferred being between doors: between the last door he has left and the next through which he is obliged to pass, even if they stand a scant twenty yards apart.

The *Coast of Maine* goes barely two thousand tons, yet she looms leviathan above the scrapshops and beadboard sheds along the quay. Over the roadway, the District headquarters presents a formal, granite facade; even the seizure room inside has carved plaster cornices and flying-angel medallions. On the water side, though, the offices are shanties, jerrybuilt, much in the style of adjoining enterprises—the coalhouse, a gear and tackle shop, a sausage vendor.

By comparison with the Gansevoort District, it is a backwater. So much less to contend with here. There, as soon as the Cuban sugar manifests were off your desk, the French wall-paper manifests were upon it. Crew counts, registers, bills of lading—piles of paper—and every day, some bold new game was set in motion. It might be expensive kid gloves stuffed inside the sailors' boots, or a fabulously conceived steamer-trunk with its maze of false compartments, or the little German who imported wigs of human hair, taped neatly to the ribs of his crewmen. And all the rubber bags of fine cigars, like schools of fish bobbing untaxed past the shadman's net.

There was never a day without "opportunity," as that old scrutineer Grant White so nicely labelled it—a chance to stuff your *own* boots and not one soul to blame you. A victimless crime, plead the men of the New York Custom House. Herman expects and understands this petty knavery (after all, he has authored a virtual manual for the New World confidenceman) and as often as not, he finds it amusing. But he does not participate.

He never takes home the pretty blue cut-glass bottle of French perfume, or the cedar box packed with Havana panatellas. He has never enjoyed a night on the town with a fist of free money, even though he cares nothing for public opinion and little enough for the laws of man, which he knows must change from time to time and place, horologics and chromometrics notwithstanding.

No, it is the same here as in other matters; he has a close watch on himself. Lives for his own opinion, seeks his own regard, and often falls short.

"So it's carpets?"

Servalle, the ship's captain, has an itchy look about him. Eager, one would have to guess, to get the business behind him.

"Carpets, and a few of half-decent Madeira, which you may wish to sample, sir? A small cargo, all quite visible and clear apparent. Shouldn't have to occupy you long atall."

Ah, but there is no particular rush, Herman confides (by means of the miniature smile), not for an honest man prepared to do his job. It is a quiet day, just one ship swaying in the tie-up, and besides, your Turkey carpet will forever roll out a pretty challenge, a source of amusement unrivalled by a dozen dozen of London trousers, or crated bananas by the pound. You know what those are worth, but who on earth ever knows what a Turkey carpet is worth? Who can solve the everlasting intrigue of its sundry warps and woofs, the indissoluble mysteries of every such carpet declared through history at all the borders of the world? A Turkey carpet on shipboard is like a blank check, drawn by a stranger, against a bank that moved west under last evening's cloud cover.

Herman will not bother himself with a microscopic examination of dyes, or a close count of threads-to-the-inch. No amusement in that, even for a fellow once charged with a monstrous propensity to detail. He will take his measure from Captain Servalle's stance, from his squint and his tone, never from his bill of lading.

"We had an honest declaration on these things once," Herman tells the bluff Virginian. "Right around the time U.S. Grant came in office."

"Wellsir, you have got yourself another honest one here and now, guarantee you that."

"Come, let's go have a look at them, Captain. Mr. Barclay will stay aloft and await the sanitations discharger."

"The rat man, do you mean?"

"Ships are but boards, Servalle, and sailors but men. There be land-rats and water-rats, land-thieves and water-thieves."

"What are you saying, man?"

"Shakespeare, Captain—from the *Merchant of Venice*. Likely as not find it in your own ship's library."

Two blocks to the north, across a muddy lot, stands the lumberyard, Simonson's, with its sweet-pitch and nutty smelling stock. There are pallets of planed pine boards, bins of maple shorts and dowels, and thicker hemlock planks, stickered up under a lowpitched tin shed. This square-edged order is in sharp contrast to the messy lot alongside it: oily rags from the wharf, blowing garbage, glass, loosened schist. No one ever cleans the lot, so the lot is never clean. Maybe no one owns it, apart from Mister Rat.

Where the feeder lane to Simonson's circles back toward 76th Street, hemmed in by a wire fence, is perched an oddly fanciful coffee-stand, crowded with architectural touches. Staggered quoins at the corners, a panelled alcove set back for the entry door, and windows (flanking the alcove) which are Gothic-arched at the top and subdivided into dozens of sash-lights the size of your jacket pocket. The little building is as pretty as the Taj Mahal, albeit on the scale of a sophisticated toy.

This is Fenton's Best & Freshest, where all sorts of men take their coffee. This new neighborhood has nothing like the cosmopolitan face of South Street, or even West Street, yet in the past week Fenton's has served visitors from Pakistan and Prussia.

At the moment, though, with one exception, Fenton's has fallen into the hands of our men of the Custom House. They have taken the outdoor tables, with a clear prospect to Blackwell's Island and the East River channels that skirt it. Barclay, McBride, Wilkinson, and Carnes at one table, and Herman alone at another. This is a privilege he is sometimes accorded with minimal ragging, given his status as an ex-literary man who wears his highbrow lightly, yet will occasionally want to scribble on his sheets.

Sitting alone too, at the third and last small table, is an unattended woman.

There are unattended ladies on every commercial waterfront, of course, plenty of them, and how readily they will come attended for just the right coin, or a penny less at slack tide. The good and only half-corrupted Barclay will be attending to just such a one at four o'clock—"my Tess" he calls her—as he has done every Wednesday at four o'clock for about three years, during the course of which he has come to know her better in certain respects than he knows his wife, while naturally his wife does not know his Tess at all.

Tess and her ilk are never unattended long, that is the point. If she is, she must move along to some place where she will be attended the sooner. "I'm not a hard one," Tess will tell you frankly. "I won't be caught out-of-doors after dark." So she must earn her living steady-on through the daylight hours.

Another small point. Tess, careful as she goes, a daylight creature exclusively, has nevertheless in the line of duty been nicked near the eye with a blade (that's the dry patch of skin, where the eyebrow came away and stayed away), lost two teeth to which we can attest at duelling distance and four more we attest to when she smiles close-up. Lovely as she is, then, Tess is not quite *intact*, not an entirely graceful apparition.

The woman seated here is not of the docks or the streets ("Clear skin marks a clear conscience," as the saying goes) and she seeks to attract no notice from the men. She keeps to herself and, like Herman, reads a book as she sips absently. They are mirror images, in a way: sitting solo, bumper of coffee, leatherbound book. She seems perfectly comfortable

where she is—but can these rough-and-ready gentlemen
allow her to remain comfortable?

Carnes starts toward her on instinct alone, as a dog will
amble toward a scent. He is somehow turned back by her
exclusive downward gaze, though his lips are trying to
move. Barclay merely leans forward and stares at a bared
scrap of wrist, as though it alone has summarily convinced
him he could know her better than Wife and Tess combined,
given the merest hint of an invitation. Something alerts him
she has her every tooth in place, and the rest of it as well.

Herman has noticed her, too, of course. He owns the reputation (stemming in part from a sometime habit of silence)
of a man all-seeing; ironic in light of his chronic eye strain,
yet not altogether unfounded as metaphor. He has seen some
things, and certainly he can see ten feet in front of his nose
in the clear May air. He sees the slim wrists, the tresses of
chestnut hair stirring under a kerchief. It is a little surprising—moreso than a Pakistani, less than a Laplander in his
snow-shoes—but then most likely she is here to meet
someone.

Herman is no threat to her. He would never address her
as stranger to stranger, or frighten her. Even if he did, if
grace would grant him one sentence to say, it would not be
cousin to any sentence the rat man might produce. Above all,
Herman has noticed her book. He is a bookish man (moreso,
perhaps, than when he was a man who wrote books) and he
is curious about it. It looks just like his copy of Tennyson,
with the same dappled boards and diamondback spine, yet it
cannot be Tennyson. It must be some popular novel, *Barriers
Burned Away,* or *Under a Hot Southern Sun.*

Nothing could make him simply ask. He stands in constant awe of the world's imbecilic workings, and all its self-
confounding regulations—and no less so at his own transcendent folly from birth to this morning—yet would never
no more override them.

★

Generally he walks home by way of Central Park, veering "inland" at 59th Street and up a hill to his favorite spot, a large bluestone outcropping that serves him as bench. There is plenty of sunlight left today, an hour at least, and it glows softly on the solid, modelled hills beyond.

Solid modelled hills. Yes.

The tableau strikes him as a perfect Claude Lorrain, a classic landscape on the classic scale. He frames off this painting in an imaginary pantograph, then wonders just how large this landscape is. Surely it is the world's largest painting, but Herman wants to know exactly how large (for no particular reason) and guesswork need not do. Marking out his boundary trees, he resolves to step it off.

And given his age, and the day's labors, he is pretty spry at stepping it off—though given his age and the zigzag nature of his research, a few passers-by are more impressed by his eccentricity. He doesn't mind. If the research has an outwardly eccentric aspect, he is in roughly equal parts pleased, oblivious, and indifferent. To the extent that these three responses might seem to be mutually exclusive, Herman does not mind that, either.

His canvas is half a mile wide, a quarter-mile to the middle distance, four miles straight up to the cloud above the water tower. This last dimension he must reckon by sketchy trigonometrics, though he would gladly step it off too, could he but step on air. Herman does not lack the time or the interest to measure it up.

Solid modelled hills, though. Earlier this afternoon, Herman had borrowed from our government a scant half hour to work through a stubborn problem of versification. Just a short line in a short poem, but he had beat against it two hours last night without a scrap of satisfaction, and then today at the District the line came perfect. "The hollow of these liquid hills" was just how he saw it and needed to say it, as precisely as he sees these solid modelled hills. *Quod erat demonstrandum* to be sure, with regard to this question of solid versus liquid undulation.

He had also found, inside the same half-hour, the elusive end-note adjective, the one to punctuate and unify his interlacing themes, and the word was rosmarine. Of course it was. Why did it take so long to locate? Why was clarity a one-way lane, so dark in the going out, so brightlit coming back? Can a business be both obvious and obscure?

Once I wrote (and meant it too!) that there were more words than things—too many words, in other words, so the words serve most to complicate.

But do we complicate a hat when we name it beret, derby, crush, or fez? Grab-rope, guess-rope, guy-line, halyard? And come to ideas, so-called, complex they are and complex remain, whether stubbed at monosyllabic or fleshed in full verbalia.

There are things of this world with no word for them, ready-made, and others that call for half a hundred pitched and patched together, plus those which may want four adjectives at high noon yet cannot stand a single one at dusk, when the inkwash sunset drives all words away. And so on, to the replaceless rosmarine . . .

Or that "basilisk glance" in the bye-canal poem. That one came thundering by brainmail on a Friday—where was it Monday through Thursday?

Nor forget the opposite extreme, of wordlessness. My scrivener's thesaurus, after all, his vast vocabulary of silence. To stand verbless at breakfast and verbless at supper, verbless in between. Silence as the vestibule to all the mysteries, silence in its many usages and forms.

Along the fringes of Madison Square, the lights are coming on, garish new electric lights shining down through the antecedent gaslamps. Thirty blocks have made Herman ready for another respite. A glass of punch at Aiken's Garden, on the Square, sounds good.

Indeed, it sounds as perfecto as did the liquid hills, or if not so perfectly perfecto (should perfection admit of degrees) then only because "hills" be plural and "glass" merely singular. This can be fixed, however, and Robert, the waiter, fixes it by arriving almost unbidden with a second glass. "Plural!" says Herman, approvingly.

Gliding past Masonic Temple, definitely on the homeward strophe now, he claps his hands and exclaims, "Thank Heaven for poverty!" By the time he reaches the run of stout cast-iron balusters that mark his own familiar frontispiece on 26th Street, he will have begun declaiming (to the hordes of culture seekers, 37 seats sold in Cincinnata, 29 or so on Buffalo's windy shore) a spontaneous new lecture on the topic of poverty. "For it is poverty, gentlemen and ladies, and poverty alone which prevents us asking for glass number three: poverty therefore which maintains us virtuous and soberous and wonderfully *promptous* at home. Much to be said for the fine state of pennilessness."

Still bluff and risible at his own front riser, still hale and outgoing two strides inside. "To poverty, Lizzie," he says, lifting his stick. "A dry toast."

What, if anything, does he mean to say? Lizzie does not know and will not ask; certainly Herman will not explain. Perhaps he believes she can hear the long and rumbling train of his thought, or perhaps it is something he would call humor. Perhaps he is making fun of her.

No matter, so long as he is in reasonably good spirits, and such would seem to be the case. He stows his hat and stick with a flourish and follows Lizzie into the parlor, where they sit in the facing Chippendale side-chairs. Even if Bessie comes down to dinner, they will be alone here for half an hour now.

Lizzie hands him the day's mail with a look of significance, and at once he sees why. Stanwix has written. The other two envelopes he slides inside his jacket, a vessel where each pocket has its own unvarying office, one for the scraps of verse, one for invoices, for wallet, pipe, and so forth. The breast pocket inside right is for mail. Herman carries no other portfolio, no bag or leather case, only the pockets—four in his trousers, six in the jacket, three more in the top-coat—so that his hands are always free. If the man with a dozen-plus capacious pockets cannot go forth unencumbered, who the devil can?

Stannie's letter is addressed to both of them, and it is of greater interest to Lizzie than anything in the last month—the month, that is, since Stannie's previous letter. But she will not have cut the envelope open. A precipitate reading, a unilateral reading, never sits well; not if Lizzie's the unilaterian.

The side-chairs; the sherry; the letter-knife. It must be done just so, and she must search his eyes, and wait. "Is he well? What does he say?"

"He is, Lizzie dear, well enough. He has left the unnamed ailment behind him. It seems he may be leaving his employment behind as well, though perhaps I read between the lines."

"The lines themselves, Herman. Will you read them?"

He will not.

"My eyes are a little tired, Lizzie," he says, and at last hands over the famous page.

And surprisingly (or not) he does look pale and slack. The vigor of his recent boisterous entry is nowhere visible in the slumped unmuscled heap of clothing on the chair. A brighteyed sailor came charging through the foyer, a spent and longdrawn lubber landed on the Chippendale.

Lizzie has seen it before, this collapsing. Never has she thought to associate it with Aiken's punch, effect or after-effect, because Aiken's Garden, however close by, is not a place she notices. She does not know the people who patronize such places, or presumes she does not.

To her the shift is self-explanatory. Herman's walking invigorates him, but it also takes a toll. It catches up to a man of his age. So she is neither surprised nor concerned to see him give way; in truth she is a little proud of him and his rigorous habits. Lizzie may disapprove in principle, but she does not imagine very many men his age could get the miles. And however oddly Herman may strike the world at large, after thirty-five years Lizzie is used to him. She knows what to expect, and to a great extent she has made her peace.

She knows that he will be extremely quiet now; quiet at the dinner table, too. If Bessie does dine with them, he will go directly upstairs to his desk afterward. If Bessie has remained in her room, he will stop off there for a minute—more, if made welcome—and visit with her. In his room, he will empty his pockets, arraying the contents on the mantel. He will still be standing there at the mantel when she comes up with his pot of coffee.

All this Lizzie knows and likes knowing, as she likes having got to this juncture of the day, where he has his mail and she has hers.

The note from Britain is our third such since Easter. It is either conspiracy or grand coincidence that they all cull their phrases from the same dictionary, beginning not with "aardwolf" but with "genius." There is a wonderfully uniform sort of praise shipped out from England's sceptred isle.

This other note has not travelled so far, only a few blocks it seems. It issues from within the watery walls of our own Manhatto, and begs to assure me firm seating in the pantheon of contemporary literary light. No mention of genius per se, yet here is a fellow will take me straight to the bosom of his author club with no question asked.

He knows I am living (since he sends me mail) yet none of the usual statute of limits on my authorship for him. He must have

*read the verse. To him, I am not the Man Who Lived With Canni-
bals, but the bard of brotherly strife at Shiloh, the poet of holy
pilgrimages. Here is a gent who has read the verse!*

Well, no. "Your voice has been too long among the shadows." *He has not read the verse. It is the Man Who Lived With Cannibals who attracts this invitation. The gent ran out of contemporary
literary lights before he ran out of chairs.*

*Dear Sir, replies the Man Who Lived, I haste to respondere
while still barely able. They say my voice is moribund (or that I
am, moribound in winding-sheets, both dead and buried—the latter
presumable) and therefore without a voice to speak of. But as luck
would have it, my voice goes reasonably strong this Wednesday,
indeed this is the very day I delivered my popular talk on the
Benefits of Poverty, to an unnumbered throng in the world's
largest city.*

*Now the clubman wishes to know a reason why I prose no more.
Beware, though; go careful, young clubman, lest whole heavy
leatherbound volumes of prose be writ in explanation and apologia
for writing none at all. We explain our apologies and apologize for
our explanations, for that, gentlemen, is how we make Literature in
America nowadays.*

*So attend our short answer, and all the more since we offer no
long answer. You do not steam a book from the thin air around
you. A poem you may well draw down from the cat's paw breeze
about your cranium; to write a poem, you go upstairs. But to write
a book, you go to war, or to sea.*

*Lastly, on the question of literary-dinner. I have a policy, and
my policy is to say No to those, because then I do not need to attend
them. I likes good talk, I likes roast beef, and upon occasion I likes
a glass of whiskey as well. The three taken together, though, in
the form of literary-dinner, I do not like so well. (And cannot tell
thee, Doctor Fell/ Why.)*

"Herman?"

"Come in, Lizzie. Thank you," he says, taking the glass
of brandy from her. "So, you are pleased?"

"Yes," she says, making a space for herself on the trunk, while Herman rises to stretch and pace, after two hours in his chair. "To hear from him is such a tonic to me."

"And to hear good news!"

"Good news?"

"To find Stannie well. Or not unwell."

"You are right. But it is such a brief letter. A note, really."

"A painless note, Lizzie, this is the vital thing. Better a brief note of all's well than three thick volumes of grief."

"Something in between, though. Three pages, say, of what he does and who he sees. How he is spending the days of his life."

"Three pages? Pouring from the pen of our boy Stanwix? It would be an historical document in the annals. He hasn't turned out a letter that long since he was a little boy writing to his Granny."

"He tells us almost nothing."

"Mebbe his voice is in the shadows," he says, passing her the other letters of the day. "Mebbe he deals in a sort of verse, or cryptogram silence, who knows? I believe he has a voice, that no one hears. Truly, I know he has."

"Well isn't it very sad, both for Stannie's sake and ours, that we cannot hear it."

She glances at both of the letters, and is pleased for him. Praise and invitations have both been rare. "You will attend the dinner?"

"No." He tilts his head as though to reconsider, only to reiterate through a wan smile: "No."

"Oh Herman. Weren't you just complaining how much you missed having people like that in your life? This might lift your spirits."

"A literary-dinner? It's kind of you to suggest my going, but I think I am in dangerously high spirits even without such strong tonic as that."

Lizzie looks askance. In her expression he reads the charge of unsmilingness (of dangerously *low* spirits) but then she does not know what a wonderful day this has been. He ought recount it for her, smile by smile, beginning with the uptown strophe in cool May sunlight, surely the loveliest morning of the year. Even at the District there was some fun to be had, with the would-be Turkey-carpetbagger Servalle. On the promontory at Fenton's Best & Freshest, two small pear trees announced their miraculous presence by blossoming inside the sumac grove, and surely the Tennyson woman was worth a smile—yet another miraculous dispensation. Then, rosmarine!

All that in half a day. Plenty more smiles and pleasures to decorate the afternoon, like the westward trek to Central Park, and the Claude Lorrain; like Aiken waiting downtown with his fine refreshments, and, come to think of it, a service-able chop from Mattie at home. A memorable day, even before the happy mail call, before Stanwix' delightfully un-eventful note. Not one hint of illness or discouragement in the note, not one word on the sadness life so easily could bring. Oh treasure such minimal mail as this, with "nothing" to say!

Could Herman but tell out this brimful catalogue to his wife (could she but hear it of him), he would have done the job of refutation, straightforwardly. But he cannot. He can only offer up a joke—"Mebbe my smile is in the shad-ows!"—and take her hands in his, solicitously.

They are so cold, though. Lizzie has always had the cold-est hands.

Something drumming at his temples—blood?—something keen-ing in his ears. And it is nothing like thought, but raw knowledge, blind certainty, that grips him by the throat as he rams through the bolted door. Certainty that he has come to the worst moment of his life.

There is Mackey. So white, so still, so irreversibly dead. The sweet boy's face gone pale as paste, one eye sad as Jesus, the other

bound in blood. Blood dried plum on the coverlet—and the gun.
Where dat old man?

*There is nothing to do and nothing matters. Nothing can help
this or change it—help the helplessness, or change the awful change-
lessness—it is too clearly real and final.* Where dat old man? *It
is the worst moment, and you must live inside it, inconsolably,
ever after.*

*Tears have clotted like honey in his lashes, blinding him, as he
collapses forward atop the boy, bedsprings squalling, as though to
hide or protect him, to cover the slender defenseless body.* Where
dat old man? *Herman is resting on top of his son, light as air, gentle
as feathers.*

*Tears keep coming loose and dropping like small bitter fruits; his
throat is too tight for breath to pass. The baby he loved, now buried
beneath him: now eighteen and dead. The little boy he had somehow
lost, now truly lost.* Where dat old man? "Here I am," he sobs.
"I am here, Mackey darling."

*All this in less than seconds, this epic of grief, and now Lizzie
is in the room—screaming, screaming—and Herman has never
heard such a sound before, and the terrible screaming pierces him
to the quick anew.*

It is very late. Herman has finished the brandy, and Stannie's letter is spread out before him.

Mail intrudes always, as visitors do. A letter implies response and, like conversation, it wants to flow therefrom as
directly as possible. He has already answered the Englishman
and the American who wants to feed him dinner. Answering
Stannie is a trickier proposition.

It is almost like crafting a poem. To write a son like Stanwix, a sensitive boy like that, every word must be mined
like bits of gold from the busy flashing stream. Every passing
phrase can make a crisis, both for what is said and what held
back. Stannie is so like Mackey that way—one wrong word
(or a right word, misconstrued) can total-eclipse the sun.

He had them both, in the hills above the house one time. Not far from the blueberries, though this was a winter day. They had borrowed Sarah's old toboggan and were screaming with happiness all morning. Uncommon for them, such loud delight; so rare for them to let it loose. They had him shouting too.

Both of them, though—they were probably eight and six—and walking back down to the barn they asked him about the sea, and bravely mused about sailing before the mast. Sweethearted boys of six and eight, innocent children playing games. Surely you play the game with them and help them render their little dreamscape, their pretty thought. After all, the dream was only a dream of love, a dream of the child and the father, little enough to do with the forecastle.

But he stiffed them. He was a blowhard, and a stiff old fool. You wouldn't like it out there, he told them, out on the miles of watery highway. It's scary and you would be too homesick. You boys will do better things than that.

Oh, he had meant well. He meant that he had been frightened and homesick himself; meant he was not the man they saw, but rather the same child they were. He meant that under his loving protection they would have no need to fear. They would not be sent to sea.

The voice was not right, though. It never was right. The love was not in it, somehow, and the fierce urge to protect them could sound more like a punishment. Like something being snatched away from them: not something given in the name of love, but something confiscated in the name of authority. He saw them shrink back, but there was nothing for it. He could never find the words, or the tone, to set it right. Something about him: a big flaw, a failing.

Even tonight, as a mellow old voice in the shadows and would-be genius, he cannot manage the trick. Perhaps it is simply too late to write, or think. The letter had distracted him from a poem, now he is distracted from the letter. Pulled away by objects in the room, by the dryness of the air, by faint sounds in the house below. Aimlessly, he scribbles a few familiar words on the page before him: *we know what to be, yet cannot be it.*

True enough that the voice was wrong, and true they danced it out of step, too many times. But not always. Some memories come freighted with pain, yet others offer consolation, like the recollection that comes to him now (a gift, really, filtering into his languor through the pipesmoke air) of one morning when they danced it together. Oh sweet consolation.

Malcolm had determined on going to church. They all went, generally, unless Herman stayed home, but a storm blew so wild that Saturday night that not even Augusta was pious enough to venture down the road. But Mackey was fourteen. Bored silly, housebound, snowbound—and outward bound. He was all for going and no one would go with him, until Herman volunteered. The year he hurt his arm, it was, so Mackey had to play the man throughout. Mackey shagged Old Riley and rigged the harness, and Mackey took the reins as they bumped and slipped toward the village singing "How Great Thou Art" in the flying snow and laughing.

Oh, thank Krishna for broken arms, and deep snows, and brandy-in-a-flask as well, whether Mackey knew it or not. Likely not, for he was fourteen after all, and barely knew he had a father! Some days he barely did, but not that chilly Sunday morning.

Herman's gaze moves across a row of books: La Rochefoucauld, Spinoza, Hugo, Sheridan, Balzac. How different, he muses, was his desk at Arrowhead, a vast and windswept plain of a desk across which, through the window, Saddleback was constant. Beyond the green corn or the October stubble; beyond the golden apples or the barren dry-ice branches of January, it was always there.

Here he "looks out" on damask wallpaper, on books and plaster busts, a candlestick, a bentwood whatnot stand. He must step to the window if he wants to look out, but all he will see is darkness and bricks. When he stops to rest at this desk, he instantly shuts his eyes to rest them too.

Herman sets aside his pen with a sigh; it can only be called a sigh. On other nights, he has posited many a wretched line—then scratched it out and tried again, and again, before giving up for good. Tonight he knows enough to stop. True that you go upstairs to get a poem, but you must also remain awake.

"Is your mother in bed, Bessie dear?"

He touches Bessie lightly on the shoulder. Absorbed in her reading, Bessie half turns and grants him a shrug. Not a charged or unfriendly shrug, more a pleasantly weary shrug—rough equivalent, he makes it, of a note from Stanwix that springs no loud alarms. But their conversation is done.

He goes out the front door of the house, down the five steps, and strolls to the gate-post. Gaslamps glow like sentinels along the block, as he inhales the lilacs' sweet aroma. A few dandies are laughing with a self-conscious heartiness under the Putnam House awning. Down in the Putnam House lounge, he knows, the last whiskerandoes are sipping their brandy. But it is too close to home—Bessie would sharp him out again—and it is late.

Above the Hippodrome, over the topmost tower and pennant, the moon is lying on its back. A mere crescent, small curved fraction, though the longer he studies it, the clearer comes the portion eclipsed. There is the shadow moon, the *rest* of that round and distant mass, and Herman feels grateful that his eyes will still do such work for him.

But he is done for the night. Too weary to stand (or to formulate any more lines, or thoughts, or letters), Herman is ready to go up to bed. Spent. Or well-invested, better say, for even here, at the drowsing edge of the day, he cannot leave a figure of speech short of its beckoning potential.

He will stop at Lizzie's door and listen briefly—for what, he never knows. Then he will wash and dress for bed; peel back the faded afghan, and blow the candle out.

"Herman, it's six."

The first time he woke, he was standing on the dock at Pier Number 7, watching the lumpers work. They were passing gigantic timbers of yellow pine, timbers two feet in girth, down onto Crayton's flatbed. The famous team of snow-white horses there in harness, and Abe Crayton barking like the dog he was; but Herman was not on duty. He was not on call to discharge or to weigh. He stood on the pier a free man, at large in the world and unencumbered.

And it must have been one of those powerful, climbing seas in the harbor, seas that sledgehammer the bum-boats and shower the low circling shearwaters with a cold green foam—for here it came, ripping up the river, and Herman knew (from the sing and tang and taste of it) that this selfsame mountain of air was fresh from the sea, that just minutes before it had torn off the sea-top, watery page after page.

That was the first time, when he had not fully awakened, and it was mostly a picture, though vivid and sensual—better say a moment, a picture of a moment, taken from the inside. The salt wheeze of the wharf, that raw blast parting his hair. Herman knew it was a dream, even while he dreamed it. It was so very *like* a dream.

The second time is more confusing, at least half real in the shallows of sleep, half dream on waking. "Ten after!" he hears, and so presumes he must be waking to a Manhattan day, a Thursday in 1882, until he hears Sarah's voice *and now he can feel the muscles jump in his arms, as they fly along the Gulf Road, dodging branches, jumping roots, the horses grunting, gliding, steam pluming; and Sarah's hat is gone some-where behind, her hair flies loose, and now her crazy laughter.*

"Sir?" *she is saying, and it is clearly later on. They sit like facing Buddhas on a crimson blanket thrown down over the grass. Brightness showers them through a million hinged leaves.*

"Madam?"

"You have ridden hard. Some brandy to revive you?"

"Yes. Something is needed, by way of restorative."

"Not brandy?"

"Brandy is good. Something more, though."

"Good talk, as always. You will tell me more about the world."

"The world, certainly. One of my many holdings, in real estate. But something more—"

"Something like a gentle reviving touch?"

Tentatively she presses the back of four fingers lightly against his cheekbone, barely touching, below the eye and just above the start-ing fringe of beard. His heart clots a little, but he holds her gaze.

"Woolly-bear," *she says, unfazed—bravely—as she strokes down into the tangle. He takes hold of her wrist so lightly that she keeps on stroking; as though a moral will has been expressed, or represented, yet not so strongly as the physical will.* "Or perhaps a kiss would help. Do you suppose a small kiss could fit into the midst of this woolly mass you present me?"

Briefly now they are riding again—riding back?—and the soft irregular turf keeps catching a hoof, bobbling their stride. Blue sky flicks and sketches at them through the over-arching greenery.

"We can't afford to lose our heads," she says, though he knows where they were when she spoke those words. It was weeks later, in the lean-to. Herman is sure of it. He remem-bers running with the joke (getting up to search for their missing heads) and remembers her calling him a child, "my gigantic irresponsible child."

And it is true, they are in the lean-to and Sarah is under the quilt, neck and breasts gleaming in a cobwebbed bar of sunlight. She pitches the quilt on her head like a tent and calls him inside ("Come into my tent") with those sudden spots of rose on her cheeks, her whole face both embarrassed and passionate.

He can feel himself sliding over the sheets toward her, on his belly, almost like sliding into the sea (like a dead man getting the dead-launch into the swelling foam) but he hears her silvery laugh, feels her arms clasped round his head, and he is inside the tent of the quilt, tracing the knotted tips of her breasts in the darkness.

"Ten after!" she shouts, so strangely in the midst of their tenderness—until he glimpses her face in the doorway, a kindly dutiful face, and knows at last he has been dreaming.

Wakes at last full waking, and knows precisely where he is.

III

BERKSHIRE

(1850–1852)

July 7. It is remarkable to have come here, as summer boarders, and find ourselves boarding in this fine old house we hope to own. Rowland has determined the roof is sound and the chimneys do not sway in high winds—though his amusing idea of engineering is that you kick the cellar wall with your boot and say, "Not bad." But the place was very well built and has been well maintained over the decades, so as to be more than ready for our fifty-year siege.

For my part, I have fallen in love with the broad prospects and the grounds. Orchards on two hills, a teardrop of a pond large enough for skating parties, and a grand avenue of elms to the entrance. We came to escape the march of ugliness, and we have escaped it emphatically.

All these mornings I awaken to the wonderful notion that our summer suite here on the second floor of the Inn will become our suite for life! The window-seat in the dormer is as large as a room, and has a spectacular lookout toward Mt. Greylock, or "Saddleback," as it is known locally.

Downstairs, there is a European-style ballroom, a large drawing room, and a sunny library overlooking the gardens. I can easily foresee such winter waltzes, tea dances, and costume balls as to make the Berkshire winter if not "short and sweet" then at least agreeable. All the talk of snowdrifts high as horses' necks will not deter us; we shall ride over those snows in a beautiful sleigh with Willie shouting out his childish joy.

July 8. Last night I omitted one very interesting detail. The Inn has long been in the family of none other than Mr.

Typee, the author who once "lived with cannibals." It is his uncle's old home, now run as hostelry by his cousin Robert. And "Typee" himself is expected to arrive momentarily for a stay of his own. So we will not be able to say that Berkshire lacks for culture. The distinguished Dr. Oliver Wendell Holmes is a near neighbor, and one virtually trips over famous men in the Post Office.

July 16. Rowland has now been to the city and back twice, and he swears to me it is as easy as getting out of bed. (Indeed, he testified that getting out of bed was much the hardest part of it.) You walk off the platform at Pittsfield, sit down on a plush couch for a smoke, a coffee, and your newspaper, and walk off at Canal Street perfectly rested. The travelling will not be the worst part, he concludes, but rather the best.

Meanwhile, up from New York as advertised, is the man who lived with cannibals—a lively robust gentleman now living amongst us civilized with no apparent strain. He is here as a paying guest in his uncle's home, though we expect he gets the special rate.

The man has perfect manners (after all, he was not himself a cannibal) and is extremely lively of conversation. His one-year-old son was of great and immediate interest to Willie. And he comes with a shifting troupe of ladies, sisters I think, plus wife Eleanor and a mother who is staying close by and soon to arrive.

They have the parallel accomodation, beyond the stair and chimney.

July 18. Some compliments today from our landlord Robert and his cousin Mr. Typee, who were impressed that a city lady such as I could saddle my horse and ride her. Away I galloped in a storm of dust, a shameless case of showing off, though I know their compliments were silly.

Mostly I was reminded of the debt I owe to God, for lending me such ability when two years ago I barely had the strength to latch the front door at night. Now here I am, my lungs clear, breathing without any difficulty the sweetest air on earth.

Mr. Typee turns out to be a volcano of amusements and a great source of knowledge about the surrounding hills and meadows. He took us to an old cellarhole, then through the woods to a place where there are Indian mounds and many relics of their wars and ceremonies.

And though freshly arrived, and on vacation, he has also put himself to work. He dusted off an old ancestral desk from the attic, and set up office in his dormer, looking toward Saddleback for inspiration. For him, the view is rife with the freedom of his boyhood rambles, plus memories of old haying days, as he calls them—for he has sometimes done the farm work here.

He is very kind, in general, though prone to having some rough fun at his cousin's expense. They seem to understand one another well enough, and in fact are off together now on a tour of the provinces. They intend to go around the farms of nearby villages and write a report for the Agricultural Society on the state of the crops. No one can discern whether this assignment, or the spirit in which they undertake it, is altogether serious.

July 25. Willie and I have been abandoned, to solitary riding and flower picking. Rowland went down on Monday and the distaff Typees are off visiting in Lansingborough, on the Hudson. Meanwhile the touring cousins returned, but flew in the door, stuffed a knapsack with biscuits and flew back out, to haunt some boyhood landscapes. Then this morning, Typee was off again, down to New York on business of his own.

I do not object to solitude at all, nor am I without important occupations, thus far neglected. Rowland left me with a list of all the lists we must make. Our anxiety that we would for some unseen reason not manage to get the place is so rapidly displaced by our newest anxiety at the fact we have got it, and have so much to see to in a hurry. All too soon we will be travelling to England and everything must be arranged and settled first. It will be midwinter before we arrive back, and there will be confusion enough moving in at a time like that.

July 30. Back at the Inn and very delighted at being back. Though our home is still in Carmansville (though our belongings and our histories are still there) I have not been homesick for it and was not happy we had to be there this past week. I felt a visitor there, and a resident here.

Well, says Rowland, it is summer, so the case cannot be fairly weighed. To me, however, the case is closed. The contrast between the allure of rural Pittsfield and the clangor of the city is no longer hypothetical. Upon our return, I literally ran up the staircase and threw our windows open, to admit the magical air. My husband calls me a drunkard, as tipsy on this medicinal vapor as any tosspot on his bottle, but is nonetheless pleased to see the results. I have never felt better. There is an enormous difference between lacking symptoms, on the one hand, and genuine robust health on the other. I now understand this difference very well.

We tended to some business in the village, afterwards took mounts and rode in the hills, and no distance, no hill, could tire me out. Instead, my husband was out of breath more than once. "It is my health we shall have to attend to next," he said.

Typee is also back, with yet more Typees in hand. The rumored mother, for one. That is an irrepressible gentleman, I must say. When I remarked that it was an honor to be so closely quartered with a literary man, he responded with a shout. "Wait a day or two, madam, and you will have enough literary men on hand to start the Revolution." (Some eminent friends of his, from New York, expected soon. This is something to shout about, perhaps, yet so too apparently is his breakfast egg.)

Our summer stay continues on high notes only. Could I postpone the sailing, I surely would, at least until the last leaf were fallen, at a minimum. Fortunately, we do have many weeks yet to enjoy before the first leaf falls, and before we disembark from this place which I already call home.

August 5. Mr. Duyckinck and Mr. Mathews, these are the literary men from New York. The former is refined and elegant, the latter is not. They are equally convinced that the countryside has been but recently discovered and find it exotic as the moon. Decanting sundry libations into their beards the first afternoon, they talked and talked downstairs, an extraordinary talking party which one was envious to join.

In the end, I had to intervene for the sake of their healths. They had filled the house with pipesmoke, filled themselves with champagne, and were growing paler by the minute. They needed to bestir themselves at once, I declared, and took them and their luncheon—with a promise of more champagne as bait—to Pontoosuc for some lazy fishing. (Fishing of the sort I specialize in, where to catch a fish is the most unlikely outcome. My sort of fishing begins and ends once you are in the sunny boat, on the bright water.)

Mrs. Typee came with the party—the wife, that is, not the mother. She is a Boston girl, more of a nodder than a talker. Her name is Elizabeth, it turns out, not Eleanor as I had understood. Luckily I caught it right before I had the chance to noise it about.

August 7. Last evening in the parlor, I had a conversation with Sophia, who is the pregnant wife of Typee's brother, Allan. She and I were left behind, she for being very pregnant and I being uninvited. She told me how Typee has found himself another brother, a new one, right here in Berkshire. He made acquaintance with Mr. Hawthorne (the equally famous Scarlet Letter author, residing in Lenox) and they struck it off at once, hiking and climbing Monument Mountain, brothers and warriors philosophizing together against the darkness of our century. When you add in the New York men, they must have made quite a literary locomotive, chugging over hill and vale with their champagne baskets and stale crusts. They became lost for hours, too, which only added to their fun.

This morning, Mr. Duyckinck and Mr. Mathews drifted into the parlor early (from their lodgings half a mile away) to collect Typee and go on to see the Shakers. I awaited my invitation—politely and in vain—but watched them go out the door. Then resolved upon an independent expedition to the same destination, with my sisters, who are now with us. So we hitched up and flew, the ladies' auxiliary, with myself at the reins, and found them by the famous round barn in Hancock. "You drove at us with such speed and spirit," said Evert Duyckinck later (by which time we were old friends) "that I thought a war had been declared. What a relief to learn you were on my side."

We were by no means unwelcome, it seems, merely absent from their plans. In high summer spirits, we formed two teams and ran races around the barn. (Here too, I was on Evert's side.) And I ran my share, shouted my share as well and experienced no pain at all, no hint of coughing.

"You can ignore this business about feeding the cows conveniently," remarked Mr. Typee. "The barn is clearly round to make a perfect race-course of it, that's obvious now."

The three of them are constantly on fire with their sallies and retorts, but Typee is the natural center. He has a unique energy, or enthusiasm, that turns everything quotidian into a sort of party. This is the same gift, curiously, Rowland has accredited to me; yet where I am well organized and full of effort to accomplish it, Typee merely laughs, and clanks his glass, and rambles up the flanks of mountains. He lives, and accomplishes it strictly as a by-product of living: effortlessly.

August 8. The eminent men continue on their rounds, having been once more to Hawthorne, to Dr. Holmes, and to dine with other local writers in Stockbridge. They are like a club of young boys; it is summer and they have a place to play.

I had proposed for today a pic-nic on the grand scale (a dozen guests, wagons on hire) then scaled it back when some declined on grounds of short notice. This was curious in the case of the Typee distaff, as they are all of the great sitting-and-knitting tribe of women, whose plans never seem so terribly inalterable. But others declined as well, including "Mister Doolittle" as Typee humorously styles his cousin Robert.

In any event, the Lord declined to have us today; he sent a great downpour, which is pounding still on the dormer roof above my head. So we will try tomorrow, with only one wagon and only eight guests. Meanwhile, I compensate the willing with a sudden masquerade, announced at tea time, to begin in about one hour. All round the neighborhood, costumes are being patched together.

August 9. It is very late, but I did want to note before bed that the masquerade has been a roaring success. Not only for the costumes themselves, but for the thespianism they inspired. Evert, in a waiter's vest, served from a tray all evening; Typee, in flowing robe and turban, made a frightening Turk.

We had dancing in the hall, and a midnight supper. Like one of those enthusiastic impresarios of amateur theatricals, I took on half a dozen roles, from the smudged match-girl to Cleopatra of the Nile. What a lark it turned out to be.

One odd note on the subject of our dangerous "Turk." There had been some sort of drama played out at the depot earlier, whereby Typee seems to have kidnapped (or humorously abducted I should say) the pretty wife of someone Evert knows. Evert and the husband pursued the Turk and reclaimed the bride, but I gather the joke was not entirely funny to the young couple involved in it. Everyone at the masquerade had heard a version of this bizarre tableau, each version wilder than the last. One result: Typee's scimitar-wearing Turkoman gave off a whiff of real danger all night, being armed and highly unpredictable.

August 10. Today we launched our pic-nic early, in a pretty mist. Soon enough, the sky was blue and the fields along the Housatonic as green as Eden in Willie's illustrated Bible.

Joyous from start to end, apart from one single mishap— an accident involving Elizabeth. She fell from her mount (remarkably, as the mare was standing nearly still) and rolled down a gentle grass hill. She was not hurt but very embarrassed, I think, and Typee was necessarily solicitous of her and nervously protective for a time, before returning to his humor. Elizabeth had taken riding lessons in Boston it seems, and Typee eventually joked about having their money back as the lessons did not work. Elizabeth was sporting, but blushed, and I was very much in sympathy with her. Or feeling sorry for her.

Not to be unfair, she does seem dull, or doleful, for him. (I was not the first, or only one to say this.) She is very pleasant, kindly, and shrewd in her way. Still, here is a man

once oiled and fanned by a Polynesian princess, a man full
to the brim with his vigor, who barely speaks without rumbling the mountainside and starting avalanches. He has a
laugh to make one laugh along, even when one does not
fully comprehend the joke. For he has a magnetism—and
she a sort of Boston dullness, that the magnet does not draw.

Though people often speak of my having a magnetism, or
a spark, I know they intend a different meaning. (And I
always suspect that no matter how I shout and dance about,
they see through to Sarah Knockknees in her ringlets and
jumped-up nose. How Ellen tortured me about that.) In any
case, I am merely a woman, and never sailed but one of the
seven seas. I have never burned dark as a Fiji from re-
morseless tropic sun, never required bushel baskets to carry
my beard around. Perhaps there are large worldly magnets,
and smaller domestic magnets too.

Postscript : This house has a definite magnetism. I lie in
bed and find that it fills my thoughts, it excites me. We have
learned it was built in the later days of the Revolutionary
War; all the timbers hewn from oaks on the south hill, and
all the bricks struck at the old millrace. This may account
for what I call its unpretentious grandeur.

Second postscript: Once or twice today, I caught Typee
watching me (or imagined I did). Remembering that he is
an author, I had that terror people get when they fear they
are being framed for a role in a story or novel—that they
may so easily be laid open to ridicule.

August 16. Given all his travel, and paperwork at both
ends of every journey, it is no surprise that Rowland cheerfully calls our life these days a "swamp." If it is, then it is a
lovely one—as they say of the Okeefenokee Swamp, with
its dark liquid mirror of the rising cypress trees.

Admittedly, there is too much to organize each day, cou-
pled with the profoundest disinclination to organize anything
at all. I saddle up at the drop of a hat, and ride out to see
our own willows come mirrored Okeefenokee-like in the
slow flowing Housatonic. It is insupportable to be housebound at this time of year, especially for those of us whose
very purpose in life is breathing. Learning how to breathe
anew.

Nor am I this neighborhood's only shirker. When it comes
to resisting confinements—and dodging assignments—Mr.
Typee is at least my equal. He shares a love of air, and of
moving through the air. He and his sisters, Helen and Augusta, are ready for any outing on the hills. There is a general
freedom here at the Inn that reminds me of happy child-
hoods, summer images I had near forgotten.

September 4. Rowland home with fresh news. He saw
Typee in the village and they rode back together in the carriage. The news: Typee is won over by Berkshire, no less
than we are. He intends to buy the farmstead bordering ours,
a small old-fashioned house with charming views. We have
ridden past and seen it, and wondered aloud who lived
inside.

They plan to live year round, and Rowland at once clumps
them into his category "the fools of summer." These are
people who come when wild strawberries cluster in the lane,
and peaches float in the greenery—people who forget that
soon the snows will begin, and will not end until the distant
time of mud and Mayflies.

But wait, I said to my esteemed, If this is the H---you
describe, then what in the world are we two doing—unless
we are the fools of summer too. Of course, I know the
answer. We come because we do not mind the snow; because
we hate the dirt and noise; because our lungs, particularly,
will love this mountain air. We come for Sarah, though all

the burden of our coming falls on Rowland, who bears it with such grace.

What a fortunate turn that the clan Typee will be our closest neighbors. It suits me very well. Augusta said to Rowland, separately, that the wellsprings of their decision lie in Typee's tie to Mr. Hawthorne. He has found his brother, literary and spiritual, and must go where he finds him. I suspect there is more to it. They all revere these ancestral hills, and none moreso than Typee, who finds his youth in every woodland patch.

And perhaps we figure in a little, too. We have all been such easy friends. On the day of our pic-nic, Typee and I talked for half an hour—so easily. As we both tossed stones onto the water (more surprise, more compliments), I could feel us becoming friends. Not brothers, mind, nothing so vast as that. Just friends, of the sort that draw together quite naturally, and always look forward to one another's company.

September 18. There have been so many comings and goings, and in a very few weeks, like it or not, we will be gone until February. Neither Willie nor I like it very much. When we explained to him (about going on the boat to Daddy's old family home in England, and visiting there during the bad weather) he simply threw his head back and forth, saying "No no no no no no." Compared to that, my response is mild indeed: a realistic sigh.

Yesterday it was so stunning bright and airy that I was in a sort of trance. I looked up and Typee was standing there with his reins in hand. He was in a melancholy state, he declared, and invited me to have a weep with him down among the weeping willows. So off we went together in a high stirring wind.

"It almost pulls the hair right off your head!" he laughed, and his laughter had the effect of making me strangely vain.

I knew my hair was flyaway (having leapt up quickly from the sorting of china, I had hardly bothered with it) but I surely did not wish to appear bald as an egg on horseback. He read my mind—saw my concern—reached over, and said, "It is very pretty when the wind takes it, Sarah—that is all I meant to say."

Later, I asked about his melancholy. Was it real?—because he seemed as lighthearted as ever. Yes it was real, but hardly serious. It was something that accompanied the autumn season and felt "right" even if it would feel wrong in spring or summer.

Typee is so full of plans, most boldly the addition of a high tower to his house, with windows on all four sides. "I shall sit in God's lap, and take the view!" I told him that for our part, we have chosen to postpone any major changes at the Inn, so as to suffer them through firsthand next year. "I shall suffer firsthand, secondhand, and thirdhand, whenever the wrecking ball arrives," he said. His tower will be underway as soon as the winter wood is in and all fields ploughed under.

He was sorry we would be gone for such a long time (he and Willie) and I agreed, I was sorry too. We sail so soon.

September 23. Everything has been seen to, I think. Most of the things that have been shipped from Carmansville will remain in crates until our return. Robert will stay on here as caretaker—no paying guests henceforth. He will see to all the stock, his and ours being commingled in the barns.

This way, we can expect to find a life at the ready when we arrive mid-winter. The sorting, packing, and shipping is behind us, though we do realize it will take months to sort out our lives, the old and new, and re-establish order. Only Rose will accompany us to Pittsfield; the rest of the staff we will have to advertise for locally.

All our neighbors are bringing in wood and bracing for winter so it is slightly odd to be unconcerned with all of that. Typee had planned on building his tower and writing his book in it; instead he has been so yoked to the farmwork that all literary work is off limits, including well-paid work for Evert's magazine. "Bits of cheesy cloth anyway," he says, "to be cut and fitted to the magazine public." He speaks the word magazine as though it were an unholy oath, while Augusta quietly implies it might be well to cut a little of that cloth.

The new book will take all his time, once he has some. And it will take three reams of paper from the mill at Dalton. Perhaps, I suggested facetiously, he had better get himself a fifty-gallon barrel of india ink to cover so many pages, to which he readily agreed. "Come!" he called to me. "Let us go straightaway to India and fetch a barrel back, just as you suggest. My pen will soon be flowing heavy, and won't stop short of life's last page."

He seemed terribly eager to have his reams of paper and the ink barrel. Perhaps it is like a farmer with a crib full of pumpkins for his cow, or a soldier with his rifle cleaned. It is an important book, he fulminates some more, then quiets down, a little sly—"Important to me, and to no one else."

Well, we must leave him to it: book, field, and tower. We have one day here, the rest of the week in town, and then we embark. Rowland is right that my reluctance to leave has much to do with having had no symptom here, and with knowing that in England the months of cold rain await us. "It will be all right," he soothes me. "And if it is not all right, even two days' worth, we shall reverse field and abandon England without hesitation."

As always, Rowland is eager to get on with the plan. His one concern is our understanding with Robert. It evolved quite naturally, from our needs and his own, and there is no question it is a sensible solution. Rowland is only afraid (and with cause, from the look of it) that Robert will be dug in and stay on, as our "guest" for a decade or so beyond the terms.

December 25, London. Some unhappy news came yesterday, the day before Christmas. We had asked that the Pittsfield horses be allowed to run free now and then—seeing no reason why they should not, and many reasons why they should. We were wrong, however, and with tragic results.

Lydia Weems is good enough to write, as she has done thrice now. The story is that Robert was racing down the Gulf Road in his sleigh-and-one, while our horses followed on. When he crossed the tracks, the horses crossed behind him—but somehow he had not seen or heard the train, which somehow managed to hit them all. (Our three horses that is, not the incompetent Mr. Doolittle.)

I can imagine them all too clearly, shivering in the dirty snow and cinders. Black Quake and William Tell are both in splints and under a haze of morphine, or they were at the time Lydia wrote. It appears that Jenny is in the clear.

Rowland writes it off to the likelihood of afternoon alcohol. Since Doolittle lives up to his name so well, he must have come by it honestly. Typee he grades higher ("Good man in a crisis," being the full and all of it) for it seems that Typee fetched Mr. Bernardston at once, and did what he could for Jenny and Tell. So, as ever with my husband, grateful and generous where it is due, and not one bit of nonsense where it is "due little."

Only the distance in miles and the fact there is still hope shelters me from this terrible episode. I almost expected to hear some bad news, as for months now it has been only cakes and ale. Nonetheless, Berkshire has been in my thoughts, and now I fear it will enter my dreams as well: a picture of Quake caroming against the siding; in the cinders; listless upon his straw.

I will cheer myself (and lend cheer to these pages) by recording an historical milestone—Willie Morewood can read. So he has said and so he believes with all his heart. What he means is that he now and evermore recognizes every letter of the alphabet and recognizes by name the person who goes with each letter in his little book. He goes tripping through from Alice to Zenobia, without a moment's hesitation. (His clear favorite being Miss Olivia, with her seven lovely chins.)

January 5. Lydia has followed up with a note that cannot have been easy for her. Black Quake has died, there is no other way to say it. Destroyed in the end, the poor creature; he was only eight years old.

William Tell has come through—thus the ledger, for Heaven and earth. We will delay informing William Morewood of our loss until it is closer to sailing time. And we agree it is a lesson in the perils of absenteeism. If you are elsewhere from your responsibilities and rely upon others, it is your responsibility when others fall short. Your guilt.

Naturally I feel a need to be there at once. Rowland points out that it is too late, there is nothing to be done. He wants to extend our stay into the spring, both for the business he has been gathering here and for having heard such tales of the risky winter passage. It is the worst time for those of fragile health, said his friend Mr. Heath last night at dinner— as though he came here hired to say it.

I reminded my husband I have graduated into the ranks of the robust, yet I suspect we will not be sailing soon. A lesson in democracy. The truth is, I would lose on votes in any case, because Willie, recently so eager to stay in Berkshire, now is just as eager to stay here. Of course, he does not know of Quake's sad fate.

January 7. It may be too late, but I have written to Robert my request that Black Quake be buried in the small field behind the stables. Our first Berkshire mortality.

Rowland told Willie last night. Something came up so that he would have had to lie to avoid telling. "If you have pets, my dear—animals—you must always know you will bury some. They do not live as long a life as we do."

Willie appeared to accept this logic and frankly it helped me too.

April 10. We are safely back and in the new house a little tentatively, after a frightening passage. There is no end to the lessons we learn this year. To avoid the buffeting of February winds, we sailed two months later than planned and were buffeted by April winds instead. Bitter winds that rolled the ship, as sleet flew for three days.

Nonetheless, we are safely back and on our calendars, at least, the season is spring. In the woods, the trees are packed in snow; around the house there are blotches of snow; the sky is gray with a coming snow. Otherwise it is spring.

We have enough to do indoors. So fully occupied, in fact, that I have yet to call on neighbors. Time to roll up our sleeves in earnest—Rose and I are the fulltime help, though Rowland has been busy arranging. A girl comes from the village tomorrow (as day staff until further notice) and it appears that Harry Moffitt will take on the grounds and stables.

April 12. It turns around so quickly at this time of year. It did snow a bit on Tuesday, now today everything has melted and gone. The grass begins to darken, trees are budding, and a lovely sunshine comes pouring down. I feel a deep contentment that we are truly here and that we are staying here. It will not be taken from us soon.

April 14. Augusta and Typee came to chastise us for "laying low." They have done naught these months but await our return, and here we do not even deign to call.

To this friendly sarcasm, he added a sarcastic bow, and kissed my hand, sarcastically. ("Madame of the Castle.")

I fell in happily with this game. Addressing myself to Sir Typee of the Tower, I asked for an early tour of that no doubt extraordinary perch. "You will be the first to tour it, once it is begun and finished. Meanwhile, alas, it has again been postponed in favor of pragmatic considerations."

Typee looks older to me, perhaps because his beard is larger. Or perhaps because he has lived here, as a veteran farmer, where we are now latecomers. Despite this aging (and no doubt we have aged a little too, in the interim), I experienced a tinge of youthfulness when he kissed my hand. However sarcastic and social it was, I felt for an instant like sweet sixteen, at a tea dance. My silly schoolgirl heart still goes where I go—Sarah Knockknees leaps back to life, and so readily!

This is of no significance, though I note once more how the process of maturity can rarely be marked on your calendar. There does not come a day, even confirmation or wedding day, when one is magically wise or saintly. It is a little more interesting than that.

Lydia visited in the afternoon, as I had hoped she would, and she, if anything, appeared younger. (And did not in the least mind my saying so.) Both visits made for welcome intermissions in our relentless quest for order. It was good to be back among faces and voices of friends.

April 17. I did go calling today with spring baskets in an attempt to rouse our community from the long winter's nap. Some of our neighbors in less than perfect fettle. Mrs. Satterlee has been weak since Christmas, and looks lingering to me; she is seventy-eight. Mrs. Coleman had a very difficult birthing, from which she and baby daughter have each clearly suffered. Terrible to see an infant so dark around the eyes, and with skin the color of paste. Who knows better than I that health is the first blessing and the last?

The road to Lenox was well maintained, and I thought hard on all the backbreak work that went into making it so. Found the Hawthornes not entirely inhospitable, which is to say that they let me in the door. It has been said that they locked the world out all winter, or used the excuse of snow-drifts to lock themselves in. Certainly they are a sort which does not much venture out, nor ask you in, yet are fine company once their security is breached.

Put another way, they are more able than willing, socially. This stems in part from their also being the type of love birds who are woven so closely together that one coughs and the other covers her mouth; one trips and the other falls. Sophia Hawthorne is an interesting case, for being such a sturdy, brainy sort (with a clear position on every issue of the day) yet at the same time a fawning wife, who stares in admiration upon her noble, all-important husband. Rowland, on the basis of a single hour's observation last summer, resolves the contradiction for me: it is strictly on account of who the husband happens to be. The crux is that Mr. H. is the great man, or is at least perceived by Mrs. H. to be the great man. To him alone, therefore, she subjugates, while standing up every elsewhere. No doubt he is right, though he did not observe, at the welcoming last year, how Mrs. H. subjugated a little for Mr. Typee, too.

Well, but I see what is not there, Rowland tells me. He says I am too ready to impute all sorts of flirtations and conflagrations. I say he is too solid, with a man's attention to acres, and dollars, where I have a woman's instinct for posture and glance.

There was nothing to impute today. Mrs. H. gave me tea, and an apology for having no cakes in the house, and then, after half an hour's polite talk, gave me another apology in conclusion. Regrettably, she and the great man would not be able to attend our rites of spring celebration on Saturday; his literary work under hand is too close to completion to allow for social pleasures now.

One supposes it must have been part of the literary work, then, and not a social pleasure, when Mr. H. ventured from his profound retreat to sit with Mr. Typee in the window of the Post Tavern a week ago. Lydia has testified that they looked profound and then some. *Well-oiled* was her word, I believe.

April 19. Our celebration will include twenty guests, nearly half of them from neighboring "Arrowhead," which is the charming name Typee has given his farm. I went there today seeking a head count for the party, and found the man of the house away. He has gone to Brattleborough with a friend, Mr. Fly, leaving the diminutive boy Malcolm behind in a dark forest of large women.

The large women all pledge to attend our party. Elizabeth was most in question, having been so long in Boston and so recently back. She is there so much that it hardly seems she has moved here; more as though she has moved there. People have their reasons, though. Rowland is mostly absent too by necessity, and few know that we could not be here at all (and thus my lungs could not) did he not accept the sacrifice.

I am very glad she will come, for I wish to know her better, and it is genuinely a challenge. Helen and Augusta are so easy to know, so friendly, whereas Elizabeth is always polite, but never seeems to warm at all. Nothing radiates from her. She lives life as a factory girl lives out her factory day, minute by hour all the same, day by week an eternal go-round. It does not change, and she does not want it to change; she only wants to polish the days with a certain New England pride, that has no value or meaning beyond the polishing itself.

But the matriarch, Maria—Herman's mother—I am not so certain I wish to know. Young Malcolm finds Elizabeth warm indeed; he clings to her. Yet see him draw back from his grandmother. How often do we see a sight like that? A granny should be all sweets and sweetness, a fount of steady affection, not a dragon.

Of course, I hope my instincts all are wrong, and that time will make us better friends.

April 24. I have been too busy to deliver any news here. Arrivals and departures by the hour. Eva came, Mrs. Henderson came, Rowland came and went. I have rolled to Albany to meet the boat, rolled to Stockbridge for the stage, and frequently roll to Pittsfield for the trains. (I think our remove to Berkshire may prove very good business for the train cars of the Housatonic line.)

The party was friendly and jolly throughout the day, though my scheme to have the Brothers Bell align and dance with the Sisters Typee proved a mathematical dream and a pragmatic failure; none of the six would budge from chairs.

The celebration had none of the *spontaneous* delight which marked last summer's ball (an occasion since made famous, and infamous, by the good Mr. Mathews in his magazine account) but it was judged the liveliest time since that night, which will have to do.

Much of the credit is due to Missy. We are very fortunate to have found her, and fortunate that she has gained Rose's approval. Rowland has been extremely generous with her. He believes in securing a mutual trust from the start, and I agree. If they are to make our lives easy and agreeable, then why should we not do the same for them?

The Typee women so greatly outnumbered the silent father and motionless son, at dinner. The latter two seemed surrounded, and muffled. I thought how Typee, once surrounded by naked brownskinned nymphs, is now left to drown in a sea of crinolines, an ocean of taffeta and toilet-water.

During dinner, he maintained a steady, silent *twinkling* across the table, as though he were perched upon a nest of nice secrets. His countenance is secretive to begin with, one realizes, for his eyes are not large and his Old Testament beard most assuredly is. Once he told me a tale of "de-bearding" at sea, when every sailor was shaved clean (as a punishment) and perhaps it was nothing less than the awful trauma he makes it, because now he cultivates this impenetrable thicket on his face.

Meanwhile, the puckish silent *twinkling* proves to be temporary. Once he has lubricated his vocal cords at the Beaujolais, he proceeds to chanticleer all afternoon, thereby transforming himself from the recalcitrant guest who must painstakingly be drawn, to the opposite extreme, the guest who cannot be contained. Before he had done, we were treated to the low humor of a heifer's mating dance, to songs and stories rendered with a hefty palm whacking the board for punctuation; and to some extremely impolite charges about Minister Fletcher.

"The good shepherd Fletcher anoints his head as one anoints a salad," he observed, and that was merely the beginning. As I say, the wine was never cut off, and neither, once begun, was Typee. Rowland's lone sanction was that expression which I call his evil smile, a subtlety which no one else would notice in the midst of his flawless graciousness and tact.

Tact, I suppose, is what Typee lacks, or more accurately, disdains. This choice of manners lay at the base of Rowland's discomfort with Typee, for he later allowed that what was said of the minister was true, and not a little amusing.

Rowland was most surprised at Typee's boisterousness; I at his earlier silence. We agreed that a trace of eccentricity adds to the party, gives it a sort of signature that serves to highlight the occasion. In future years our guests may think back on Typee's antics and also recall that the turkey was perfectly roasted, the house bedecked with early flowers, the piano in very good voice.

A final word, which I would not add had it not been Rowland who mentioned it first. It is this: were I Elizabeth, I would not so steadily apologize for my husband, even in jest. Such apologies call attention, they are more awkward than the gaffes themselves. I would never reproach Rowland in society and I am confident he would never reproach me.

It is to the credit of Augusta, my favorite, that she prefers to laugh with her brother. She is open to the possibility of laughter, which I like, and never reproaches him in that awful resigned way of wives.

May 4. We have come upon a time for all invitations to be politely refused. It is an absolute social grace this week to refuse, a sort of rule. Some few may be validly excused: Dr. Holmes has gone to Boston, the Fisher Farringtons are abroad, and our literary men claim the haven of their art.

Mr. Typee has a case to bring, for certainly his days are full. It is he who drives the ox and he who seeds the rows they make together. And when he is not here, writing his pages, putting in crops, or hammering down his piazza floorboards, he is in New York to handle the details of publication.

He promises no refusals once his manuscript has been driven through the press. It is about the whale fishery, written from personal experience. I pray that Rowland is wrong when he says the reading public may not flock to his chasing after whale blubber in the same way they flocked to his chasing after lithe Marquesan beauties.

Herman assured me that he cared not a fig whether twenty people read the book or twenty thousand; his task was to write it, exactly as he pleased. Oh, said I, prancing lightly backward from this sudden Pacific typhoon, I'm sure the book will be delightful. No indeed, said he, it will not be delightful, nothing of the sort. Then he softened, and twinkled, and began to speak of *elm trees*—or of the countless hours of youth he spent staring at our elms, in particular, and at another massive elm that stands without the garret windows of their Lansingborough house. Those trees "have landmarked all my imaginings, between the mountains and the sea."

There is not always a response to make when my friend goes so quickly out to sea, and no response for the philosophic silences that often follow. The always wise Lydia has instructed me to anticipate such silent passages among all our writing friends. They stem from the habit of being solitary, and then solitary some more.

Very well then, let them be less solitary and come fishing this afternoon. Let Herman defray his polite refusals as he defrays them for Brother Hawthorne. For the evidence against them mounts. Last Sunday, in the afternoon, they were seen with sons Malcolm and Julian respectively, climbing in the hills.

I urged Rowland to take Willie out and join them, but my own husband sent me a polite refusal. "Those two," quoth he, "are literary men. They don't want us."

It was only an excuse, of course. Five minutes later, he was sound asleep in the Boston rocker. Willie and I left him there and rode out two-in-the-saddle to the Gulf Road. He wanted to see the tragic spot and I decided it was all right to take him there. He is such a sweet and sensible boy.

June 1. Summer is at last confirmed, in the details. We have seen the last of the May flies, the first of early strawberries.

Indoors we meet most gravely (and frequently) with Mr. Cole, the builder. We play with hypothetic doors and windows as if they are so many of Willie's building blocks, and Mr. Cole makes it all so simple, and so assured of final beauty. Nor do we doubt him, until he gives his figures. Then we go round again.

Rowland does not worry over the money, he only worries about fair honest dealings. "If a dozen of brick costs two cents, then two cents it costs and we'll pay it. Just don't tell us it costs three cents." This has been his little refrain: the two cents and the three cents.

June 2. More signs of summer: the extra trains are running, the hibernating genius Hawthorne has gone forth upon the high road voluntarily. Suddenly the world is cloaked in green.

Herman reports that his "whale of a book has been harpooned, subdued, and all but hauled on board." He is due for another spate of reading proofs in town, so we will see him little this month, as indeed we saw him little last month. Next month, however, he promises mischievously, we will see him so much we will live to regret it.

There is a wonderfully ponderous humor in his turn of speech, as he winds his way toward the carefully rounded final clause. He speaks with such elaborate metaphor—as with his harpooned, subdued, and hauled on board—yet something has me smiling a clause or two early, from anticipated pleasure. I have learned to trust the final clause. I know it is on its way, trickling steadily under the ground, and will arrive.

June 6. Herman has already broken his word, by being available for a pleasant talk in the lane. This breach I forgave him, only to become the target of his quirky humor, and the recipient of his lively worldly blather.

He is relentlessly playful with words, and with names in particular. For no reason, he called me Miss Brittain—called me by my maiden name. I quickly corrected him on both counts. (*Mrs.* for one, *Morewood* the other.) And he hopped about with delight, repeating these syllables like a foreigner learning our language. ("Mrs."—he bowed—""Morewood.") One hour later, as we parted, he brought the little performance back intact, even retaining the comic pause, and the bow.

Concerning his high spirits, and his extraordinary vigor in general, Rowland has a theory, as usual. He posits that a literary man must get all pent up, if he is always "living in his head, while sitting on his arse."

I do not disagree, for wives must not be disagreeable, yet I do wonder (for wives must think for themselves) whether literature is any more or less wearying than the next line of work. For apart from a laborer, most men of accomplishment must to some extent be working in their heads while sitting on their arses, not excluding my dear insightful husband.

"It is different," he assures me with a gentle pat, indicating perhaps that I have struck just the right balance between thinking for myself and submitting.

If Herman is indeed pent up, all his careening about does not appear to pent him down; he remains in perpetual motion. This particular literary man spends quite some hours on his feet, for today alone he has walked in the hills, chopped away at next winter's wood to take it off the stump, and made his daily constitutional to the village. He ranges far afoot and even farther in his talk. Most of us can add to the conversation something we have read, or overheard. Herman can offer magic lands, where fresh water springs up through the shallow sea and the natives capture it in cocoanut shells. He has seen white people starve in London, not twenty paces from a performance of *Macbeth,* and seen dark people reign as kings. Consider the relativities, he exclaims. Consider for a moment when they switch their places, when the dark man comes to London and the white man ventures to Marquesa, for surely they will switch their fates in the bargain.

He dares recall a pretty Tahitian maid who quite flawlesslly recites the Lord's Prayer (in the tropic chapel where she learned it) then steps outside to invite a debauch in the nearest bed of fronds. "Christian in the heart, heathen in the carnal part," observes our Mr. Typee, who has been on intimate bantering terms with such creatures as these.

I am hardly the Boswell for him, but my point is simple enough. He has seen the world, and the world is inside him; you see it taking form in his eyes as he speaks. The rest of us see such a shrunken world. We travel to London in a velvet-lined cabriolet; we walk down quiet marble halls. None of us go where Typee goes, for even from London he comes back with muddied boots, and with an inner life surcharged by the outer.

Enviable. I am often called energetic, but my energy is to Herman's as a candle to a blazing bonfire. Or as our little Sasha is to his outsized Jack, a loose-faced Newfoundland who stands beside him wherever he stands. Even in his choice of "puppies" his taste runs to the scale of leviathan.

June 20. I had an extraordinary meeting on the green in Stockbridge today, with a companion no less likely than the reclusive, exclusive Sophia Hawthorne. Herman was her topic. "He is your nearest neighbor, how fortunate." She was so full of pronouncements, all to do with my "nearest neighbor." I heard about his son, his horse, his dog; soon enough I would have heard about his mice, in his hayloft.

It is only my opinion, but it still appears to me that the doting Mrs. Hawthorne has kept back one small chamber of her great heart, and into that chamber she has moved most of Mr. Typee's furniture. She goes so far as to testify that

her boy Julian has taken Typee to bosom as a second father—
presumably in case the first one evaporates?

In her presence, one has the constant feeling of being
watched. Closely watched. She may be speaking, she may
be listening: *you* are being watched. As though it is all an
exercise to catch you out, or trip you up. She makes me go
carefully, which is not my way at all.

June 28. Herman has been twice to New York (his
"scalded Babylon") to see this endless book through the
press. Somehow the process has become as tortuous as if he
were the very pressman, setting every line of type. It was a
very simple matter, I recall, when Bryce was engaged with
his poetry volume. One day he wrapped a parcel, next day
the stage carried it away. Then, two months later, the stage
carried it back well-dressed in leaf and leather. It gestated
into a book offstage.

Herman allows for all this, allows me to make fun of him,
and then explains: "Everything comes hard to me."

Not to us. We have enjoyed a rare summer treat, with
Rowland staying on. Mercifully, he has not been to New
York even once this fortnight of blessed vacation. He lingers
with Willie in the strawberry beds, side by side for hours.
They pick and eat in a steady motion, like strawberry-eating
machines; yet with such blissful human expressions on
their faces.

The arrangement has its difficulties, but Rowland insists
he is truly content with it. He has the best of both worlds,
he says, and makes good use of the train time in between.
Far from being a wasteful bore, it is restful, and productive.
He catches up both on sleep and paperwork in the quiet
hours of travel.

Meanwhile, we grow confident of my health. Why not be
optimists now, if my only symptoms are joy and vigor? I

ride as much as I wish, I hike around the lake with my fishing
tackle, and I only feel the better for it.

July 10. Mrs. Leacock's visit has been pleasant, if somewhat taming, as her quiet preferences limit my time out of
doors. The entire neighborhood is quiet, with Mrs. Leacock
here and Mr. Typee in New York City.

Elizabeth's parents came for the 4th of July and both are
fine company. Mr. Shaw is a charming, impressive gentleman of the old school. The entire time, however, poor Elizabeth was pressing a wet compress into her face and making
sad dovelike sounds inside it. The cause is allergy, they say,
combined with the heat, and perhaps unmentionable difficulties from her condition. But apparently she suffers this
way every summer and fall, poor soul.

July 22. Very hot now, even at night. Rowland very sen-
sibly took some extra days off to sit in the shade while July
exhausts itself. There was also work to do here, or decisions
to make. He and Mr. Cole stood facing one another in the
dining room, with handkerchiefs drawn. To me, a room
away and out of earshot, they looked like strange duellists,
or contestants in an odd game, where first one and then the
other mops his brow. Their decision, I think, was to have
some cold lemonade.

Back from town (where it is even warmer) is Mr. Typee—
or Mr. "Omoo" as I discover the Hawthornes call him. No
one calls him by his name, which could not be fitter punishment for a man who alters everyone else by a syllable or
more. (In my case by a marriage, for I am still either "Miss
Brittain" or "Mrs." "Morewood.")

He has set right to repairing his pumphouse, and sings as
he carpenters. As to the carpentry, Rowland says, "Let us
hire him, and fire Mr. Cole." As to the singing, he has one

strange and dolorous hymn, learned of the Lebanon Shakers, which he intones quite relentlessly.

"I am closer to God when singing about him, than when thinking about him. And it is so much easier to sing than it is to think."

"Perhaps," said I with a smile. "But for your friends, it is a great deal easier to listen when you are thinking."

July 25. If not for daily infusions from Herman, this entire week would have been lost to the oppressive heat. It has been so sultry, so humid, that the dogs have given up completely, and the humans stagnate. Most of each day I surrender to laziness, then we all fly away on Herman's coat-tails, and live vividly for an hour.

He is in no mood to notice the heat. Like a child set free at the schoolhouse door, he is swept away. Thus launched (and disemburdened), he is determined simply to let the wind blow through him for a month. And if there is no wind, he is determined to manufacture some.

So here he comes, like the comet, and there he goes, a sober drunkard on horseback, full of schemes. "Summer's lease hath all too short a date" is his watchword for the month. When he heard that Mr. Hawthorne's daughter was born, he went pounding down to Lenox at once, twelve miles round-trip, to demand his cigar. Certainly he is impulsive.

He is also generous, for including me so often, and kind both to his sisters and to Elizabeth's brother, who is here now on a visit. Apart from his trip to Lenox, it has been come one come all, on his daily outings. He is famously reckless at the carriage reins, and no less so in the stirrups, but I like that I can keep his pace on horseback. He is the more reckless rider, I am the more experienced, and we both like to gallop full tilt.

The others do not. They mock our speed (or our folly I suppose) and prefer to banish us rather than to keep up. "Perhaps," said Augusta today, "we will come along in time to repair your broken bones." That was hardly necessary, of course. We did go very fast for a distance, but one must be mindful of the horses too. As much as they love to run for their own sakes, they too feel the heat. It is at their expense that we plunge through the air and are refreshed.

So thanks to the horses, and thanks to Herman, for lifting me from this July languor for a vital hour or two each day.

July 25. This is a delicate note, perhaps better left unwritten, as it must surely go unspoken. The subject is Herman, and our friendship. For we have been friends, steadily drawn to one another's company, and now, due I think to this slightly intemperate passage in his life, and to the confusions of a warm July afternoon, it has come to pass we are also unwitting conspirators.

On Friday, we were out riding with Fanny and Augusta, when a playful race began. Augusta started it, in a way, when she wondered aloud whether Herman's recklessness or my experience would prevail over the race-course of the Colemans' lower pasture. So we took the challenge, racing toward the river. Neck and neck we went across the pasture, exhilarated by the speed and danger. We should have reined up, but did not. Herman did not, so I did not. We kept driving on, and by the time we reached the riverbank, in sight of Tully Mountain, horse and humans were equally cooked in the blazes of July.

It is such wild pretty land there, where the water-meadows spread, and the willows sag over purple loosestrife.

"Why don't we refresh ourselves," says my friend at this time. "Let us walk right into the river on our mounts, and refresh them too."

Surely the suggestion was made in jest, so I gave the comic response. "We would get wet."

"Good!" says he. "Let us be soundly wetted, what could be better than that? Let us swim, and the horses swim, for if ever there was a day for swimming, it is this day."

He makes it a matter of common sense. If we first can agree the day is very warm, then surely we agree to the benefits of a country bathe—as though he were not Mr. Typee, and I not Mrs. Morewood.

"We are not dressed for a bathe," I quickly point out, experiencing a pang of shame at knowing what is proper and what is not proper. (For morally speaking, he has managed to turn the world upside down.)

"Dressed?" he laughs, "Who is it that dresses to bathe? Why even princes and Popes must undress to accomplish the goal."

Next comes a rush of language on the tonic Housatonic (the bracing waters, the water's embrace) alongside assurances his proposal is perfectly discreet. We will dress, or undress, in separate quarters, and be safely inside the dark waters when next we glimpse one another's "topknots."

Certainly I was tempted by the water. Admittedly I had no wish to present myself as bumpkin, or prude. Yet again I was forced to express the obvious: "However discreet we are, we would need a thousand times more discretion at home. For we would have secrets, ever after."

The obvious does not deter Herman. "Excellent!" he roars, and claps his hands, then claps them lightly on my two shoulders.

"I *like* secrets. Let us have them, Sarah."

I cannot excuse or explain how I was blown away upon this gale of personality, but I entered into the proposed scenario. Off we went to our separate woodland chambers, and from them slithered low into the undeniably cool, honeyed embrace of the river; nor did we approach before only the "topknots" showed, plus noses and eyes. I felt naughty as a girl of ten feels naughty, for having chosen her fun over obedience. When we played the old slap-water splashing game, we were indeed like children—apart from my unshakable anxiety that one of the horses might break loose.

I could show no such concern. Having surrendered in the name of spontaneity, I was determined to be blithe and playful, and I was, until Herman's playfulness went too far. He would dive, and disappear below the surface for so long that I could swear he is amphibian. I never worried that he might have drowned, as I am sure he wanted me to. I only recalled (again from childhood) how Ellen and I would have such contests. Holding our breath, counting to twenty, or thirty.

Then suddenly I felt a wake, an underwater tide, and saw air bubbles rising to the surface nearby. Where was my irreverent friend now? Would he soon be tugging on my bare toes?—for that too we used to do.

He did no such thing, of course, but I did feel terribly exposed by now. I sank below the surface to investigate how dark these dark waters might be, and found them clear as London gin. Herman, thankfully, was nowhere in sight. I was from the water, dry and dressed for home in less than a minute. At that point, however, it did not seem possible that Herman and I could ever again face one another, or speak. And what in the world would I say to his sisters or to my husband? My mind was in a welter.

Not his. He too had dried and dressed, and he came with both our mounts in hand. What could I do but take the reins? What should he do but display his most innocent smile and say to me, "Admit, my dear Miss Brittain, that you are now as cool and fresh as mint-leaves on an April windowsill."

And what, at this point in the proceedings, would I say in response, other than the acquiescent, fully complicit, "Mrs" "Morewood." I did say it, and he had got away for the moment with turning his prank into yet another witty exchange.

Postscript: We parted, one hour later, as friends; but friends who have been too free, and now must harbor secrets so long as they both shall live. (Indeed, ironically, till death do them part.) All this was strange, and awkward. Fanny helped us through the transition, certainly, by asking so pleasantly who had won the race. And it is remarkable how easily innocence becomes just another suit of clothes, a face to wear at the dinner table.

Nevertheless, I know the truth. I am very agitated, and my greatest peace consists in solitude, the simple fact of it. I am at ease only behind my bedroom door, which seems a shield.

August 2. No amount of study has given me an answer to the question of my husband. It is my luck he is not here, and I am left alone to ponder the question. Several days' avoidance, however, serve to remind me it was never my wish to avoid Herman, my admittedly unbridled friend. I have missed his teeming spirit; there is a sort of hollow.

My embarrassment, moreover, has undergone a surprising change. Looking backward (relieved of the pressures and confusions of the moment) I seem to take almost a pleasure in my own boldness. Such behavior is doubtless wrong, yet is it not in the end harmless? And does it not entail a rare, courageous liberation?

It appeals to the side of me that made Mother call me her "imp" and that never hesitates to shake the world into a champagne punch? So it is not my own position but Rowland's, or mine in relation to him, that gives me pain.

Walking with Augusta today, just the two of us, I experienced a perverse thrill at knowing what I know and knowing, at the same time, that she must never know it. We do have secrets, Herman and I, we are partnered in a private dance, as though we had waltzed away from a ball into a room beyond all the windows. It is not fatal to anyone. Indeed, it has more to do with life than with death. And though it has some of the flavor of secret lovers, it is wonderfully without the sin.

Postscript: From Augusta comes an account of Herman's latest escapade. She tells it with a smile, for while there is nothing eccentric in her, she can enjoy her brother's eccentricities. She does not find that humor contradicts her piety.

It seems that Herman dressed himself as Don Quixote and rode his horse to Lenox. When he came upon Mr. Hawthorne (on a bench in the grove, reading a book to his son) he greeted the great man in Spanish. It was young Julian who eventually recognized him (saw through the masquerade) and Julian's reward was a trip in the saddle with his "second father," while the great man came alongside on foot.

It makes a nice story, and happily confirms me in my belief that Herman is bold yet good. That he is in a mood to play. He has been so brimful with his book; now he decants his excess of spirit into these summer eccentricities.

August 3. Augusta and Herman came today with a basket of tomatoes. There were oblique references, intended to normalize us, as it were.

When Herman refers to "this queer little settlement we call the world," he is perhaps no more than right. Certainly we must look foolish to him, with our fine lines drawn in the dust. Why refuse a cool bathe in the glorious river, which God himself has set coursing through our hills, and on a day to fry the Devil's own ears? It sounds irrefutable when framed that way, and that is the way Herman frames it, naturally.

Meanwhile, he says that Evert Duyckinck is coming this week along with his brother George, who is also his partner at the *Literary World*. They particularly wish to visit the infamous Shaker preacher, with his green glass eye and his "gaseous pornographic prattle." The bulk of the visit is yet unplanned, so I shall plan it. (Better a chief than a brave, they say.) We will see the glasseyed man, and see the back of Saddleback, and the lakefront of Pontoosuc. We shall dance, deal cards, take tea, and be great friends all. It makes me want to wake the stable, saddle up now, and ride beneath the moon and stars—in Spanish armor, if necessary.

Or perhaps, like Lady Godiva, armorless entirely. Now there was a woman to accept a dare. After all, hers is the true story of an historical occurrence. The Countess of Coventry, a noted lady of the village, gone cantering along the familiar streets of that village in the altogether! Cantering past the pillars of her church with nothing but a long blonde mane to cover her naked beauty.

She banished fear and shame. She over-ruled small-mindedness, in favor of boldness and laughter. My tiny grain of pride at the riverbank may be a distant cousin to her pride in riding "bareback," more ways than one.

I can imagine the actual Lady Godiva growing old: age fifty, age sixty. And what a rich retrospective pleasure she must have taken in the memory of that youthful adventure, and of her youthful beauty. Very different emotions would she harbor, had she, like the rest of us who make no legends, shied away for fear of indiscretion.

August 4. A lovely spontaneous party last evening, for sister Hetty and her betrothed Mr. Smith. Once again the treasure hunt was on for costumes. I made several ready, trying on youth, middle age, and old age, in the course of the celebration.

The guests came late, due to the rain, but all came cheerful, and only grew moreso as the night advanced. Indeed, one could measure the party's rising pulse by measuring the sinking level of the puncheon. Mr. Smith was a frequent visitor there, while Hetty made a great hit at the piano, with her tragic and comic ballads.

Herman behaved himself most of the night. He was not got up in Spanish armor, as I had suggested, but as a sailor boy. Nevertheless, he behaved—apart from the one wicked moment. He and Mr. Smith read out a series of toasts, allegedly sent by telegram from Mr. Mathews, including one to me as "the Pittsfield beauty, in bloom but never in *bloomers.*" Though I was disguised inside a powder white wig at that moment, I am sure my face was blooming red. Almost as sure that Mr. Mathews, in absentia, was a mere scapegoat for Herman's own ribald joke.

Rowland came late, arriving just before the stroke of midnight, and his reflexive graciousness crowned the occasion. Far from expressing any pique at finding his home in the hands of revellers or excusing himself on the grounds of fatigue, he recognized the costume theme, slipped into his red hunting-jacket, and drew himself a glass.

This morning he rose in the same blithe spirit. It was a very successful week at the factory, and he is happy to be home for some cool Berkshire nights. If I were to tell him of my indiscretion, if I were to destroy his peace with that news, how would I begin?

Perhaps this is why the Catholics have confessions. They do not confess to the injured party, they confess to an invisible voice in a dark hallway. It is less complicated, and the injured party is not further injured; in a way, not injured at all.

August 7. This afternoon an outdoor ramble with my visiting ladies and Herman's visiting gentlemen, plus Hetty's Mr. Smith at his best and his worst.

We climbed above Washington Lake, with Mr. Smith charging about, declaiming verses, to the sarcastic pleasure of the literary. They have a sort of eyebrow code for disapproval, and a sour lemon they must all have eaten, that turns their mouths down.

A heavy rain drove us to shelter in someone's barn. We knocked at the house, but could raise no one. The floor was muddy, so we climbed the ladder and sprawled in the hayloft like gypsies.

Mr. Smith happened to have his latest poem in pocket (a poem to rival Congessional filibuster both in duration and distinction, I fear) and Herman did the reading honors, verse after stentorian verse, while the lemon men puckered and mocked an approbation. I am sure poor Joseph had hoped to charm the Brothers Duyckinck, so much so they would schedule his work in their very next issue. Sensing their true response, he turned his disappointment on the farmer's innocent chickens—flailing at them, kicking, shouting Demons begone! The poor man. (A relief that Hetty was not there, to endure it firsthand.)

Herman was excessively polite to me. Polite or distant, I am not sure which. It is felicitous that this August influx of humanity comes; it may bridge us back to normalcy. For today, it meant simply this: that Herman leans to Duyckincks, not to Morewoods, with all his hearty wit.

I gave him the same in kind. If we are to remain at bottom schoolboys and schoolgirls playing at silly lookaway games, one may still prefer to win those games. No doubt our Duyckincks were baffled utterly by the storm of heartiness and wit buffeting them from both sides.

The hills were a sensation, pure and uncomplicated by human nuance. The steep gorges had filled with mist; now came the sun to steam it out. We watched the streaming vapor rise, watched the hills emerge in full summer glow.

Herman seems to allot himself a single indiscretion daily, as a sort of physic. At the lake, where it was not so warm by four o'clock, he suggested we might all like a swim. No one thought him serious, though for an instant I did fear our mad poet might fling away his frock and frolic in the shallows, declaiming.

Nothing of the sort occurred, but in the pause, Herman turned to me directly, in the presence of the sundry ladies and gentlemen: "Now you, 'Mrs.' 'Morewood.' You are fond of a swim, are you not?"

Do I put this down to humor, cruelty, or wine? If he hoped to draw out further blushes, he hoped in vain. I curt-seyed and, in the spirit of the Countess of Coventry, declared that having our bloomers on, we would happily follow him into the water, though I doubted any of us could aspire to the *depths* he would reach, in water or in thought.

Herman enjoys his games, but so do I, as it happens. He bowed me back, and smiled a coy one, with barely a trace of the lemon-sucking expression for his learned lemon-sucking friends.

August 9. The literary men have this in common with all men everywhere, that every thing they do, from the eating of breakfast to the fighting of a holy war, will become a story at supper. Thus were we privileged to hear the travellers' report from Lenox and Lebanon Springs.

Given the inside tour by the Shakers, they saw the many ingenious improvements on daily living, clever solutions like our famous race-course, the circle barn where their cattle are fed. Nevertheless, the one-eyed preacher remains the chief attraction. He and his congregation carry on, twisting and writhing, and crying out on high. The preacher warns them off the whore of Babylon in language so earthy that they redouble their licentious dances. "I have never heard such eager reference to the sexual passions, among those who make themselves eligible," says Evert, "as here in Lebanon, among those who do not."

With the possible exception of Mr. Hawthorne, who went with them, these are men with a determination to enjoy. And their ability to enjoy lies partly in their determination to enlarge—as with Evert's nice description of the Lenox clock. The full moon of the clock, he says, lay just beneath the full moon of Berkshire last night, like two bright eccentric circles.

Thus he turns observation into experience, and experience into poetry. Whereas most men do not see the moon at all.

August 10. We had music yesterday, in the great hall, the B-minor Mass very beautifully played by our guest Miss Dillingham. I had planned refreshments in the garden-close, but it rained again just as we were moving outdoors.

Then, chaos. I accepted a flurry of gratitudes, and the literary men abruptly left us. (Better fish to fry.) Away they flew in barouche-and-pair, though moments later skies were clearing, and Evert's moon was starting up over Hoosac.

Tomorrow, eleven strong we make the grand pilgrimage to Saddleback. We will stand upon the highest rock or clod in Massachusetts. Reverend Entler will be in the party, so Herman will have to behave. I trust Augusta to keep him within bounds on that front, for he would never insult the cloth in her presence. And I hardly care that he quibbles with his brother Alan. They both seem to enjoy the quibbling, and some say that is what all brothers do.

How will he behave toward me? Tonight he barely spoke a word; we had more of the polite new distance. The distance comes and goes, it is not always there but what makes it come and go?

I begin to think Herman is not the most straightforward of friends, though I ought perhaps to note how constant he is with the Duyckincks. They are his friends too, of course, and his guests this week. It may be no more than that: he has much more than Mrs. Morewood on his mind.

August 13. We are back from the mountaintop, and to say the trip was memorable is to say the very least. I truly believe we shall recall it vividly for the rest of our days on earth. It was a high point in more ways than one!

Some have found it a challenge to reach the peak of Mt. Greylock in hiking garb, with knapsacks. We reached it carrying ten pounds of ham, a dozen sacks of Heidsieck, half a dozen of cognac, chickens and bread for eleven, cushions, blankets, buffalo robes. In short, we not only ascended, we carried with us half the worldly goods of Berkshire, and more than half the visiting population.

Though we numbered eleven, only four of us qualify as natives. Two of us, Herman and I, qualified as host and hostess. This was inevitable. The guests were either his, or mine, so all arrangements were ours to make. We did take charge, and giving a party together, as it were, did serve to eliminate the distance. We were best friends again, of the best sort.

Evert had his needle out for us, though. He started calling us Mr. M. and Mrs. M., whether in mischief or, as he protested, "with simple accuracy." He was the most satirical all day, especially regarding the difficulties of the trail. He was also the eldest, being in his middle thirties, and the least vigorous, and so frequently called for the cognac to fuel him onward, ever onward. As we carved a path through wild brush near Bellows Pipe, he grandly reclined and applauded George and Herman as they slashed away. The Reverend Entler, feeling perhaps the responsibility of being second eldest, charitably joined him, "for there are always implications that fall upon a *solitary* drinker."

We reached the summit in full light and set about furnishing our sylvan home. Herman disappeared into the limbs of a tree, yodelayed from somewhere on high, then set to work at the base of the tower. He hollowed out a rotted stump and built a bonfire inside it, which he fed with logs past midnight. This was not for cooking (as our supper wanted only unwrapping) but for warmth. There is a wintry finger upon the windy Greylock summit.

We ate the first courses of our supper beside the glowing hearth, and then, at sunset, we rushed up into the tower. It stands at twice the height of our attic peak, so from the topmost platform one sees a matchless panorama, from the Connecticut River in east Vermont to the Hudson, coiling through the Catskills. The world lays out like a topographical map: field, forest, and lake. We counted a dozen church steeples, risen above the crowns of the elms at every village green. Words cannot do justice to these sights; not my words, certainly. Perhaps the literary men will prove equal to it, in the coming monthlies.

But here was a famous night, a night to never end—and it nearly never did. We greeted the stroke of midnight with a reprise of the cognac, accompanied by a quart of brandied cherries. Eat, eat, I urged them all, for the more we eat the less we carry back down the trail tomorrow. No one resisted this exhortation, nor the cherries, nor the last of the ham.

Only Allan could sleep. Augusta is afraid of the dark, and quite seriously feared that large rats were lumbering right past her head. Her brother suggested she sleep standing up, a trick he had from necessity perfected at sea: "Then the rats won't take a vital organ, only the little toes."

Poor Mrs. Pollack rolled over and over on the lumpy roots and stones, until she was virtually sharing a blanket with Evert. As he had begun the ribald theme, I gave some back to him by wondering aloud if the venue was not a little public for such nuptial rites. He grew bright cheeks at that (as did Reverend Entler) but I was only just beginning, for the night was magic, the place mythic, and the cognac inexhaustible. George threatens to release a careful "word by word transcription" of all my indiscretions, to launch his new blackmail business!

So kind a man is George Duyckinck that I am surprised he can even raise a joke about criminal enterprise. We were together through the long descent, filling our baskets with yellow raspberries; bending, picking, bumping backs and laughing. On the evidence of nothing more than these few days, I believe we will be friends for life. Indeed, we all shall be.

We slept (or did not sleep) as close to the stars as one can in the state of Massachusetts. It would make for a long night to be camped up there in January, but our ripe summer night was all too short and sweet.

When daylight broke, the mountain was swathed in that same impenetrable mist. Whatever we had seen the evening before, this morning we could not see each other across the stump. We were standing inside a cloud, I suppose; then one large gust blew across the peak and seized the shroud away. There it lay afresh: our bright green valley, through air clear as glass, for forty miles.

Herman and the Reverend made a strange pair at the breakfast pit. "Broiling Birds For Breakfast" was the song they composed and rendered, in harmony, as merrily they stoked their coals, and plucked the last reluctant feathers. Far from assailing one another on God and morality, as Rowland had forecast, they *wassailed* one another, and made a joyful noise. There was no end to the wonders of this extraordinary foot party.

A final adventure did lay in wait for us at North Adams, where the mysterious baggage contractor refused to take us from the hotel to the depot, and threw our luggage off the wagon. Happy indeed to have consumed most of the impost last night and this morning, we loaded our backs and made safari down to the railway platform, only to find the sheriff there, waving a warrant for Herman's arrest!

Herman declined the honor and his brother Allan, who is after all an attorney, fired off some sallies from the statute book, chapter this and paragraph that, until the gentlemen's necks were all grown red and half the vagabonds of the village had risen from their naps to witness the coming brawl.

It was all a ploy for money, an extortion. The contractor had piled his extra charges into fine print, and the sheriff was in his pocket. Herman demanded a bill, disdainfully paid it out, and we boarded the train. There was no brawl, only more laughter and song, and this last tale to tell.

In just a few hours, Rowland will be home, bringing the Van Winkles to supper. Good, I say. I have no fatigue. Boil the potatoes and bring them on. The rest of our party voted for total respite, but I was ready to cast lines on Lake Pontoosuc, where the bass are all but volunteering. Others may take life in bites, and rest up between courses. Not I.

Of course, I know what drives my locomotive. They have never yet lost life; never had a year fall out of their life as through a trapdoor. They have never been in a purgatory, where you may get better and you may get worse, so you better not move and *can* not breathe. They have not had that, but I have. I have rested enough.

August 14. Reverend Entler has caught a summer cold, for which I am being blamed—even though George Duyckinck caught a bass in Lake Pontoosuc and pronounced the same air that laid the Reverend low to be nothing less than "evaporated manna."

The Duyckincks left us this morning, with a parting vow to stay in touch over winter. They propose we reproduce the Saddleback excursion, in all its details, next summer and every summer thereafter, on the 11 of August.

I am assigned these details, which should be simple enough. All lists and maps are drawn, though Herman reminded us we will need to hire a new wagoneer. "We will need to hire a new porker, too," he adds, "and six new chickens."

Lydia finally met them on their last evening. George she liked at once, Evert she found foppish, yet amusing. What they thought of her, I will likely never know.

August 16. An interesting contrast, at our neighbor's farm. Allan reading newspapers in a lawn chair, Herman baking in the field, turning the hay. But Herman likes his farmer mode. The haying and harvesting rather suit him, so he takes it all on cheerfully, and tells us he is happy he cannot afford to hire it out. His horse is more reluctant, so Herman engages him in running conversation. "Take it home, Riley," he encourages, "Take it home. It is your Christmas dinner, not mine."

Meanwhile, he already has launched a new literary work. This time, he envisions a sunny Berkshire idyll, something to retain the savor of our recent "green and golden" days.

He is in such a sunny, mellow mood. Toward me, he is again very amiable, almost tender. There is less of our jousting, more of easy friendship. We are agreed to an hour of riding soon: day as yet unspecified, chaperone as yet unnamed.

Lydia cautions about overfamiliarity, announcing a mild disapproval of our magical night in the clouds. (Inklings of the co-educational campfire—of bedrolls overlapping, of Mr. Duyckinck and Mrs. Pollack as close as "horse and harness," have naturally trickled down to her.) But I was quick to remind her that our very Reverend was present, and that he seemed at peace with all proceedings. Indeed, he provided us with an eloquent and instructive historical context, in his "starlight sermon."

He recalled the tens of thousands who drifted into the American wilderness, not so long ago. Intrepid souls, who slept on skins and earthen floors, and hunted their breakfast in virgin woods. "Our nation is a mere sixty-two years of age," said he. "I have a dozen parishioners older than that. Older than the nation."

From this historical perspective, we were more than civilized up there in the clouds, with our ham sandwiches and European wine. Not to mention that the talk was all of Goethe, Schiller, and Waldo Emerson.

Perhaps, like moralists everywhere, Lydia is mostly envious that she missed the party. But like all moralists everywhere, too, she will not be budged from her bedrock. The nation is far from young, she holds, it is just as old as you like. My family (she holds) goes back to William the Conqueror, and my nation is more than firmly established, thanks you werry much.

August 20. For the first time since our river swim, I had a moment alone with Herman. He was very quiet, which I mentioned. He then spoke of the different kinds of silence— of Mr. Hawthorne's wonderfully companionable silences (which I, of course, find to be less than companionable) and of the sort of awed silence that signals reverence for nature. Then he spoke of his love of solitude, and of solitude going hand in hand with silence.

Misunderstanding, I offered to leave him be, if such was his preference. His apology came quick and warm; genuine, I felt. "No, Sarah, I did not mean that. I only meant to tell you something of the sort of fellow you have for saddle partner."

Thus suddenly, for the first time in our acquaintance, I became *Sarah*. (Neither Miss nor Mrs.) Through constant deprivation, he makes you grateful for the sound of your own name.

August 23. A brief chance meeting with Herman in the village, a sentence or two on the street, nothing of the least consequence. But I believe there is something new between us: a closeness perhaps too close, a male and female sort of closeness, with that kind of dangerous spark in the air.

This may be an excessive response on my part, though the truth is I had already felt something of this on Tuesday. In any case, when we ride on Saturday, the entire sisterhood will be riding with us, to chaperone away any sparks.

August 26. Left unsaid above was the obvious: that the spark is not merely dangerous, it is pleasant. Therein lies the danger, of course, for it is at bottom no more than the spark of life itself.

And I discover it is unmistakable even in the presence of chaperones. A kind of chill; a tightening at the breast, and as I say, unwelcome pleasure.

I am safe from it, of course. I am long in the tooth, at 27, to swoon away on forest floor, and married, let us hasten to add. Happily married. Herman is such an unquestioned gentleman that one is safe enough taking some small amusement from this callow agitation.

But does it have an outward form? Is it visible? Because today at the breakfast table, Rose said to me, "A shame Mr. Rowland must be so much from the family." Why say it now? Rowland is away by design; he is at work, as he has been all these months. Was her intent to be sympathetic, or insolent? Does she read my mind? Or worse, has she read these pages?

She would not nor could she, since I keep the key. But perhaps the phenomenon does have a solid aspect; perhaps it is not mere vapor, but as definite as chairs and tables, and Rose has bumped her hip on one.

Our New York interlude will mark an end to this matter. By the time I return, it will be the start of the second week in September, and this ambigous summer haze surely will have lifted.

September 1. By taking the train trip Rowland takes, I see for myself that it is not punitive. Not the first time at any rate. The prospects are lovely on both sides, compartments are neat and private, and the ride is so smooth you can indeed be working—or writing in your diary.

I am also confirmed in the timeliness of this short trip. Yesterday, I experienced an unwelcome emotion, and an inappropriate one. Jealousy. Not of my husband, but of my friend. I knew that Herman had gone for tea with the Hawthornes and their house guest, a visiting Swedish poet. The poet is a *poetess* (Fredricka B.) and I imagined the four of them being poetical together, hour by hour on the Hawthorne lawn.

Augusta could not tell me if this Swedish beauty was 25 or 65 years of age, and I could not ask a second time, or appear to be too keenly interested. I felt so ridiculous. I have a husband, Herman has a wife. It is for his wife to be jealous of Swedish poetesses.

September 7. Somewhat distracted still, hours out of every day. We are safe from our actions, yet never safe from emotions. Sometimes there is nothing that can dislodge an emotion—not age, nor geographical location, nor marital status, nor anything else.

Rowland is thoroughly absorbed in the timbering at home, which has begun, and in the dining room changes, which begin all too soon. Since the changes are more my hobby horse than his, he is right to presume my interest. Yet I cannot listen for long to his perfectly sensible discussions. I do not think about the timbering or the dining room, I think about those simple moments at the barn and on the hill;

moments with nothing memorable about them, beyond that
they occurred.

Is this emotion mutual, as I sense, or am I alone in my
nervous agitation?. One cannot easily picture Herman nervous, or agitated, and he is far too busy for emotion, between
crops, books, and family—not to mention the companionable silences of his brother Mr. Hawthorne.

September 12. I am quite sane. I love and esteem my husband; I treasure my son. And never do I take for granted
this fortunate life we share. So why do I wander to the window, with a hollow at my core? Why does my mind wander
from what my darling Willie is telling me?

I am so aware, minute by hour, that Herman is just beyond
the hill. I know that if I ride past to say hello, and hear his
voice hello me back, my distraction eases, my balance is
restored. But this can hardly be a solution, any more than
the opium is an answer to the opium eater's distress.

The question of mutuality haunts my thoughts. When I
see Herman calm and confident, I am convinced there is
nothing—and I am disappointed. Misery does love company.
Yet am I not calm and confident in his eyes? Certainly I am
trying to be, with all my wit and fibre.

Perhaps I am not quite so sane, after all. If this is summer
reverie, though, born of mountaintops and sunny hillsides,
it will exhaust itself as the season exhausts itself. In the meanwhile, I fear it must begin to show, though nothing bothers
Rowland outwardly. He does not react to Mr. Smith's indis-
creet dinner reference to the Mr. M. and Mrs. M. theme
from Saddleback. It seems, both to my shame and gratitude,
that my dear husband has no idea what a fool he has wedded.

September 20. I gave in today to a harmless invitation.
Helen insisted, really, saying that Herman needed and de-

served to see a face from outside the Arrowhead clan, and the face she chose was mine.

We walked among early fallen leaves, as Willie and I had done yesterday, gathering his favorites—the leaves which are half and half, one side red as an apple, the other green as summer lawns. Today, we brought a binocular, for Helen's birds, and we brought two carafes of light wine and a hamper of sandwiches. So here was, said Herman, a midget version of the famous ascent.

With that in mind, we trained the binocular upon the tower, and traced a path along the eastern face of Greylock. There is a chance Evert Duyckinck will return next week, and Herman proposes we go again in the fullness of autumn: not next year, but next week! Why not, he says. There is a man who runs up Mount Monadnock each and every sunrise, just to run back down.

Helen was all for it, having missed out on the original. Augusta was quick to console her, and assure her that the legendary occasion consisted chiefly of sleepless exhaustion and rodents innumerable. Herman and I maintained a "companionable silence" on the subject, exchanging a lightly conspiratorial glance.

Later he argued the case. Now is surely the time to take that eagle outpost; to float across the foothills of Heaven, above the Byzantine mosaic of colors. (And on he waxed, with his Pisgah views and flushful grids of gold—"sunrise and sunset melded together in the hissing leaves.")

As he flung his verbal salvos, and as we trained the glass on Williams' tower, I felt a dangerous mutuality. We were outlining a grandiose scheme for a party of ten in wagon train, yet were we not both secretly envisioning an escapade for two, a sort of chaste elopement?

All unspoken, to be sure. Unformulated. This was only the ghost of an emotion. We locked our gaze and knew;

that is all. That, and something lingering in our parting handshake.

I will not dodge yet another of my famous conclusions: that were our circumstances different, were I at liberty still, and he just back from the world, both of us eligible as we sat together on that warm autumn hillside, our friendship might logically proceed to a courtship. Why would it not, when our spirits are so naturally drawn?

Circumstances are not different, but surely people cannot believe that in all the wide universe there is one and only one who might thus occur to your senses. For what if that unique soul should reside in Georgia, and never venture north to make your acquaintance?

Meanwhile, back on this earth (where we all do so happily reside) I am resolved to be so tender with my dear husband that he will be convinced his train has stopped in Paradise, not Pittsfield.

September 26. Another magical day. We took a pic-nic to the balanced rock, and afterwards explored Pontoosuc's shore. Bright wind swept the lake. I have never seen it so rough, or so beautiful.

A most successful prank at the balanced rock. I had secretly brought along Hetty's music box, and stole away to creep beneath the rock with it. I was not afraid, for though it is delicately balanced to the eye, it is in fact unyielding to the sturdiest shoulders. I went underneath, quite far, placed the music box, and hurried back to join the others.

We reached the rock and sat, and then the "miracle" occurred. They took it for exactly that, at first. I shall never forget the way Herman's face opened with joy at the sound of music from under the stone. As for Joseph Smith, he was prepared to create an epic poem on the spot; indeed he called it his duty to do so.

Then I confessed. They were no less charmed (and greatly impressed) though I am sure a hundred children have crawled inside. And Herman assigned a higher duty to Mr. Smith: "It calls not for a poem, but a new Bible. Here is the start of the new religion, no less!"

To which we drank several toasts, in jest. It would be the Church of the Saturday Saints—the Morewoods to replace the Mormons. (We even have our own Joseph Smith!)

September 29. For two nights now I have held my silence close, reluctant to seek relief even in these private pages. But one can never be so private as to hide oneself from oneself.

It is nothing less than the unthinkable. An act committed almost casually, as though it were no sin at all, so very naturally did it flow from the hour preceding.

What sort of person am I, when even now, after the fact, my character fails every test? I begin and end with justifications. Is it not true, I have told my bedroom walls, that such behavior occurs in every epoch, and in every class of persons, including the highest? Is it not, therefore, behavior to be expected? Not condoned, but acknowledged; as opposed, say, to burning in Hell forever.

Oh, I know this is facile, and that it goes straight past the question of one's obligation to *others*. Yet still, I say to my ceiling, is it not the case that Herman and I are decent, moral, intelligent people—and that if we do this, is it not possible for decent, moral, intelligent people to do it? If such things do happen, in other words, why would they not happen to us? I feel these false justifications as strongly as I feel the guilt and the remorse.

We were not to be trusted, yet they trusted us—or let us go our way, trust or no. For it is true that we each, for different reasons, are granted a wide berth of freedom compared to others, Herman as a writing man, myself perhaps as a famously willful eccentric. So we found ourselves near

Sessions Pond, alone—or as Herman said, "strictly on our own recognizance." But we could not have been more alone.

We noted the extraordinary quiet: how one heard the foliage stirring, heard small animals in the fringe of brush. The water was as still as water in a dinner goblet. We caught the echo of an axe at work, two miles off, or perhaps ten. When shoes and jackets came away, it was surely unremarkable. Yet even when the rest began to come away, pin by pin, button by button, it continued unremarkable, as when birds fly or fish swim. And then very quickly we were two people holding close, with such genuine affection that it could not feel evil to us. We did not anguish, we laughed. Rejoiced aloud at the absence of mosquitoes, relished the uncovered mysterious flesh. We were calm, and friendly throughout, strange as this may seen

Truly we fell together as though old-married; touched shoulders as though these were the very shoulders we were licensed to touch. How can this be explained, the strange ease of it? How indeed, when even now we lack the proper remorse, for even now the memory is as pleasing as it is disturbing?

The aftermath was just as natural. We sat and talked, then walked. We rode homeward, and the topics were our usual topics: renovations and the cost of lumber, novels and the cost of ink. We did not mention Rowland or Elizabeth, or the children, but then I do not think we ever mention them. And here is why, one might well say!

Nor did we take up the future as a topic, the question of tomorrow. What is tomorrow to be, and when? It cannot be tomorrow on the calendar. I am at sea, completely. I should know what to do, or think, yet I do not know. And here I am, a despicable sinner, while being the same person I was when so recently affirmed as spotless and good.

It is so very strange and above all is the strangeness of the position. I tuck Willie into bed and tell him that Papa comes home tonight, just as though all is right with life.

October 1. One can be so thoroughly upset by events, so taken in shock, as to lose capacity for response. Perhaps this explains my calmness; for I am calm.

We drove to the village to see the wallpapers, and I pretended to care about wallpaper; but I was as easy as they come, sell me anything you like. Rowland concluded I had at last grown mellow and wise, had overcome my fussiness. He looked almost disappointed, like the soldier who girds for battle, only to find his enemy has stayed home in bed.

No part of me could begin to tell him the truth. My moral character is worthless. It is too late for sound moral choices and, in a strange unaccountable way, it was too late even then, at Sessions Pond. Choice did not come into it.

So I reason as the pragmatist reasons. Rowland is content; he is relaxed, and hale. He is happy to have the wallpaper question settled, and happy for these glorious days. It would be cruel to tell him this particular truth: so says the pragmatist.

Tomorrow, however, we must co-exist as families, at the Cattle Fair. We must do the two things at once: be families, and innocents, and be lawbreakers, guilty with sin. How can it be true that I look forward to the Fair? But I see it as our first "tomorrow." What is wrong with me? When will I find my remorse?

October 4. I have survived the weekend, and the Fair. There is no better word for it. Rowland has gone back to town unscathed and now comes the rest of life. Now comes tomorrow.

In among the contests and prizes, there were long walks in every permutation of the company. There was lighthearted conversation, and we wore our poker faces perfectly. I am shocked at how simple it is to be completely fraudulent— but then the alternative is self-destruction.

October 5. I would have been surprised by a word from Herman yesterday. I am a little surprised now, to have no word by today. This necessary communication is something I am not empowered to undertake, it must be he. Though why must it?

In any event, I have lived inside this paradox: that surely some word is coming soon; that no word will ever come. I must remember that my agitation is not the whole world, even though it feels that way to me. Can Willie sense my distraction?

October 7. I had sent the Bulwer-Lytton to Herman weeks ago, and today he came with a reciprocal gift, or such was the whitewash. The gift was Mr. Hawthorne's tales. I am happy to have it, happier still to be given it, along with belated explanations.

I took the occasion to stroll him back to Arrowhead. There, at his gate, Herman turned and smiled, prepared to stroll me back to *my* gate. "Thus back and back we might go, ad infinitum, in an odd sort of togetherness, full of good fresh air."

We dared one brief embrace along the way, and that one not before looking four ways five times, and laughing at ourselves, *very softly.* Clearly there is confusion, but there is great affection too, without which our transgression becomes worse than wrong, it becomes grotesque.

Elizabeth had contractions, or believed she was having them, so the doctor came, amidst chaos and flutter. It proved to be a false alarm. The doctor has gone, the teakettle is back on the hob. And the *delay* accounted for.

I had honestly forgot her condition, but Herman cannot have forgot it, too? Because he did appear a little shaken. The false alarm, before it was a false alarm, "felt very like a telegram from Heaven" to him. You, sir, are a father; now get ye homeward. It has the Hawthorne note, this telegram, a message from the God they doubt.

He did not say we must heed the message. Perhaps he left that task to me. I did not say it either, however, because, God help me, I do not wish to heed it entirely.

October 9. We are terribly suspended between our shared yearning and the more natural call of family. At moments today, Herman was whole: sweet, tart, so alive. Other moments, his face was as vacant as a man who has fallen off the roof.

I am precisely as confused and torn, only far more mercifully arranged. Where he has an expectant wife in bed, crying her discomfort, I have a husband dining contently in New York. How very shameless I have become, though, to hide behind such rationalizations.

October 12. Why do I continue to trust in these pages, and compile in them all the evidence against me? It is a known truism, I suppose, the relief one gains from giving confidences—like a pressure valve releasing steam. I feel a powerful wish to tell the truth, not only on paper, but to some living soul. George, perhaps, if he were here—though no one really, no one can be told.

I tell everything else. My mouth reliably prattles on like some grotesque contraption, a machine of sociability. It ranges wide, as I say, omitting only every honest thought in my head.

Nor do I tend toward early repentance. I can only think of repentance in the future tense. The damage is already done, I tell myself, and repairs may take a lifetime. What is a week or two delay, against a lifetime?

This is a wicked proposition. It is like saying that once you have robbed a train, why not go and rob two more? (As though sin, or crime, does not compound.) But where I should be seeing visions of H---, I see the prospect of an hour with Herman, in October sunlight.

Once you have crossed the line, it is not so difficult to cross it again. The way is marked. I have learned how simple it is to break the laws of God and man, and how much simpler a third time, or a fourth.

October 13. Herman said today that he has always been shy. Boy and man. This surprised me completely. Shy people, he says, can be concomitantly exuberant, precisely for lacking the comfortable registers in between.

I pointed out he has never been shy with me, going back to the first hello, and he agreed. Something in me gave comfort to something in him, from the onset. Thus we find ourselves entangled—given that the converse is equally true, and given our too free spirits.

But I was deeply touched by this conversation: touched by the notion of his shyness, and touched that he values me so. Afterward, I thought of Elizabeth, and wondered how it all comes joined together, and how it falls apart. I tried to imagine an exchange of lives: what if Elizabeth lived in my house and I in hers, as it were?

I do not want to be the sort of woman who calls such a turn impossible. We know it is possible, and that it is done. Mr. Morgan and Mrs. Wells have done it, simply by moving to New Jersey. Does one cite George Sand? Every heroine she gives us will at the least consider doing it, as I gather she has considered and done for herself. But her characters are French, fictional French at that—and they do wind up killing themselves.

I do not mean to be flippant. It was only a way of thinking about our real lives. Would the exchange of lives work? Rowland and Elizabeth, sitting in their garden? Life begins to seem so arbitrary, and it is difficult to imagine such scenarios.

October 14. It is remarkable how many shifts and turns a single hour can accommodate. Of course we are far out on a limb, and vulnerable. Every nuance is magnified. To each minor crisis, laughter is our answer, while the larger crisis goes unattended. There has been not one word of discussion. I am reminded that we never did say anything: never debated, never decided. We acted without a plan, and without definitions, and we still have neither.

Herman is so unpredictable. So still and silent did he lie that I worried he might never speak again. Then, one minute later, he was bursting out in gales of laughter, and making the boldest, freest jokes about our passion. ("We thrashed in our flurry like a harpooned whale going down to death.") I have never heard such remarks in my life, and thought I never would.

I am not offended by his freedom of reference. Nothing he says offends me even when it is offensive by every social standard—but I do dislike the silences. They might be "companionable" if we had all afternoon, but we do not. We are fortunate to have the hour.

"Silence is the vestibule to higher mysteries," he responds to my gentle complaint, and gently touches my face. But what care I for higher mysteries? I want to hear his voice.

October 16. The entire day compressed into one hour, once more. All other hours point toward the single hour of unity. Two o'clock.

Off I go for my daily "airing out" and Herman for his Jaquesizing ponder. We hold to harmless and familiar patterns, and no one makes a correlation. Why should they? No one charts my day or his—though increasingly he is a slave to his manuscript. He is so devoted to his imaginary Pierre and Isabel that we speak much more of those two than of ourselves.

I brought hot tea, and Herman made a fire. (Damp and chilly all today, and the lean-to where we meet has only three full walls. We had concerns about the smoke, naturally, but in time we grew peaceful enough beneath the blankets. Herman's recipe for cottage love is "birch logs, brandy tea, and plenty blankets." Only the blankets have been a challenge.

I am even grown more comfortable with silence, when it is comfortable with me. Quiet sometimes fits the forest.

Yet today I felt the dark side calling. Rowland comes early this week, Thursday night, and I sink a little, at heart, where I should rejoice. Pain begins to spread, after all. And then, Elizabeth is due. She will give birth to their child, a fact which must alter everything. It must.

I felt the season changing, too. December soon will wedge between us. All night tonight I felt them coming, December and the baby, coming on like a lowering storm. I thought of Herman's recitation: "Tis dark and the wind sings hoarsely in the cordage."

October 17. No negative thoughts today. I have banished them all, by mandate, on a day of cloudless Indian summer, with impossible beauty all around.

The wind in the "cordage" sounds like the creek rushing round Cuthbert's Bend. Oak leaves come flowing down like a golden snow, and acorns bounce waist-high in the lane— you can wait and catch them in your hand. Red and yellow leaves float in the pond, as though the water has freshly extinguished them. It strikes one dumb with wonder. What is there to say? Look here! Look there! That is what one says.

I saw Augusta in the morning and she urged me to organize a walking party, as Herman "always loves your company." (Look here! Look there! was my best reply.)

She says that Mr. Hawthorne has praised the whaling novel lavishly. He has appreciated it, and his appreciation will satisfy Herman. I did not know, but Augusta told me, that the book is in fact dedicated to Mr. Hawthorne, so it is well indeed he should appreciate it.

November 1. Some days of journal silence, with agitated nights for me. For Herman, a son is born—eight days ago. I have only spoken once with Herman, understandably. A son is born, a wife is far from well, and a literary man is very much put upon. So I am left to wander in my cloud.

Five days of cold rain have left the grounds barren and soggy—perfectly cheerless—and the interior is worse, with the changes finally under way (or I should say under foot). It is as though cannon shots have hit us, reducing our home to rubble, the ravages of war. The chimney comes down brick by brick, the partitions stick by stick. Between the mortar of one and the plaster of the other, we have at all times a lovely fine white grime in our eyes, and our teeth, and our teacups. And, grins Mr. Cole a bit triumphantly, the work has only begun.

There is nothing for it but to be cheerful by mandate. I must get myself into motion in the usual way, by getting others into motion. I must take this gray and dirty passage by the ears and shake it. We will give some parties, and if we are in ruins, then we shall label them chaos dances, or rubble teas, and incorporate the theme.

I must be myself again. Wandering within my cloud, I have once or twice forgot my role; forgot to play the part of Sarah. What must Rowland think? Or the sisterhood? I have scarcely seen them, between the baby and the bad turn of weather. Now I must make them all come to a rubble tea, including Elizabeth if she is willing and able. I must gird for her, and do more than merely countenance. They must all observe me in good high Sarah spirits, and so they shall.

And Rowland? That saintly soul has decided I am a little under the weather. Nothing too serious, no cough, just the effects of raw air, and construction dust, which sickens us all somewhat. Rose walks around pathetically, with a damp bandanna pressed to her face.

Rowland is solid as oak behind this infirm spouse of his. Either he has no love for me at all, and hence objects to nothing, or has so much love that he *therefore* objects to nothing. I do what I do, and my husband smiles upon it, regardless. Of how many men can this be said? For how many women? He is so extraordinarily kind, so emancipating.

I have abused the privilege and sullied the good in that word, yet it remains a good word and he a very good man. Nor do I say this from guilt or remorse, but from a loving heart, paradoxically or not.

November 4. With guilt crashing round my ears, I undertook a very small good deed—and now criticism crashes round my ears, instead.

Elizabeth has been poorly, and naturally I wished to do something, at least a gesture of some kind. (*Not* to make a gesture would be abnormal, unneighborly.) So I had a blancmange prepared, intending it for suppertime delivery. It would not gell for hours, though, and the night raced a little faster than I realized, so that Rose and Missy went quite late to Arrowhead, on foot. When they returned looking frightened and chagrined, I was afraid they had come across a wolf, or a bear. It took a lengthy cross-examination before I learned what had actually befallen the two of them. It was not a bear, it was Herman's mother.

Maria pronounced my gesture dramatic and foolish—and tried to send the blancmange back! Yes, it was late. That is why I sent them both. They had lanterns, and they went less than a quarter mile on a mild night. Nevertheless, Maria wanted me jailed and hung, on the spot.

But let us allow that life there is difficult just now, and leave it at that.

November 6. Our purposes today were all cross-purposes.
We fought, and were distant.

I understand about Elizabeth, and the baby, of course, but
it has not been home life standing in his way, for it turns
out he has scarcely laid eyes on wife or child. He has been
hacking away at Pierre and Isabel, a little obsessively, I fear.
Between awaiting the splash of the whale and plunging ahead
with his country lovers, he has had no time for anything
else—or no inclination.

I will take second place to Elizabeth. I only ask a second
place, and only offer such in return. Must I take a third place,
though, and a fourth? I was cold to him, and then I met his
perversity and silence with perversity and silence of my own.
And I very nearly said to end it.

End it in deference to the coming winter, or growing families; end it in deference to books, if we must. At the very
least postpone it, to a time when we are in between books,
or when the tulip trees come back in flower. We could meet
again by cosmic appointment of the blossoms.

It felt to me almost symbolistic that we have moved from
soft September evenings with fruit pies on the sill, to the
sight of men rigging sleighs in their dark barns. Just so, we
have gone from the flush of union to the distance and anger
we felt today.

Are we not the same two souls? Do not our hearts still
hang in the same chambers where they hung one month ago?
We are; they do. Yet we are pressured apart, as surely as we
were pressured together. The mystery of it is so rich that if
I could write a book of my own, it would be this one: the
man and the woman.

November 7. Some of the mystery has come unravelled.
The Hawthornes have made a sudden decision to leave
Lenox—not for the winter but forever. Herman received this
most unwelcome news at the Sedgwicks' dinner party,

which unbeknownst to him had been hastily organized as a faretheewell. Apparently he turned morose at table, and was no doubt morose when he woke the following morning— and when we spoke that afternoon. So it was not Elizabeth, nor Pierre and Isabel, and certainly it was not Sarah. It was Hawthorne.

And of course, he did not say one word of it to me. Were it not for Lydia's famous gathering and dispensing of all gossip, I would not know now.

I tried a pose of equanimity at our little supper, but could not maintain it. Lydia offered me the excuse of headache and I all but clutched my temples by way of validation. It is all a lie, of course, one large disgraceful lie, yet I sear most inside from the small white lies, with their cheap benevolence.

My brain was a mill-wheel in the dark, whirling round, driving off sleep. (It is a wonder the headache remained a fiction.) In any case, I quit my bed and came to perch here on the window seat, with Mr. Hawthorne's stilted little tales.

The tales are impossible. They are not even sleep-inducing, merely impossible. Nothing in these vignettes has any weight with me, beyond the ponderous weight of his prose. If I knew nothing of the man or his habits, I would guess that he writes from inside a snowbank, or a bunker under the sea. His sentences are not unlike him: over-wrought, recalcitrant, intelligent, and cold.

I am hard on him, I know, because I am overwrought myself, and hard because he has hurt Herman. Even in his pages, though, he does not try to make a friend of you; he wants to trouble you. I do not doubt that he has always known what I have lately learned, that when venturing in the twilight glade of moral justification, one stumbles every-where. On symbolic rocks, off symbolic cliffs, into symbolic caves.

Nor do I doubt that this is why we are asked to accept the given, to abide the law, *whatever it is*. So we know where we stand, and who we are, and so we can sleep.

November 10. I feel a constant pull to be elsewhere. Herman is contained in every minute, more or less as clay is contained in brick.

Yet my husband is present as well, even when so vulnerably absent. So many wives dislike their husbands, even recoil from them, but that has never been the case with me. Rowland was a welcome sight today. When I looked up from the platform, I saw a friend and ally coming down the steps, not an enemy or an obstacle.

I was stunned to think that Rowland is younger than Herman is. From appearance, demeanor, outlook, position, no one would guess it. But the question of age is a puzzle, to be sure. Am I young now, or old? At times I feel extremely young, and inexperienced, yet I am so much older than I have ever been before.

November 13. Herman wavers openly. And the fact that I am made a sort of marionette, who moves as her strings are pulled, gives him little pause. He lends his "systolic diastolic" glossing-over to the painful gaps in time—that alternation is the natural pattern in all things—and I merely nod. I do not complain. I have no real talent for complaining, I find, whether owing to a generally cheerful nature, or to the fact my moral posture is blown from its foundation. Are the guilty permitted to lodge complaints?

I am full of questions. What do we think we are doing, now? Or better: what does he think he is doing, and what do I think I am doing, for we have surely lost the unity of earlier days. Were we free of our histories, free to act, would we join together in the fifty-year life? Would we fit together under one roof, as we have fitted together in outlaw habita-

tions? I ask, and the answers I give myself are no and no.
Reality is ever present, objectivity unattainable, yet I do take
solace from no and no—I think it is an honest answer.

(Though perhaps my newest concern, a new *condition* I
suspect, has colored all the rest. What if it is true—what if a
baby is underway?)

And what, meanwhile, is Herman thinking? For in my
long brown studies, I ponder on that riddle much. Here is
my best answer there: he thinks of brother Hawthorne. Hawthorne is his court of last resort. "Him I write; his response
I await. No one else."

The mighty volume they cooked up together, or which
Herman cooked and Hawthorne tasted, is declared to be fathoms beyond poor Sarah's depth. He does not await my response, I am permitted only the Twice-Told Tales.

Hawthorne's presence, summer before last, was the very
flypaper that caught Herman, and held him to these hills.
Now Hawthorne is abandoning the good ship Berkshire.
But Herman will not discuss the future. He has, he said
today, only two ways of looking into the future. "There is
the far prospect of death always, and there is the nearer prospect of dinner. But between death and dinner, or dinner and
death, I see very little in my crystal ball." Meaning: do not
ask me again about Thursday, or Friday.

He accounts this shortsightedness to a youth that was
without clear prospects and to a five-year life at sea, where
you live "from sunrise to sunset, from flip to pisco—or
otherwise from embarcation to disembarcation, which may
be years away, over numberless horizons." Thus is the business of two days hence, or three, rendered moot.

Herman is at sea. There is an expression well born to its
meaning! He will remain at sea, I now believe, whenever I
need him here on shore.

November 18. Necessary that we meet today, and gird for
the party here tomorrow. So we met. This time, we were

so much our better selves that I dared to ask the dreaded question (What does he think) and he responded to it. Or verbalized his inability to respond: "It is not that sort of muddle, dear lady. With *thought*."

Very tender, though, and affectionate. And I find that I care less what he thinks than what he feels, and care that we stand on an even-balanced board. No, there is no plan. How could there be a plan? What would it be? There is only emotion. When we share the emotion, I am more at ease on my own.

We went along the rails on foot, diverging into the wood here and there. It was such easy going, with everything blown bare and shrunken. What had seemed a massive impenetrable wall of green is transformed overnight to trunks and twigs, with great airy spaces in between them—as though a fiery wind raced through the forest, and blew it all away.

November 19. Herman and the sisterhood were here as scheduled, to visit and dine. It went like earlier, simpler times: no sidelong glances, no offstage rumblings. We did have the assistance of limitless sherry. The sisterhood may be famously sober, but tonight they were sober in the face of significant imbibing.

We are still a work in progress, of course, or shall be if only Mr. Cole will bend to the task. There has been no visible progress this week, and much of the gaiety flowed from this circumstance. We "walked the plank" over chasms in the floor, and did detective work on the mantel-piece inscription.

The mantel is still outdoors, leaning its face on the piazza railing. On the back of it, never before seen, Herman found the clues. A date, an autograph—presumably from the man who nailed it up—along with his intriguing toast, "To the health of Nettie Walls."

Who was Nettie Walls? I liked Helen's guess that this was no more than a builder's homage to his own solid walls, Nettie Walls and Harry Floors. Fanny came in for Nettie as the fellow's wife or, given the hidden inscription, perhaps his secret lover. (That one I allowed to pass.) Then there was a lovely vote from Augusta, for Nettie as the childhood sweetheart to whom he never found the courage of speaking up, though he loved her all his life.

Last came Herman, to relate the history of Nettie, the legendary beauty of this county, in the days before the Revolution. Every man in Berkshire loved her and they all paid her secret homage—inside a hollow tree, in coded messages on stones, invisible toasts in eaves and cellars. He spun this tale, this long sherry-drenched ode to the charming Nettie, as though all his lavish fictions were facts, painstakingly recorded at the Athenaeum. It was an hilarious performance, really, in his better mode, and so convincing we agreed to look her up in the book of births.

Then we had the naming of the house. It is to be known, permanently now, as Broadhall. There were no other nominations. We drew ballots from my straw hat and the winning ballot bore Kate's initial. But it was a plot: they had all put Broadhall on their scraps of paper. The house had long been known by that name, they knew it as such when they were children. It was from the family that Mr. Mathews took the idea, when he used it in his article.

I am confident that Rowland will like it. He was so thoroughly charmed by Herman's Arrowhead that he said at the time (with his typical generosity of spirit), Let Herman name ours as well. It is one benefit of literary neighbors, he said, to put the right poetic word to a place.

December 1. First of December, first of snow. A fine ground powder fell through the night, like flour. We woke to a scene like a pretty engraving from Harper's Magazine.

Herman came calling in his sleigh, quite openly, and he came with the nicest intentions. A ride across the hills, no questions and no answers, only the ring of our laughter. That was the bargain struck.

But Herman could not stop himself and soon unfurled the list of woes. The corn cribs and bank accounts are low; the household is in chaos; the novel goes badly yet he races ahead with it because the bank accounts are low. (And Mr. Hawthorne is not in Lenox.)

And I thought to myself, what about my own list of woes? Willie's cough, and the laggard Mr. Cole, whose men are far better at making holes appear than at making them go away. What about the fact I may very well be pregnant?

I do not wish to bicker (nor plead), so I thought I should depart. I am not so bad at departing, it turns out. But I regretted it, almost immediately, and brooded over it all afternoon.

Herman is not cruel, after all. He too is confused; he too is suffering. This morning, waking to the fresh snow, he clearly thought of me. Rigged his sleigh, worked free of the sisterhood, and arrived with his carefree promise of adventure.

That we could not be carefree is no more his doing than my own; that he has no inkling of my most serious concern is entirely my doing. I failed him today, not the other way around, and I very much regret it.

December 3. This afternoon, we somehow set aside constraint. Nothing from the list of woes, only tenderness, and the solace we take from two souls touching, which have so strongly wished to touch. The time has come to declare an end. This I decided last night, this I confirmed to myself today at breakfast. If I am with child, we must not delay. What, though, if that child—? Perhaps it was this conundrum that stilled my declaration. All I could declare was my affection.

It flows from him, always. I am the constant, affection has been my only purpose. Throughout the confusion, I have tried above all to remain affectionate. It is both my nature and my premise. What is the point, otherwise? From Arrowhead, then, comes the tornado—or else the trade winds—or perhaps the awful stillness, windless and foreboding.

Herman had a note from Mr. Hawthorne, who asserts the whaling book is "of an unrivalled originality and power." Well, these are words to improve a mood, are they not? On the strength of such felicitous mail, the wind blew sweet from Arrowhead. The list of woes was in abeyance.

What of tomorrow's list, however? Tomorrow's weather? And what of my tomorrows, if I am indeed with child?

December 6. For three days now, "tomorrow" has not dawned. The wind has shifted, one supposes. Apart from one warm gust which brought Augusta here with some news, the wind has not blown from Arrowhead at all. Yet I have felt an ease about it.

The selfsame rattling mail car that brought in Hawthorne's welcome praise has now brought Evert's doubts. Evert's notice is decidedly mixed, says Augusta, though Herman's reaction surprised her pleasantly. He laughed and said, "Et tu, Brutus?"—turned the other cheek, and went about his business. And perhaps this stoic cheer is an honest response; perhaps Mr. Hawthorne truly is the first and last barometer.

But Evert is his friend, there is no doubt about that. His friend and ally. One hundred and one literary men will soon be weighing in, many of them less than allies. However large the whale may be, one hundred one critics make for a serious impost. However white the whale, will he not be blackened, inevitably?

There is nothing for me to do. If Elizabeth and the baby are moved to the margins of his list, I am well beyond those margins. Herman is concerned with Herman, as he watches the daily mail. Our fates are steadily wedged apart, but I believe I can regain my balance. Until I see the doctor (indeed after I see the doctor) I too must be a cheerful stoic.

December 9. Elizabeth interests me, naturally enough. How could she fail to interest me? Though I have never been jealous of her, I ponder more now than ever how it is with her. Who is she, really? (And who am *I*, she might well ask.)

What does she feel, though, in these days of duplicity and confusion? What trickles down? I give it so much thought. Does she read a story to Malcolm as I am reading one to Willie—and do distractions color the reading?

Apart from the fussing Mr. Herald, the workmen have all left us. It appears that Mr. Herald, who shaves away at every tiny piece of wood, may *never* leave us. Nevertheless, chaos slowly yields to order, and Rowland is very pleased. He glows at me happily—and I weep. More than anything, this owes to my new condition. Does Rowland sense something, though? Does something trickle down to him?

Reverend Entler was here to view the changes, and drink his cup of Darjeeling tea. With his searching gaze, his wise smile, he said: "So, dear Sarah, you can at last return to your nest." Was this the rote social warble, or did he intend to fling a dart? Can he know the truth? Where does the trickling stop?

The walls close in upon conspirators, the weight of secrets must accrue over time. What starts out light or pleasing will soon enough come tangled, onerous, and dark.

Most likely the Reverend's simplehearted meaning was that the disorder has been a hardship on us. Thank goodness for disorder, then, if it throws a cloak over sin and guilt.

December 14. Never before today have we addressed the situation; never attempted to solve the problem. We wished to keep the problem, of course. But it wears upon us.

One solution proposed is a winter retreat: await the merry month of May. This was in a humorous vein, yet earnest. "'Tis cold as Blue Flujin, where the sailors say that fire will freeze!" So declared Herman—humorously, earnestly.

Then we had a fright, as there were noises on the lean-to wall. Kicking and scraping. Probably a stranger, Herman whispered, and indeed it proved to be a stranger, a pretty doe nosing among the withered apples, in the blighted orchard.

Surely we could laugh at this, and enjoy relief. Relief, more and more, is our goal these days. There is nothing larger. We are most fulfilled when we experience a relief that nothing so terrible has happened yet, that perhaps the larger disorder among us all can still be fixed.

At the start, one must always be blind and heedless. Then the blindness heals, and into view come confusion, guilt, and fear. Soon the goal of love (a word we never say) yields to this goal of relief, as walls come closing in.

We have never wished to harm the others. It is for them, of course, we have these fears: fear they will be harmed. How much longer can our good fortune hold? How much longer until the hungry doe turns out to be a curious human? I do not deny that a hiatus would be soothing.

December 17. Elizabeth consents to attend our first Broad-hall Christmas, and I am genuinely glad of it. It is always unseemly having the lot of them and not having her. Lizzie is in Boston still, they will say, or Lizzie is not up to it— whatever "it" may be. It is so odd to think how present she is, at the heart of Herman's life.

Well, I am glad that she is here for the holiday, and glad that she is up to it. I feel that I have been responsible, in part, for wishing her away; now I will begin to wish for her presence.

December 23. No communication since Monday and, however strange or surprising to say it, no anguishing. Relief, again. It is Christmas—a time to close one's doors and be snug behind them, with so much family about. There is no time for dalliancing, as Herman calls it, and little inclination on my part.

Where has Godiva gone? My state of mind, my domesticity, has more to do with new conditions. Once there was winter and Elizabeth's baby to consider; now there is winter and my own baby.

Clearly there are phases. Just as the traveller is content at coming home, he will go abroad again in time. (Herman's systolic diastolic.) Meanwhile we must make ready for this party. We must make our Broadhall gleam, outwardly at least.

December 26. What a complicating day it was, a wrought and overwrought sort of gathering, so full of Herman's "intertwisted turnings."

Right from the start. Herman comes breezing in past me as though I am a coat tree, and fixes all his charm on Rowland. It is a barbed charm, however, with a nice sharp edge. Speaks up when he perhaps ought not, silent when he ought to speak. "Flavorish this," he remarks of Lydia's soup, "but where's the bullock broth?"

And never before have I seen him put his famous needle to Elizabeth in public. "She tasks me to stir the pot, and earn a nickel pronto!" he announces to one and all—not smilingly. It is a thin blade, thrust in with a curl of the lip, the work of a pirate.

For me he launches his respectful squire act, with much bowing and deferential wit. He is always quoting lines.

Lately I have grown aware that he mostly quotes himself.
"Few matching halves do meet and mate, my dear," he tells
me, tenderly it seems. Indeed, my heart is stricken by this
hard truth; it is a truth we have ferreted out together. It is
also, he sarcastically reveals, a line he has scratched into the
margin of a book on tortoises.

As to needles and "intertwisted turnings," the highest
honor of the day must go to dear Elizabeth, who came to
our Christmas dinner with the express aim of hurting me.
So I now believe. Never have I heard from her lips a single
word that was ought but purely social, pleasing, trivial. But
as she tasks her husband, so she tasks me too, and in no
accidental fashion.

Draws me into the vestibule (her wine-glass full to the
brim, her lips as dry as her discourse) and all but confronts
me there. Or did I dream this?

The operation was performed with such consummate skill
that I scarcely felt the scalpel passing through my skin into
the soft vulnerable organs. A conjuror's trick it was, almost.

What exactly did she say? "Sarah, you have in you a great
deal of good." That was her opener. How did I know it was
a backhand slap? Because you do not tell a person they are
good, you presume it; unless you are prefacing an insult.

The insult: "You have so much time to live and grow. You
have as yet no real character, no sense of value or purpose,
but those will come, I am sure. And soon, because you do
possess such a wonderful spirit."

She poses as a sage from some bygone era, an austere sort
of godmother, yet what?—she is one year older than I am.
True, she does appear, and behave, immeasurably older than
she is. Doubtless she was Elizabeth the Correct when I was
Sarah Knockknees, and none of that will tend to change.
Nor ought I complain, in any case. According to law, for all
I know, she may have the perfect right to shoot me.

How shall I respond to her? She continues smiling on, and patting my arm throughout, as though ladling out fond affection and not this vinegar bile. Do I shout a self-defense? Do I claim for myself some raft of virtues (prominent among them "real character") when I suspect that she suspects the very worst? What cards is she holding, while holding so firmly to my arm? Surely Herman did not confess? Surely he would not do so without a word of warning to me?

Now, as though to heal the wounds so freshly opened, Elizabeth smiles and speaks of our spending time together, in the coming months. "I will do more exercising in the spring. You can show me the best lanes for horseback riding."

Oh indeed I can. It is as though she came along and swallowed me up!

Likewise with Herman: swallowed up. He darkens inside her shadow, shrinks in her presence. It is very clear the matter of income can shrink him. How he shone, on pic-nic day, when he took the crooked hostler's demand and counted off bills like so many sticks tossed in the brook. He is neither rich, nor poor, he is proud. His pride is what leapt at her, because it remains, even when he is darkened, and hammered fine.

And he is. His health now concerns me most. Augusta fears these recent weeks have sapped his strength. He has stowed away in his garret, pouring his all into Pierre and Isabel, and it has poured right out of him. Augusta fears for such a catalogue of parts—his eyes, his heart, his lungs—that it begins to seem a bizarre obsession. What about his liver, I nearly asked.

Herman is not a child. Let him walk outdoors and breathe, if he is suffocating upstairs. In truth, my impulse was to intercede. Let *me* see to his health. Give him proper rain or shine, for goodness' sake, or else let me do it. More than once I sought his eyes, but they were gazing far away.

Postscript: There is too much weight to carry, and courage surely breaks a little. We are neither of us the sort to decamp a family, so there are limits: it becomes impossible to carry on, just as it was earlier impossible to stay back. Perhaps that is all we needed to know.

Or will it become impossible again, when summer's in the meadow? Do we call a halt, or only a hiatus? We will be the same two laggard souls—or will we? It is so soon, so recent, that one disinclines to say we have changed, yet it seems we may have. It seems that Herman is changed, and it seems that I am changed as well. After the New Year, I will have confirmation from the doctor. Not knowledge, or fact, merely confirmation of the fact. The dating will be most vital (and quite possibly a bridge to cross) yet I am optimistic there.

Meanwhile, I can come to myself for comfort, myself alone. My hands keep settling upon my belly, finding the comfort there. It is as flat as a washboard, to be sure. As with Willie, it may still be flat as a washboard when I am six months gone and more. But I feel the change. I feel a round bow-window growing, to soften the blows and shelter my baby, and it begins to take me over.

January 2. Herman is in New York for the week, and I find it throws me slightly off my balance. Very early this morning, I walked along the flooded marsh banks, and watched the wide brown water racing, and more than anything I felt that here was a landscape to see with Herman. It has been his place in my life, somehow, to share such scenes with me.

And it has been a part of my comfort, in these recent weeks, to know he is close by—just over the snows, at Arrowhead. But my missing him was not unpleasant; it contained no trace of the panic. I wished to have him by my side in the older way, as friend, and good company.

As for the rest of it, the rest of us here, we grow livelier by the hour. On New Year's Day, Rose and Missy served up refreshments from late morning to past the stroke of midnight. We saw every face we know in Berkshire, plus several dozen we had never seen before, as by local custom all doors stand open.

We were too fully engaged at home to wander in the direction of other opened doors (Taylors, Roots, Van Winkles, Van Leers) or to the open portals of every inn and coffee house. Nonetheless, a festive party spread itself across the hills for twenty miles and twenty hours, flowing on beneath the boldest full moon.

At the stroke of midnight, our carriageway was bright as dusk. On a wager with the Reverend Entler, I stood in the garden and read "Lonely as a Cloud" by moonlight. The Reverend has leveled no charges against me lately and now, as a result of our wager, he owes me the first quadrille at our gala in May.

Rowland has twice pronounced me cured. He is more certain than ever the dust was the cause of my malady, and now the dust has settled.

January 4. Word of Herman. They plan to stay in New York through Wednesday next, when Elizabeth again leaves for Boston and Herman will manage on his own. But where? Where will he be managing? And will he truly manage?

Meanwhile a noose is off our necks. The child will arrive in June, with conception dating from early September. I call this luck, or grace, and do not know how I deserve it. On the contrary. Over and above everything else rides the luck that I have my health; that I am *able* to bear this child into the world—a beautiful sister or brother for Willie.

January 5. We are going for a week in town, ourselves. (Rowland's suggestion.) I can see firsthand to the fittings, he will be spared two round-trips, and it will serve to interrupt the winter nicely.

January 10. Three eventful days in New York. This city has changed so dramatically, in a short time. It is as bright and bawdy as a carnival. It is worth your life to cross Broadway, where the stream of humanity comes rushing and curling round every corner and carriages come clipping the heels of other carriages. It is all so *squeezed.* Hotels, block-long piles like fortresses or castles are flying up in the midst of this traffic, filling every slot of sky.

No need to travel far, no matter what you need—it is all in arm's reach, or if it is not, it will be by noon tomorrow. They beckon you in with song and dance, with bright placards handed out by harlequins, with pretty girls or dandified mustachioed men. There is one shop with nothing but toys for sale, and their barker is a man in a lion's suit, with a lion's head and tail. A far cry, all this, from the winter tranquilities of Broadhall.

There is something so odd in the way Rowland and Elizabeth have pursued a connection here, something almost eerie. We are neighbors, understood, but they never pursued a connection before. Now they nod, and agree, and make all our plans. Meanwhile, Herman and I were bad, now we are good. We do exactly as we are told to do and smile.

We have kept so busy together—undergoing coffee, undergoing wine—that we must seem like those foursomes from Pittsburgh who tour the continent together, checking off museums and cathedrals. I only hope that this is beneficial to Herman. One sees that he is cheerful when drinking, a bit morose when wholly sober; cheerful in company and, one gathers, morose at home.

One gathers this from Elizabeth herself. She has cornered me purposefully on several occasions. But am I her project, as stated, or the object of her soft secret wrath—the hammer swathed in velveteen?

This has been daunting at times, and it is clear that Herman and I will not manage one honest moment here. Still I am glad I came and saw him, though I see him burdened. Outwardly we have been jolly enough, and never gloomy. We have been to the theatre and twice have dined among Duyckincks. We reminisced for hours and I imagined Herman's mind at work, recalling how it was and again could be, once some clouds had lifted.

What clouds though? Am I a cloud? In truth, I can only guess what he wants or thinks. Augusta may be right that he is simply worn, from too much work and pressure, but there are pressures which Augusta, hopefully, has not taken into account.

Tomorrow Elizabeth travels to Beacon Hill, while Rowland and I travel home. Herman will follow on Thursday— we have signed on to fetch him from the depot. And then will come the rest of winter, the hard part, as Rowland says. But he adds, with that sweet frown of his that is not a frown, really, "It is a good time for enlarging families." I can only be delighted that he thinks so. Had we been alone at that moment, I might have told him, with the appropriate flourish: "Done, sir!"

Just as well to save my news. There is an obligation to settle first with Herman; I owe some loyalty there as well. Both these obligations, the unspoken and the unsettled, tug on my nerves every minute. I must see to them soon.

January 18. I am well, and calm, except that Herman proposes tomorrow at three. Why does it make me shiver? I am come to a resolution, one which requires just such a private meeting, and now that meeting is arranged. Yet I am thoroughly agitated by the prospect.

I am not weak-willed, I do not fear his response, and I can smile at the old wives' tale that early term is a time for female passion. I feel quite relieved of all passion. Quite calm. For months my decisions have been impulsive, like the decisions a horseman must make in the heat of a race: they are right or they are wrong. And you live with them. Now, there are no more such decisions.

It did occur to me (Sarah the innocent) that Elizabeth has been *hors de combat* in the conjugal bed since sometime last summer, or earlier. Now of course she is in Boston, and given her system of family living, she may well be in Boston when the crocus blooms. Can this circumstance have played a part? Will it play a part tomorrow, when we meet?

I have not thought so. I have believed we two were different. Still, Herman is a man and it is likely that every woman ever fooled, or used, has believed the same. Surely this is the most famous difference between the sexes. I do not subscribe to such a pessimistic view, I merely note that the thought occurs, among a hundred others.

Above all, I want no rancor. Such affection do I feel for Herman, such sympathy, that it will be unbearable to cause him suffering. Perhaps he will approve and shout, Good riddance. But that will be unbearable too.

It depends on who he is; on where he has dwelled in these weeks of darkness. Herman must know what is best for him, as I know what is best for me, now that the road is forking.

January 19. A sad accord reached. Herman agreed at once we must put a stop. "In a way," he said, "it has happened already." Then he retreated into humor—"We do not have to give it up yet; we can *decide* to give it up, and cut our loss at that."

I replied in kind: "It is easy enough to stop, when you are not stopping. If we are resolved upon giving it up, then we had better do so at once, or our resolution has no force."

At this he smiled, and proposed delaying resolution. "But let us decide to plan on so resolving *soon.*"

Herman survives best when he can reduce difficulty to humor. Or reduce our differences to mere semantics, as though whole new moral systems are invented through word play. And perhaps they are.

To this point, we were friends agreeing, or sparring in their private style; at worst, compatible businessmen setting out their terms. Suddenly it turned painful, and sad. We locked back tears, both of us, for we both could see that what was theoretic at first is real at last: we are to lose one another's hearts.

What Herman said next was deeper and wider, and agony to hear. "The moment has passed," said he, so deeply sadly. Morbidly, almost. What do you mean? said I. Everything, said he. Us? said I. Everything, he repeated, absently. As though mortally wounded, yet not, I felt, by me.

Life has a shape to it, he asserted after a pause. It crests and falls, like waves, like tides. It remains the selfsame world of water, yet a rising sea is one thing and a falling sea another. Between them, very briefly, comes the crested sea. Are you talking about us? I asked. And he looked at me heavily, and took my hands. "No, my dear, I am not."

The expression of his eyes! My heart could have burst for him. We were not businessmen now, bargaining in good faith, we were God's tiny helpless creatures, struggling desperately in His bittered meadows. I wept so hard, Herman did too; each for his own reasons no doubt, though also in mutuality, for this loss we agree must now be taken. The moment has passed.

I am only twenty-eight, and still I feel the awful truth of it. Perhaps it is unwise to have started a baby now, or inauspicious. Then again, perhaps it is the one salvation. Perhaps God does wish for me a second chance. If so, I pray He grants one to Herman too.

January 25. No word, of course. But it is strange and hollow-feeling to have no word, and to anticipate none. Strange to hope for gossip, in lieu of intimate exchange.

To "stop" is not unlike having something large removed from your body—an operation, and you wake up legless. You must, at times thereafter, simply forget you are legless. You wake and instinctively begin to stand, to travel to the window.

The analogy is too strong, I know.

January 30. A string of clear, cold, vacant days. I had almost forgot there were people in the world, outside our walls. Then suddenly, Herman and Augusta were here, they materialized in the snowy dooryard.

We sat in the parlor, Augusta and I with our pot of tea, Herman and Rowland smoking by the fire. You cannot play with fire and never get burnt. Elizabeth said this to me, as part of her encoded little message. Proverbial Elizabeth. And I thought of it now, as the flames licked their feet.

From the start, I thought it would be me, now I fear it is Herman. But the future is long and in time she may be proved right: both burnt. So be it, I say. I am burdened by the splitting of our fates, just as I was with the Hawthorne abdication. It runs against our unspoken premise. For a moment in time—be it week, month, or year—two people inhale the same tornado, they behave insanely under the pull of the moon. Why? They cannot resist the chance to share one heart. It is love they seek, though they have never said love, and though they are not free to seek it any more. The moment may pass, but should not the pain from it be equally shared?

A curious sort of skit played out as they were going for the door. Rowland took a piece of cheddar from the tray, for Sasha. She is a gravity-fed dog if ever there was one, always ravenous for whatever is on the floor, let alone her favorite treat served up with a whistle and a toss from Master. But she never roused, and though urged on would not eat the cheese!

Rowland puzzled over this, while Augusta could not conceal her dismay that we would waste good cheese on our dog. Herman gave us some philosophy, of course, with an edge. "It is the law of all great natures to disdain a scrap. To have the whole pudding or go without any."

I must have colored. His reference felt brutally direct, the pudding almost obscene. Hopefully I was mistaken; certainly I was alone in my interpretation. "Don't mind Herman," said Augusta, "he is only quoting from his own work, as any great nature must." (And as she, his most frequent scrivener, would surely know.)

I joined in the laughter, though mine was not so different from being tears. When I quizzed Herman with my eyes, he smiled for me a hideous social smile. I turned away and there was Sasha, wolfing down the "scrap."

February 10. Saw Herman on the road near dusk tonight, by chance, and we went a mile together in our great coats.

It has been well below freezing and dry as dust. In fact, there is rock-solid ice on the river. Walked upon it Sunday, with Rowland, Willie, and Sasha; also with, I realize, the other one, who will complete our family. He or she was also there!

A frost in Herman's beard, something melancholy in his soul. The book has turned continually darker, he says, and the process lonely-making. "We have invaded the text," he told me. "You and I, Sarah." It is only a book, I nearly said, but restrained myself. I have gained at least a little wisdom.

His family is still away, and for the first time he spoke of this problem. Of missing Malcolm and the frustration he feels not knowing little Stanwix, who by now is three months old, yet has been bundled away so much of his young life. Herman confesses he lacks strength to overcome these constraints, or walls, put up within his family.

A bit mysterioso there, but I was careful not to probe too deeply. Certainly I gave no voice to my suspicion that his very real emotional desire to be a good and loving father is more real as emotion than as a call to action. It harks back to his own father's early death, I have gathered, and his awareness of a void; but does not always hark so sharply when it comes time to give over the actual hours of a busy day.

His loneliness, though, is palpable. Standing close by him, one experiences it as one might experience rushing water: it knocks one back. He does not speak of loneliness, or ask for help. Nor did he ask that we bend our resolve. We chanced one tender moment, pressing together briefly for a little warmth, but this happened naturally. It seemed, (and perhaps will always seem) faintly absurd for it not to happen, for I do believe we have loved.

The road was darksome, with no soul in sight, but I almost did not care. Knowing our liaison is over has made us somehow innocent again, with our friendship resumed in a rich new key. I would love to maintain this key, through all his changeability, the seasons of his heart. To have this friend again, now closer-bound; flavored by something like love, yet innocent.

February 21. A fresh snow, new fallen, has its own special luminescence. For a day or two it glows from within. And with this perfectly transparent air, the landscape is seen to most extraordinary effect. Still very cold, but I could not stay indoors this morning.

In the afternoon, Rowland saw Herman in the village. Elizabeth is due home Saturday, he learned, and I am hoping the return of wife and sons will uplift his spirits. Something is needed soonish. Spring will arrive, and there will be an end to this extremely taxing book; Pierre and Isabel will leave him, and rise to the literary heavens. But those solutions are months away, they lie with the lobelia and the columbine, where here the case darkens daily.

No details (all knowledge secondhand) but it seems he is very angry at Evert. Feels betrayed. When Hawthorne turned his back, he at least retreated under volleys of fulsome literary praise. Now Evert, in a second notice, has harpooned the whale severely, and Herman takes the barb into his own wounded side.

This is a terrible figure of speech, I realize, but in truth he has made himself just such a martyr. Where is the triumphal swaggering soul who clanged and clattered through Berkshire in such a recent sunny past? It seems like years ago.

March 7. A mere fortnight to the calendar spring. The chickadees in the woods seem to know it, from their lively song. And every day I grow stronger; every day happier with things as they are.

I am as full of questions as ever, and never more so than when I open this book to report on my emotions. I will not inscribe these questions, for I am confident I shall know them by heart all the rest of my life. And I know they have no answers.

I do not disown what we did. But we conspired to release a demon, and the demon is released. In this we were partnered and, having secrets forever, will be partnered forever. I see us purified. I see us henceforward and always meeting with a secret inner sweetness, because we loved (though we do not *say* love) and did not precisely cease to love, but ceased to act upon it. Is there not a high, sweet, secret union in that?

Today I feel no pull; no true sacrifice in ceasing. (Because the moment has passed?) I fail utterly at understanding how an emotion so vivid and compelling can become so completely dispersed. Perhaps it does not. Perhaps it is this phase that is temporary, and in some far season we will backslide into the tarn; after all, the way is well marked now. But it seems, it *is,* a closed chapter.

This is much harsher on my friend. He speaks of "the disenchanting pages of matrimony" where I do not. He wishes almost to plan a backslide, or at least excuse it in advance on his usual humorous grounds: "We know, we humans, what to be; yet cannot be it."

I can, however. I can be it, now. I readily own to inexperience and youth—possibly to the very shallowness with which Elizabeth has charged me. It was I who made this happen, or did not prevent its happening, and I did so not frivolously—that would be too harsh—but experimentally, I confess. To see what it would be, to have what it could give me.

And yes, because I truly could not stop myself. I have not forgotten those impossible nights, when panic would seize me by the ears. I recall the symptoms of that disease. But I was never ready to lose all, as Herman's wild young lovers are intended by him to do. The book has darkened indeed.

Hopefully he will not lose all. Why should he? His family is reunited at Arrowhead, and he begins to regain his balance. He has been seen upon the snowy hill, with a small one in the crook of his arm, and a larger small one glove in glove. Silently, silently, yet there they were.

Nothing is ever complete, and little enough is neatly tied, in life. The winter is long and dark and cold. But the housatonias emerge, and the trailing arbutus; the lilacs will come in May, our baby in June. This valley will again be what it can be—a deep basin filled with the wine of golden light.

Perhaps I am grown up at last: perhaps my adolescence is
ended. Or perhaps, more generously, I was grown up all
along and am merely human, and fallible, loving that which
I would lose. If I did love Herman, though, I must never
forget my love for Rowland. I am so very grateful to him,
grateful beyond words, and grateful to God for my health,
and my child.

IV

SUMMER

(1882)

July in New York has been hot and filthy, as always. A matter of degrees, so they say, and this one is worse than most but not so bad as '72, when the thermometer went past 100 degrees Fahrenheit every day all month. People took to dining in their cellars that summer, slept on rooftops under dampened sheets and kept on dying anyway, nearly two thousand of them. Falling in the streets, falling off their tavern stools: they wheezed and expired.

One day, an anonymous Samaritan parked an ice-water wagon in Printing-House Square and gave it away, if you did not mind waiting for the cup. Two fifty-gallon slack-barrels of water and one tin cup! Even so, five cents to look through the telescope there and two cents for a shot of Billiken's Elixir, yet free of charge the philanthropist's water.

Herman, who liked the price but did not fancy waiting for the cup, went and cupped his hands instead, and drank up country style. At first his innovation attracted stares, then soon enough imitators, until too much water was spilling on the paving stones.

Today's 92 degrees won't kill you, not by a long shot, and here along the East River bluffs the air is always stirring, even if it sits as thick as chowder down on Broadway. Today, with Lizzie and Bessie safely installed in New Hampshire, Herman is managing easily enough. He strolls into the District office, stows his jacket and pushes up his shirtsleeves, vowing to enjoy the heat if 92 degrees is the worst it has to offer.

Bessie will be reading in comfort on the Plaisted House piazza, Fanny and her baby will arrive today (and the Hoadleys tomorrow), so there is plenty to occupy Lizzie, and nothing much to worry Herman.

It might hit 92 up there, in the rye fields by Israel River, but those are a devalued 92 (oh sweet and soft the hilltop air) and will never *stick* at 92—nor stick you to your sheets. Lizzie will take a couple of light blankets to bed tonight, and pull them gladly to her shoulders.

Herman launched them yesterday, down at Pier 28, then strolled to Cortlandt Street and launched himself, on the Staten Island ferryboat. In the harbor, with the sun spreading low and a wind coursing, it was a bright, cool summer morning, with a free day in hand. As they throttled down to the dock house at Snug Harbor, he saw Tom and his Kate waving and his heart moved with a boyish start, a sort of general happiness that persisted as they made their way up the flagstone path to the Governor's house. Tom's house.

They lunched on fresh oysters, a big wet basketful brought over from the inside shore, and played a game of chess with the selfsame walnut pieces handcarved for them by Carl, the carpenter on Tom's clippership *Meteor*. That was 1860, the year they sailed around Cape Horn together. Every evening, on the dogwatch, they had played a game of chess, and ever since that voyage they had argued over who won the match (one month long and twenty-some years ago), with Herman certain it was Tom and Tom insisting it was Herman.

"It had to be. You were my big brother."

"Yes," Herman smiled, "but then there is the keeping of scores to consider."

"It's a nice sort of argument to have," Kate interceded. "And has the same result as when two braggarts argue—one vote for each side."

After the oysters and the chess, the brothers set off walking and went for hours, side by side like twins, identical beards and hats, though ten years apart in age. They rambled over Richmond's back roads: oyster-shell lanes, clay-ditch lanes, peppergrass lanes that edged the creek; past pear and apple orchards, tangled berry patches, everything twice as ripe as Eden.

"No one starves here," said Tom. "You put your net in the water and it's dinner. Potshot into the bush and it's rabbit stew."

"The land of milk and honey?"

"We have no poor. Does that make it the land of milk?"

On the whole, they had little to say. Two clouds of pipe-smoke, drifting. Herman nodded at Tom's formulation, and silently affixed to it the additional evidence that even the free Negroes at Sandy Ground were plenty well off. Living comfortably off the teeming oyster.

Later, after Kate had fed them again, they relit their pipes and visited with some of Tom's charges. The inmates, as Ben—the eldest, since old Jake gave it up at age 109—called his fellow seafarers. In one of the dormitory rooms, some former shipmates had rigged their hammocks, and slept as they had in forecastles of yore. And almost to a man they wandered to the water's edge at dusk, like a strange tribe of sunset-worshipping whiskerandoes.

In the night Herman dreamed he was back in a shipboard hammock, rocking in the trough of the waves. The crush and stink of overcrowded flesh were vivid, but the rolling water lulled him.

He woke clearheaded to a whiff of coffee, and caught the first boat back to Manhattan. Heel-toed it from the Battery up to Ann Street, then jumped on a Third Avenue car and rode the six-cent limit to 65th, heel-toeing again from there to the District.

He got in barely ten minutes late, which qualified him as the earliest arrival of the day. His colleague James McBride, who had a mere five blocks to traverse, came in half an hour later and they both got off scot-free, since the big chief, John Clyde, would not be sighted until noon.

"It's a waste of shame to be too prompt," says Bridey now, as three of them are leaving the shed and starting across to Fenton's coffee stand. Over the planks; across the rocky lot.

"And how would you know a thing like that?" Will Barclay grins. "What it is, or isn't, to come in prompt?"

"You roll the dice, Young James," says Herman. "Most days you come up sevens, but tomorrow you may roll snakes."

"Herman's right," says Barclay. "It's your peace of mind you purchase when you stay timely, that's all it is."

Peace of mind? Doubtful. You can do the job badly and stay thirty years, or do the job well and take it in the neck. Did Swackhammer deserve to be pickled and shipped home? Herman was hired, and Swackhammer fired, because the politicos changed their musical chairs. Arbitrary, to say the least.

Sitting at Swackhammer's desk that first year, wearing Swackhammer's badge and carrying his locks, Herman was tempted to look the man up in the city directory, and go make sure the Swackhammer young were well enough fed. Not that he could have fed them, when he was barely feeding his own.

"Indoors today?" says Barclay.

"Why indoors? It's hot as Hades in there."

"Go ahead, Herman. You want to take out your sheets and air them. I shall sit in with William, who is ever such charming company."

"Ho," replies the charming Barclay. "At least I can eat with my mouth closed."

Herman never minds, and generally prefers, the company he keeps alone. He knows his Schopenhauer. Which is not to say he lacks the social strophe. He likes camaraderie too, as a man who likes a bump of bourbon can choose Glenlivet's scotch; or turn his mind to the news of the day and his soul to Pushkin's art. No single matter precludes another, unless it *does*.

Nor is it an infrequent outcome that those two should sit indoors with Fenton's overgrown horseflies (and Fenton's half-dead cat upon the crate in the back doorway), believing themselves to be nicely shaded, while Herman is happily ensconced on the scrap of terrace. It is warm, though; the breeze flies lightly by, and only intermittently. He draws closer to the high thicket of sumac, but it blocks more wind than sun.

"Sometime too hot the eye of Heaven shines," he recites to himself, softly. Absently.

His gaze is trained on a colorful tugboat churning down the channel. Her mahogany rails are varnished clear, the boards are painted red and green. Just a garbage barge tug, but beautiful, without question. He is absorbed, distracted—and slow to perceive that someone has addressed him, though she is not ten feet away.

"I am sorry," she says. "I suppose you were only thinking out loud—when you spoke. And I asked what it was."

"It was a tugboat, mademoiselle," says Herman, turning to face her. "One of New York's loveliest, in my judgment."

"I meant the line of verse. Too hot the eye—?"

"Was that out loud? From Shakespeare's famous sonnet, numero whatsomedever. A poem, as I comprehend it, on the merits of dining indoors versus out."

She greets this impenetrable witticism with a polite frown, an expression which catches Herman's eye; something fetching about it. About her in general. By now he has realized he has seen her before. Twice, in fact. Once, on her own, months ago, and once again, when she sat with her young son. They settled into chairs on Fenton's rude patio as though it were the Café du Beurre in the Boulevard des Boules.

She is the Tennyson woman: anonymously present, nicely baffling. Honey-haired.

"I must apologize," he says. "I have left you standing. Please take my chair."

She has misunderstood him. Before he can manage to stand up and give her the table, she has sat down and joined him at it. Herman cannot verbalize a response to this; he merely waves her into the seat she is already occupying.

"Unless you disapprove?" she now says. So perhaps she has not misunderstood him.

"I prefer to believe I am the target of disapproval—never the source, mademoiselle."

She sighs. "I should not have spoken. I am always told I am too direct, and I am always apologizing for it."

"No need to apologize here. I do not mind directness."

"Still, I am sure you find it unusual."

"I do not mind that, either. Indeed, I have found almost everything of value in this life to be unusual."

Her smile widens less tentatively, under that same winning tilt of the head, and Herman smiles back. But it may be that their talk is ended. The exchange has flowed steadily and easily; nothing about it is more remarkable than that, once beyond the initial provenance of its taking shape at all. But now they must undertake a more respectable silence.

Herman sips coffee and abides the silence, without endorsing it. He liked the directness better. He cannot help but like her anomalous presence; nothing has tickled him so in years. But what can her presence mean? It is as if she wandered in through the wrong door, or wandered off a nearby stage set.

It could be the case. The explanation. Theatre women are so much freer in the world, and she could easily be in the theatre. Why not be direct, and ask her? Or at least politely introduce himself, and pursue the story piecemeal. So this he does, with the added proviso that she may prefer the silence.

"Sometimes I do," she says, pressing her brown hair back under her hat on one side. "I am Mrs. Andrew Stevenson, born Cora Jackson."

Name, plus maiden name. A deal of information to grant a strange man on an unfashionable backstreet. Herman does in fact find this unusual—not that he disapproves—and he covers his surprise with humor, always his first line of diversion.

"You were Jack's son and he, your husband, was Steven's. So your son is Steven's son, once removed."

"You are ready with a joke, for someone usually so solemn of expression. But the boy you saw is not my son—"

Direct indeed. Apparently this woman will say anything. Despite an air of perfect respectability, she places no limits upon her utterance.

And she makes no bones. Herman is plainly presumed to have noticed her on the earlier occasions and presumed to have noticed the boy, whereas he had been speaking only in jest, and generically, about sons, wishing to be altogether unpresumptuous. No flim-flam-flummery from this one!

"—he is my nephew," she elaborates, without hesitation. "My sister's son, Patrick."

"A handsome boy," says Herman, though he cannot recall the boy's appearance. "You are not afraid to bring him here?"

"Afraid?"

"I do not mind it, understand. I very well like it, as a matter of fact. But I do suppose that most ladies would be afraid, yes."

She shrugs. "I have no fear of thieves, since I have no money. And no fear of murder in broad daylight, when even the stevedores appear more or less sober."

"And no fear for Mr. Stevenson's peace of mind, when you roam forth into raffish ports of call? Not that I mind it, understand."

"You very well like it, as a matter of fact."

"You *are* a well-soldered ship, ain't you, Mrs. Stevenson!"

Another shrug, and a little smile. What does the little smile mean? That her directness (and now her satirical streak) come to her so naturally that they are beyond conventional judgment, for better or worse? But there is more.

"My late husband Andrew was never averse to my breathing God's air. So I breathe it conscience free."

"And duty free as well!" Herman bursts out. "We at the Port of New York can surely see to that. We shall pass along the air to you, without the *ad valorem*."

Can he call a halt to this remarkable conversation? His bumper is still half full—he has been so busy talking—but he stands. The reference to the District has alerted him to the time. Even the reprobates have gone back to their stations.

"I believe with you, Mrs. Stevenson—believe it strongly at this moment—and I have said so many times, that men are jailors of themselves. And women, of course, even moreso."

"I hope you do not think ill of me. I know that I am too outspoken."

"Au contraire, I guarantee you. But my fish-eyed friends, who generally make a religion of tardiness, have already gone back to work. You will be all right here on your own?"

"Thank you, yes."

"Then I bequeath the table," he bows, lifting a pantomime hat with his right hand, just enough flustered not to know that his actual hat is in his left hand at the moment. "But do not be trusting of every man," he cautions. "Only the vintaged few."

This was a most amusing encounter, and not one pin-shrimp less so for all Will Barclay's teasing. Herman is perfectly aware of his reputation. He knows what they think, though they may not say it. And he knows what they say, though he may not hear it.

It is a mixed reputation, in fact. On the credit side, he is accounted a good enough fellow: witty, sturdy, and no teetotaller. On the debit side, however, he does tend to be capable, punctual, and absurdly incorrupt. It is only because he imposes none of these three weaknesses on his colleagues (and will never rat them out) that Herman survives their critical gaze.

Mister Do Right. That was his undivulged nickname at the Gansevoort District, bestowed by that fine young serpent Highgas. He feigned ignorance of the joke until the very day of his transfer uptown. "Be sure and watch your back now, Mister Do Wrong," he bade farewell to Highgas, and watched the fellow's face drop to the floor and bounce three times.

"What was she after, Herman?" says Beasley Crouch, for by now the whole battalion has come in for a piece. "That is the question: what's she want?"

"Love and money, like them all," says Parkinson. The youngest man in the office at twenty-four, he is perfectly comfortable airing out his cynical surmises.

"If that's the case, then what's she want with Herman!"

"Ignore these chowderheads," says Barclay, though he is the one who has brought them back the story. "But go careful. She does hang about like a buzzard, this one. I've seen her more than once."

"Fear not, William. I am old, but not yet carrion."

This edgy ribbing, kept within bounds, only adds to the day's amusement. It provides some comic relief from the heat, and there is something youthful in it today that makes Herman feel as far from carrion as can be.

Later on, when the hearties of the Custom House scatter south and west, Herman's thoughts return to the widow. Was she in the theatre? He had forgotten to ask. Might she have taken some drink? That might account for it, too—a wide flask of pisco to put her poor widowed head in a loose consoling spin. Who can say she won't reappear on Fenton's battered bricks and stand off sober, with her nostrils in the wind like a proud thoroughbred racehorse?

What you must always remember to expect of life, Herman reminds himself over a glass on Madison Square, is the unexpected. He shares this pearl with Robert, who is on duty at Aiken's Garden at this hour. Like all New York waiters, Robert has a quick firm grasp. "So do you think we will awake to frost on the windows?" he grins, as he sets down a second glass.

"Three feet of snow upon your stoop, Robert—unless, of course, you expect it."

The house is worse than empty. Nothing wrong with empty. But to help him out in her absence, Lizzie has engaged a silent old woman to "straighten up" twice a week.

What this translates to, in practice, is everything lost, misplaced, or casually tossed out with the trash. The matches are hidden somewhere, the morning newspaper (half read) has been used to wash the windows, and the brandy is fully decanted—for cleaning fluid, no doubt! This inexhaustible agent of disorder even hides the coffee beans. *But where? A nice month-long treasure hunt she makes us, in all meridians.*

Upstairs, the desk! The harridan has had particular instructions not to lay a hand, not to lay a strip of breath on it. Do we conclude the desk was wracked by high winds, which blew these papers from under the paperweight? Blew a dozen pagemarked volumes back onto the shelves, in random order? The old dear is thorough, by God.

Dear Lizzie, in her wisdom. Here I am, over-warm and overworked, and ever over-tilted toward despond in her iconography, and so she makes me this little game. You never smile, she says. She will say it when I'm jolly as a beachcomber in his cups, and smiling Mississippi-wide. I can place on display more teeth than you find in a cannibal's necklace, and still she will find me sombre.

But wait, so did Mrs. Stevenson (née Jackson) say it this morning at the Best & Freshest. You are a joker, she said, for someone

*more generally sombre. Or solemn. Sombre or solemn? Well, they
are only a little different. Hark ye, though, that she makes a "generally" (or was it a "usually"?) upon our first acquaintance. She has
got me out in cameo, with caption and description.*

*Is my smile invisible at home and abroad? I launch it yet it does
not sail? Or perhaps the case is more akin to the problem of portrait
photography, that odd confrontation with oneself wherein appears
the visage of a stranger grimacing in pain, two fists whiteknuckled
on the antimacassar. And where went the gay and frolicsome fellow
who so recently sat to make his charmful pose?*

Can it be she? Yes, without a doubt it is she; and why
should it not be? Mrs. Stevenson raking through a crate of
onions on 72nd Street, at First Avenue. *(Gleaming in coruscant
skins—incandescent in their bins . . .)* Herman stops and observes her quest for the perfect specimen.

The costermonger observes her too. Suspiciously? No, fa-
miliarly, for it seems they are old friends, on a names basis.
He is quick to congratulate her now on her prizewinning
bulb. It is the very one to have, and surely she will also
want some Maine potatoes, down on the morning train from
Aroostook County, or a quart of his new strawberries?

Mrs. Stevenson seems content with the onion. It stands
alone, it is supreme. "Strawberries tomorrow," she says,
with a sudden unguarded smile, as she accepts her penny
change. Her smile is pretty and so is she; prettier by far from
a distance. Graceful and slim in a forest green dress, a small
black bonnet with forest green trim. Her hair is the color of
tung-rubbed oak and her cheeks, brightened by the heat, set
off the hazel eyes. She must be a bright picture indeed if
Herman, with his eyesight, can take her in detail from
forty feet.

Questions occur to him, as she turns, her small purse and
string bag in hand. Has he passed her in the street a dozen
times (as would now seem likely) but never noticed her in

her anonymity? Or might their vectors be intersecting for
the very first time, making this an occasion of fate, or at
least benign coincidence?

What to do, is the real question. Should he race to catch
up with her and create an accidental hello, or should he turn
away, to avoid an awkward moment? But she has seen him.
He fiddles with his tobacco pouch, while quickly considering
the social parameters. She cannot hail and wave—not even
Mrs. Stevenson will take that liberty—so the burden of ac-
knowledgement falls to Herman.

He offers an exaggerated bow, his reflexive jest on polite
formalities, in keeping with their banter. And now she is free
to wave, and fix her head briefly to that characteristic angle.
Such a charming gesture, if indefinably so. Something is
achieved by it that could never be contrived.

The impasse has been managed. Mrs. Stevenson starts
across the avenue and Herman resumes his southerly course.
(Aiken's for sure, he is thinking now.)

When they spoke at length, the week before last, it had
been such a nice diversion that Herman had revisited it more
than once in his aftermusings. Then Sam Shaw had passed
through town, and Abe and Kate Lansing came down for
two dinners, and the widow's gay soprano voice receded,
her striking face faded a little from his recollection.

This time, though, on the strength of a brief and speechless
encounter, he has her firmly imprinted. Perhaps it was the
green dress in concert with the light brown hair; perhaps it
was distance that enhanced the image. But she is ineradicable
now, her features burned onto the innermost film.

In the District, and at Fenton's, he has taken to looking
for her. Not in any significant way; not with any purpose in
mind. But since the day they waved hello, he has consciously
allowed for the possibility they might wave (or talk) again.

Put it another way. When the unexpected Mrs. Stevenson
does appear at Fenton's Best & Freshest several days later,

she is not so unexpected. Herman heads straight for her table, and mimics his 72nd Street salaam.

"Once more you materialize, from the heavens."

"Only from 69th Street, I am afraid."

"If you do not find it overly direct, I will apply for that empty chair—being fully vintaged as I am, and harmless."

"Please." She watches him settle in before delivering a line she has rehearsed: "I should confess that I know who you are."

"Even as I know who you are, recalling our introductions of some weeks past."

"I meant that I recognized your name. I am a reader."

"I have seen you be a reader," he says. "It was a small volume—pale cow, with a red and white diamondback spine. Not Tennyson's poems, by any chance?"

"By no chance," she laughs.

"Oh? Do you dislike Tennyson?"

"Only his poems. Tennyson himself I have never met. But how interesting that you notice these details, while appearing to be so oblivious."

"I do notice books," he says, after a short pause. He is getting used to her, and to her candor. "Some say it is a disease I have. Now you, Mrs. Stevenson, are such a noticer of things that it seems you have noticed me *not* noticing them."

"Appearing not to notice, is what I said. That is the interesting part of it."

One summer evening on the Square, years ago, Herman chanced to take a bench facing two ladies and at once a miraculous freshet of talk had opened. At first he had them for nuns—or witches, in their black cloaks and cowls—but they proved a pair of cheery spinsters, and under no vow of silence. The talk went effortlessly back and forth for two jolly hours that night; there was a compatibility at conversation among them. Such natural connections do occur, and another such has apparently occurred between Herman and Mrs. Stevenson. But the spinsters came two by two to a public square, not solo to the rugged heights.

"Your friends—"

"Colleagues," he says.

"Your colleagues, then. They are also skillful at pretending not to notice. But I imagine they make judgments."

"They are hardly worth your worry, mademoiselle."

"My interest, though. I wonder, do they say I am—"

"What?"

"You know. . . ."

"I assure you, they do not. Even my addled colleagues can observe that you are educated."

"No more so than thousands of idle women, who have no way to earn a dollar. Were it not for my dear sister, and her husband Jack, I would be very hard pressed and quite alone in the world."

"Your being alone is a tragic accident. But I do congratulate you on any idleness you may have procured. To be at leisure is to be free."

"I am not so much at leisure, or idle, as I am unpaid. Unpaid in dollars, I should say, since I am amply rewarded. I help with my sister's household, and I have helped Jack with his figures at the shop. I have also given some lessons."

"Sounds well worth a dollar to me. Not penmanship lessons, by chance?"

"Sums," she shrugs. "I am good with numbers."

"I have done a round of penmanship lessons, with a tutor considerably less extroverted than yourself. Until he gave me his bill, I thought the man might be altogether mute."

"Then how does he impart the lessons?"

"By example, and through repetition. You do it wrong, he rips it from your hand and does it right—then you try again. And the page goes back and forth between us until my fists are ink. Not his, however. They remain as white as hotel linen. But oh my tails and loops, Mrs. Stevenson, the man will press his point on you by suppertime."

"It is impressive that you sign on for lessons. All of your accomplishments aside, you are older than most of those who go to school."

"Oh, I am older than most of those who are dead."

"You seem so young. So playful when you are not so solemn."

"That is nice to say. It may be that you bring out the youthful side of a person, Mrs. Stevenson. Truly, you leave little room for any other sides."

She laughs, a quiet inward laughter, and reaches for her coffee cup, momentarily arresting the rush of their repartee. Their sallies have such a breathless quality that it seems any slight cessation might risk the continuum. But no, as Herman now unfurls what is for him a virtual stump speech, not another mere sally:

"Do you know, Mrs. Stevenson, I have come to Fenton's Best & Freshest most every working day for five years. Sometimes I sit with my infamous colleagues and sometimes I sit alone—wearing a face that I gather must appear solemn, and neglecting to notice all movement and color around me—and think the least utilitarian thoughts I can manage, I assure you, while sipping my best and freshest. And now you come along to tell me that this behavior has met with your approval. I can only say, by way of closing out this overwinded description of improbability, that I am left speechless."

"All evidence to the contrary!"

Herman can only bow once more: bested, and happily so. "You are one of a kind, mademoiselle."

"So are we all, no?"

"Jones' Wood is gone, I know, but there are plenty of rough spots in this neighborhood. Shanty blocks, muddy prospects, drunkards. Admit you are one of a kind hereabouts."

"Over time, I am sure you would see me clearly, for the very ordinary person that I am."

"What if not, however? What if the heavens fetch you back before I can manage to see you clearly?"

"Given your gifts, perhaps you could just imagine me."

"But who could imagine you *ordinary?*"

August had begun with a relay of subtropical downpours. At first this was welcome rainfall: filling the Croton Reservoir, cooling down the streets, rinsing the fetid slop and grime. But it has continued on day after day until everyone has had enough of damp suits and shoes, everyone has seen enough of the saturated rats on Bowling Green.

The luckiest, Herman among them, go away on vacation, hoping for clearer skies in the Catskills, the Adirondacks, the White Mountains, and the Green. Blue aloft and the sweetest air afloat: such has been the weather report from Lizzie at Jefferson Hill, and Herman would like to see it for himself. At the moment, though, he is peering out through the boathouse window, watching the rain as it pelts the deckboards of the steamship *Bristol*.

The *Bristol* goes close to four hundred feet. She is the largest wood-hull boat plying the Sound and the gaudiest, with lavender paddles and smokestacks yellow as nasturtiums. As he waits to board her, Herman's mood is dreamy; the rain a little mesmerizing. Those suffocating July days at the District are already a dream to him, a wisp of smoke. Until the time of his forced re-entry, the District will not occur for one second in his thoughts—apart, possibly, from the widow Stevenson, who might be called a dream herself. Though she may very well occur in his thoughts, Herman is extremely doubtful of seeing her again—doubtful at times he has seen her at all! He may have been hallucinating.

A woman ruled by candor, even on casual acquaintance? A woman who would uncover her personality as recklessly as a Nuka Hiva maiden uncovers her limbs? *Landmaid and mermaid, with intent to uncover intention: to be knowable, this way or that.* Hallucination and recollection blur a bit, in the gray blur of this blowing rain, for he is imagining Faywa now, not the widow: he is imagining reality!

Fay, with her soft brown feet, the blunt comical toes spread apart like fingers. Wringing out her veil of hair, with nothing on her maple-butter skin but the salt-water and strings of tapa. How heedlessly she looks us flush in the eye, laughingly looks us up and down, as if to say this dance of male and female could not be rendered any more simple or direct.

Herman envisions the curve of pink-white sand, and the girls filled with their tropical laughing gas. Giggling as they dive into the surf, giggling as they climb the bobstays and fling themselves on board. *Can it really be forty years ago?*

An hour out, he is still staring through the rain as it disappears steadily into the waves of Long Island Sound. When he hears the dinner gong, he realizes he is starving. Has not had one bite to eat since breakfast.

They seat him beneath a dangerous chandelier—a hundred chunks of cut-glass dangling over a carpet broad as a cornfield. To the clatter of plates and trays, to the romantic weep of a violincello, he eats his lamb chops and vegetables.

He picks up scraps of talk on all sides. The roast beef is tender; the better ships have by now been fitted out with electric lights; the severe heat is due to return. To refresh himself pre-emptive against the returning heat, Herman calls for a cool drought of punch, and takes it with him back to the taff-rail.

No heat yet, however. More of this Newfoundland weather, a cold blowing mist to soak your beard. The land is close by—visible, but poorly defined. A phantom land, that may yet prove to be a fogbank. No trees, no buildings, no movement discernible: only the hulking mass.

Boldness. She shares a boldness with those island nymphets, as she shares it with dear departed Sarah. There are females who will act; who are willing to live. *Only a female of that tribe will try the likes of me, after all. Only the sort that come swimming right up to the boat.* How many times has he stood by in passive futility and watched a lovely woman—watched her come and watched her go—yet stood paralyzed and wordless?

The woman in Taloo, the English beauty Mrs. Bell, so commanding in the bridle path. Now there is a picture imprinted forever, forty years or no forty years. Oh I snapped my shutter, but meanwhile the cat had got my tongue.

Or that day in leaky old Venice, my lamp-eyed balcony Venus, imploring me in frescoed faded sunlight! But what is a man to do? Leap from his gondola and climb the drain-pipes? Shout out frantically, "I see you coming and I like what I see!" Are there men who allow themselves to behave that way?

There are. There was the Doctor, for one. Oh most definitely the Doctor. He must have behaved that way a hundred times, and won the day at least a dozen. Nothing ventured, nothing gained, the Doctor would pronounce, when faced with defeat.

But have you no shame, I would thunder at him—and soon enough we both were roaring with mirth. For to him the answer was obvious: what is shame? Why is it shameful to speak the truth? Must we take on silly airs (dignified, upright, eyes avert) that dogs and grizzly bears disdain?

Yet we must. Or I must, whysomedever. Once in a quarter century, then, by astrophysical chance (so many meteorites circling and falling), a lone bold creature may come crashing down upon our decks. And I stand paralyzed and wordless. I ain't the Doctor, after all, nor even the stripling that once stood beside him. New York ain't the South Seas, either, 'tis a different kettle of fishes for sure.

★

Without light, it is not so easy to reckon time. The wash of the sea constant, rain driving on the planks, the shipboard clamor faint but steady. (Floated voices, piano chords, the squeak and grind of the ship's equipage.) To the north, coastal lights glow faintly. Mystic? Westerly? Or it could be Narragansett.

Eight o'clock? Not that it matters, really. He could take out his watch, if it did.

It occurs to him now—Westerly? Narragansett?—that these weeks upcoming may well be subdivided into two compartments, his vacation a sort of Saratoga trunk, with two broad drawers to stow all gear. Into the topmost drawer will go the visible, the expected, the approved—all those moments assigned to the category Well Earned Rest. Outings and palaver with Brother Hoadley; cigars, wine, whiskey, and punch with Hoadley; a duffel full of pleasure texts to read. What else? The matchless air, the mountain alembic— and Lizzie. Lizzie and the ladies, to be sure.

Time will pass too quickly, the ides of August will loom a rocky shoal in his narrow sea of restfulness. A vacation, by the very word, bespeaks its own inadequacy, for it is a tiny minority of time, just enough of freedom to whet the appetite for more.

The lower drawer may change that, however. It may even make the time seem long, and slow in passing. That will be interesting to see. For into this invisible whisket (let us entitle it, after her own suggestion, "Imagining Mrs. Stevenson") will go some other moments, now foreseeable. Tedious blankfaced mornings, stilly endless afternoons, yawning suppers. There will be moments, hours, when he might gladly leave this long-awaited, well-earned rest behind him!

He is surprised to learn this, standing dogwatch in the brackish downpour. The widow intrigues him, and the task of imagining her, so lightheartedly assigned on the East River promontory, has begun far sooner than they had jokingly speculated.

At Fall River, the *Bristol* glides into its berth and the gang-ways are thrown. Passengers are herded gently onto the short-track cars like quiet, sleepy sheep.

Herman is so damp and bone-weary that the ninety-minute run to Boston feels like two nights in the brig. By the time they change trains in Back Bay Station, all questions of time have been settled. It may be ten minutes of two, or two minutes of ten; it is time for bed regardless.

He drops the latch, draws the curtain, and stretches himself to the limit—a limit sternly imposed, for these bunks are made for midgets. He adjusts the small hard pillow, at-tempting (without success) to make it bigger, or softer. No matter, he will sleep. He is cramped and hungry, but just hungry enough to savor the prospect of a large breakfast tomorrow on Jefferson Hill. And not so cramped as to delay this first sweet chapter of Well Earned Rest. . . .

With his characteristic blend of concern and amusement, John Hoadley oversees Herman's descent into the uphol-stered chair. He has told his brother-in-law how this process must strike a random spectator, for the expression on Her-man's face is like that of a man surrendering his papers to the prison warden, at the gate. No one would surmise that the man was surrendering instead to the luxury of a roast pork dinner with fresh picked summer greens, rinsed down by a crisp humming ale.

Not exactly torture, though it has for Herman one in-tensely torturesome aspect. For the next two hours, he will not be free to walk about. Herman is looking very well, however, even Lizzie has admitted as much. One week ago, when he stepped off the New Hampshire Special to begin his vacation, he looked old, gray, and dyspeptic. His entire first day he spent posing as furniture on the hotel piazza.

That was all it took. By the second day, he was the dynamo he could so abruptly become. He dragged Hoadley all the way around the lake (for it would never do to see only half) and then around again to firm up the experience. The old appetites were fully restored, for rambling, highminded talk, beef and ale, cigars and brandy. In very short order, Herman had juvenesced from the graying sexagenarian to the tireless, sea-parting leviathan..

But now, for two hours of family dinner, he was leviathan among the pinfish; leviathan quiescent, in the hotel dining room.

"We have a secret for you, dear Kate," says Lizzie to her sister-in-law, Kate Hoadley. "You must try and guess it."

Kate cannot begin to guess the secret, but she is one of those who do like to work at it, to puzzle it through. "Has it something to do with the dinner? The menu?"

"Not a thing."

"Is it something I can see?"

"Oh, you are seeing it. Bessie and I are both involved, that is a clue. You must look to us both, to see it properly."

Kate looks to them both and fails to see a thing, other than them both. John Hoadley wears his affectionate smile like a necktie. Herman steadily assails his soup.

"Let Father help to guess," says Bessie.

"Leave Father alone," says Lizzie. "Kate must solve it on her own."

"You and Bessie both? Maybe I should give up."

Kate is not permitted to give up so quickly. More clues are supplied. The secret is in stripes, yet also in solids. It has been remade. And it was a gift to them both from Kate herself.

"From me?"

Hoadley tries to catch Herman's eye with a sympathetic wink, but Herman's eye is fixed upon the chandelier and squinting hard, as though he begins to see in that marvelous

twelve-candle fixture some of Heaven's own secrets. Secrets
that had resided in the shallow soup, until that tide ran out.
John is thinking, on Herman's behalf, that they have nearly
made it to the main dishes.

"All right, you ninny, we'll tell. It's our dresses. Don't
you recognize them?"

"No, Lizzie. Should I?"

"Of course you should. You sent the lawn dress to me just
this past fall. They are both your gifts, dear."

"You have altered them so wonderfully."

"The trim on the grenadine is completely new."

"They look better than new. I am so glad you took them
on. Charlotte and Maria will never wear anything that has
been worn by another human being. They are so stubborn
that way."

"And every other way!" says Hoadley, laughing at the
thought of his willful daughters.

"You are right, John. They all are, aren't they?"

"They," says Herman, "are *We.* Always remember that,
dear Kate."

"They are we, Herman? Please do explain."

"The so-called mature are only the immature under cover
of time. If they are all stubborn, then so are we, in slightly
more artful ways."

"But no, dear brother, for *we* are all sensible, flexible, and
charitable to a fault."

"An excellent answer," says Lizzie. "Or will Herman be
too stubborn to yield the point?"

"Certainly not. I was merely airing my palate in between
courses, and agree with all that has been alleged by my
sister."

Here he performs his miniature smile (a tiny white bird
flitting inside the voluminous shrubbery of his beard) and
returns to the business of eating. The talk passes safely on
from dresses or the moods of children to speculation upon

larger matters of state, like the weather, and their fellow Plaisted House guests.

John and Herman exchange a brief glance, the meaning of which is clear between these brothers-in-law, who are fond of one another. At every family gathering, according to John, Herman will make a single foray into the conversation. Whether as a penance, the price of his supper, or merely by way of airing his palate between courses: one and only one social foray. And now he has made it.

"Is this the slowest-moving waiter on earth?" says Bessie, in her intemperate style.

"Quietly," says Lizzie, in her rectifying style.

"Yes, dear niece," smiles Hoadley. "After all, the poor fellow may have an injury, a war wound, to contend with."

"War wound! I vote we stick a pin in him to see if he is still among the living."

"Here," says Herman—and he winks at John, to mark this secondary foray. "I got one. I'll stick him."

"Herman!"

"That's the trouble with Father. The waiter is so slow that Father drinks twice what he ought—and then he is ready with a *pin*."

"Bessie: respect."

"After all, Bess, the pin is your idea," says Kate. "And there he is now, organizing the dessert tray. A sweet will placate everyone."

"Placate?" says Lizzie. "But the entire meal has been delightful. I love roasted potatoes. Bessie will agree that the food has been excellent?"

"Yes, Mother. The drink has been excellent, too."

"Please?"

"What do you think, Uncle John, of the food and drink?"

"I think them uniformly fine, dear niece. I also persist in believing our waiter a pleasant hardworking fellow, who bears up bravely under the onus of his war wounds. When I said grace, my darling Bess, I meant it sincerely."

"A good answer, John," says Lizzie, and the trivial contretemps would appear to be at an end. For of course John Hoadley has beamed on Bessie with soft avuncular affection, to cushion even his gentle jokes. He knows, as everybody does, that Bessie can be indelicate and contentious. ("What disturbs me," Herman told him once, "is not the question of delicacy or manners, but of that ill will she bears. She takes no *pleasure* from her irreverence.")

"Thank you, Uncle," says Bessie. But she is not yet prepared to let it go. "And what does Father think?"

"Leave Father be," says Lizzie, as eager to leave Herman inside his quiet cave as Bessie is to bait him out.

"Actually," says Herman, quaffing ale for emphasis, setting down his mug with a thump for punctuation, "I was trying to imagine what Mrs. Stevenson would think."

It is hardly infrequent within the family circle that a remark from Herman will stop the conversation in its tracks. He does sometimes appear to speak in riddles, or to belittle others with his private jokes. And sometimes, too, the family must choose between pursuing in good faith such nonsense as Herman has broached, or calling it nonsense and dismissing it outright, returning without him to the subject at hand.

"Who the deuce is Mrs. Stevenson?" says Kate. "Is she the tall one, who dresses like a man? Not that I get the joke, in any case."

"Oh, you won't get it," says Lizzie. "The joke will be on you, if you follow your brother down the primrose path. Do you know that once, in Pittsfield, he pointed out an elegant lady and told me she was the Countess Kerensky, of Russian nobility. This was someone new to the village, you understand, on whom I promptly paid a call. Brought her a pie and some of our apples, and greeted her by name, of course. The poor lady looked at me as if I had come straight through the madhouse gate to her door. 'Countess?' she said. 'Whatever makes you call me Countess? My name is Mrs. Smith.'"

"A wonderful story, and wonderfully told," says Hoadley, neglecting to mention that it is a recurring story, which he has heard Lizzie tell half a dozen times.

"It is simply a true story, John. And it may make for a good story at dinner, but it did not make for a pleasant moment at the time."

"I know what Mrs. Stevenson would think," Bessie suddenly declares, persisting on the primrose path.

"Is she the one in the suit?" says Kate.

"Mrs. Stevenson would think that my father has grown terribly bored with us all, and wished to say so in some roundabout way."

"Bessie!"

"No, that's all right, dear," says Herman. "Bessie's all right." A third foray? It could almost, by now, be labelled something else entirely—less a series of brief strikes into the social sphere than a casual outright participation. Hoadley is delighted to see it, though his delight is leavened, through long experience, by a mild distress as to its origins and its eventual outcome. "It is not such a terrible charge to bring. The charge of boredom."

"We ought not be bringing any charges at the dinner table," says Lizzie.

"Do you confess that you are bored with us, Father?"

"Not in the least, Bessie dear. I am never bored, for boredom must always derive from within."

"Oh must it?" says Kate, with an ironic smile.

"Look," says Lizzie, turning. "The dessert tray is coming around. I think I'll try the molasses sponge tonight."

On the stone-dust lane that skirts the hotel entrance, the Plaisted House carriage stands empty behind two stout mares, as still as houses. Between the lane and the piazza are roses, holly, and honeysuckle—a profusion of vine, leaf, and flower twining up through the soldiered balusters.

Herman and John slump comfortably in cushioned wicker settees. Above them, on the second storey verandah, two couples who have overflowed from the ballroom are waltzing politely, to Strauss. The music sifts down, faint and agreeable.

"A clear thought, what you said at dinner. It is true that all boredom must be the responsibility of the individual."

"Of course it's true, my good young man. Why else say it?"

"You have been known to tease."

"Never my ladies," says Herman.

"Your ladies were in good form tonight, I thought."

"They flourish here. Bessie has so much less discomfort. With Lizzie, it is a case of much less Herman."

"You flourish here, too," says Hoadley, letting the last remark go unremarked. "The air has done yourself some good."

"It has done the trick, most pleasantly. I am without care, utterly. On vacation, thoroughly. These my adverbs."

"A most contented-sounding group."

Herman traces a hieroglyph of cigar smoke beneath the paper lanterns. "Kate seems well," he says.

"Always. Such a good nature. And she does love the summertime."

"Kate is of the happy party. She has the gift of simplicity."

"Careful now, old man."

"No irony, John. It is a sincere compliment. I have always envied Kate."

"And she has looked up to you."

"She was just a pretty child when I first went out to work in the world. Kate and Allan would lie together on the bench in Lansingborough—point to point, we used to say, with their two heads touching. Thoughts could travel back and forth between them without the blundering inconvenience of words."

"They are very close, to this day."

"Kate was always happy. I doubt she has ever considered there might be an alternative to happiness."

"Maybe that's the whole trick."

"If your luck holds, it is. And Kate's luck certainly held firm when young Mr. Hoadley came a-courting."

"That's enough butter and sugar. Truthfully, Herman, were you not just slightly bored with all the talk of dresses, and desserts?"

"No, John, I believe in dresses. The alternative there, apart from the unthinkable, is tattooed skin and tapa, which would never do for the pallid race."

"Clearly not."

"And you know how strongly, how unwaveringly, I have always believed in dessert."

"What I know, is that I will never in my life score a point debating you. You'll change the subject, change the rules, obscure all goals—"

"But I am without goals. Without cares. On vacation, exclusively."

"Tell me, have you done some good scribbling?"

"Oho, you had me fooled. A week of respectable silence had me convinced you were cured of asking."

"I did wait a respectable time. And even now," Hoadley grins, "I ask only in passing."

"Skillfully managed, brother—far more skillful than anything I have managed to get onto paper of late. The truth is too simple, John. I am lazy, and have rarely in my life been anything but lazy."

"Ten books in ten years is hardly lazy."

"Yes, but ten in fifty years is a different percent!"

"At least say twelve. You want to stay mathematically accurate, when you are speaking with an engineer."

"Kind of you to include the verse. In those years where I was not lazy, I could never have told you *why* I was not—nor how I came to be so energized. I got going from going, and then I kept going. In keeping with Newtonian physics, I suppose, mine engineer."

"Thank God for Newtonian physics, then."

"What about your self, John? How goes it at the ironworks?"

"It goes, as ever. The same problems, same solutions, day by week."

"The business continues to flourish under your brilliant stewardship. That is your response?"

"That is your transliteration of my response. It goes well, yes. It is simply not work that matters, as you know."

"On the contrary, I am as ignorant as a newborn Hindoo on the matter of what matters. I would have guessed the creation of a Congregationalist Church would matter to the Congregationalists, at a minimum. Or that the waterworks at Ashley is a works that matters to one and all, in Ashley."

"These are tasks that any trained man could do. If I collapsed at breakfast, someone else would take charge. Whereas your work—"

"A bit of addition and subtraction, plus the endless transcribing of lists. I am confident we could find a soul to spell me, should I stay anchored to this sofa from here to eternity."

"That is not the work I meant, as you are perfectly well aware. But come to that, Herman, how goes it at the uptown District?"

"Fine, fine. Did I ever mention that after the transfer I would sometimes go in the wrong direction? Once I got as far as 12th Street. I was wandering in that forest of stanchions below the elevated, before I realized what I'd done."

"You were absorbed in higher thought."

"Naturally I was. Destinies and destinations. But tomorrow, John," (and here again he sketches in smoke against the sky) "we will turn to higher thoughts together. The highest, in fact, for we shall get the Jefferson summit by noon."

"You may need to carry me up that last half mile," says John, clapping Herman on the shoulder, a block of beef he finds as firm as a steelworker's."

"Barkis is willin', brother," grins Herman, who is only one year younger than John. "I'll carry you up, if you'll carry me back down."

Every morning a haze and heavy dew; by noon a bold sun blaring out of a limitless blue; then clear and cool by starlight. These are perfect days for vagabondage, perfect nights for well-earned rest.

Herman slips up one day, snoozing his way from lunch to supper, with no better excuse than the rich comfort of yielding to a delicious sleep. ("It shows the way age comes on us," he reports. "Not all at once, entire, but in patches unpredictable.") In general, he does not care for age, or sleep, or stasis. He is on the move, too relentlessly so for the taste of his close contemporary.

"You make a religion of motion," Hoadley tells him.

"I do believe in it."

"You need Sam Shaw to keep up with you. Or Henry Thomas. Isn't Henry coming up tomorrow?"

Henry is, and Herman's only son-in-law will be very welcome when he does. But Hoadley is Herman's first choice and they keep on the go, in summer shirtsleeves and beards of salt and pepper. Off to ride the lake steamer, to trek the Kancamangus, to recline upon schist-rich summits, taking what Herman calls the Pisgah view.

"Biblical," he explains, atop Mount Jefferson. "Looking down on the Promised Land."

"Understood, brother, you have put it in a book. Or don't you realize?"

Does Herman realize? He will not mention the books. Never acknowledge the fact of them, other than with John. If asked to provide a look at one, by an acquaintance or a chance letter, he will regret to say he has no copy in hand of the title in question.

To John, who has proved so kind for so long in this regard, so convinced of the worth in those books, he acknowledges something more is owed. No need to probe too deep with John, however. A sound reader, he has neither the quick wit of Duyckinck nor the fathomless soul of Hawthorne. He won't complain you have split your infinitive, nor clamor that you have tapped the heartroot of all epistemology. He just tells you how fine it all is.

No, he is not a critic, and his good news cannot be gospel. But the Hoadley approbation, as Herman calls it, when weighted against the world's opprobrium, can yet be a bromide. It steals on you as pleasantly as a nap in the sun. For all one's admiration of Nathaniel Hawthorne, one was rarely comfortable in the man's house. Engaged, enriched, enthralled; but never for a moment comfortable. With Hoadley, one is never uncomfortable.

"John, I feel we have achieved the ultimate, here on Pisgah. That which you have so long labored for and sought."

"Why do I sense a joke coming my way?"

"Better a joke than an arrow, soldier!" They are warm despite a thirty-five mile wind across the rock face, that ruffles even the tightclinging jack-pine. "I was thinking, as I often do, of your illustrious tri-partite agency—"

"You're too late, man. I have resigned."

"Surely not. All three parts?"

An old favorite, this one. For a decade, John has served on the Massachusetts Board of Health, Lunacy, & Charity— an agency so wondrously denominated that Herman, who cares less than zero for political trivia, is forever demanding to hear the minutes of each Board meeting.

"Necessarily. Resign one and you resign all. It is only one committee."

"Under God. Indivisible."

"Yes. And ten years of it was enough for me. *Meetings.*"

"And more meetings to discuss the meetings."

"Precisely. I am afraid my Charity came to an end."

"Still, we can raise a toast tonight to the remaining branches. To Health, and to Lunacy."

"You will start the ladies, for sure."

"I will tell them of our success. How we together, here on Mount Pisgah, achieved the trinity. I, without dispute, the Lunacy; you, despite your protests, the Charity; and both of us this crowing good Health."

"I only hope we feel half so ripe and crowing when we have made it back to base. *If* we make it."

"Place your trust in gravity, my hearty engineer, we will make it back."

For two weeks, New York has been eclipsed. Against his own expectations, with very few exceptions, Herman has failed to mount his comical program of Imagining Mrs. Stevenson. Out of sight, out of mind?

Even now, at the end of his freshening on Jefferson Hill, his picture of home is more the cluttered desk on 26th Street, where his beloved, arbitrary chores are ganged in a most disorderly order. He knows which stubmarked interlineated volumes are stacked upon the back acre of that desk; knows the sailor poems are under the tobacco tin (with the tiny inlaid compass) and the Burgundy vignettes are under the marble paperweight. He could map the layout of those delicate muntins on the bookcase doors and cite each volume behind the squares of warping glass, three vital rows of precious reference.

That he cannot work here, in the country, is established fact. There is sanctum against the heat, but no sanctorum from the quotidian world, nor from mountain prospects and mountains of food; and no way, truthfully, to nudge a weary brain. He needed rest and he has taken that rest, as per Doctor Lizzie's orders.

Lizzie does not like walking and Herman never sits for long. This is understood between them, so there is little sense plotting mutual agendas at the start of a day. Today, for example, Herman has covered ten miles (and not one step of it over level ground) while Lizzie has visited on the hotel grounds with Herman's sister Catherine Hoadley, his cousin Catherine Lansing, and Catherine Bogart—Tom's Kate, just arrived.

But today also marks an end to vacation. Herman goes back to New York in the morning and Lizzie, after a stop or two, goes on to her siblings, in Boston. So tonight before bedtime, on the balcony outside their second floor suite, they have come together for the summing-up.

"It has been particularly fine this year," she says. "Such heavenly days and nights."

"Literally—if by heaven we refer to the sky."

"Oh we do, Herman. We needn't speculate on St. Peter's gate just now."

In nightdress, robe, and shawl, Lizzie looks old to him tonight. He sees the folds below her jaw, the dessicated lips. But this aging, this physical vulnerability, draws him closer; he is touched by this living portrait of his wife. Touched to think she has gone so far into her life, into their life, and goes dutifully on, missing no chance to *make* it a life. Where he, by contrast, could watch the days die off like so many pine trees cleared from the hillside, like dominoes meaninglessly toppled, one by one by one. . . .

He takes her hand. Here are Lizzie's hands, and here are his own, still there. And with her thick fingers, her broad pan, their hands are not dissimilar.

"A shame that this must end. It does you such a world of good."

"You too, Lizzie. And I have been honored to find that none of your weightier adjectives adhere to mine brow this week. Agitated; distracted; morose?"

"Don't pick fights."

"Not at all, not at all. It has been welcome time, time well spent. Praise Buddha and his white-robed helpers for building us such hills as these, and praise my Lizzie for bringing us so near to their peaks. Oh, and praise your generous frère for footing the bill!"

"Lemuel isn't paying, Herman. That money will go for the new chairs."

"Six of one, half a dozen of the other. But let it rest."

"Yes, rest. That is the point. Though it isn't easy, with these mosquitoes. They aren't supposed to survive this high above the ground."

"They do not like it high and dry."

"Well, they like me, however high or dry I am. Look, six of them on my wrist. Or half a dozen if you prefer, Herman. Not a one on you, I'm sure."

"They know who is the more delectable."

Lizzie, with her copious sufferings at the hand of nature, her negativity. Tonight he feels a closeness from sheer recognition, a familiarity that transmogrifies annoyance into sympathy. It is only Lizzie. And it would not be Lizzie, without the rose fever, the grass allergy, the mosquito conspiracy, plus all the sundry curses of sun and wind and water.

He has depended on her. It is she who has made solid this life of familiarity and families, his strands and hers, so many Kates and Franceses and Elizabeths—not to mention the bright-cheeked tadpole Eleanor who arrived in Henry Thomas' firm paternal hold, blowing a fresh gale of excellent noise. Lizzie has tended to it and given it shape.

The old conflict is still within him, though. He can wish to clasp her hand and, at the same time, wish to shake loose of it completely. Something very like repulsion sits right alongside his affection for her. But that has nothing to do with jowls or lines, with the changes wrought by age. On the contrary, her aging has made him fonder.

When Sarah died, when she wasted away in spite of all the life inside her, Lizzie went to the service without him. Poor Sarah was so emaciated, Lizzie told him afterwards, so terribly withered away. Yet Herman had seen her just one month before, and to him she looked beautiful. A ghost of herself, with large dark eyes in a face drawn gaunt, yet such a beautiful ghost, with her beautiful smile more than intact—enhanced, almost, as a light shining out of the darkness. To look at her was heartbreak, pure and simple.

He would not look at her in a coffin, but he had looked a thousand times in their decade of restitution, and she never seemed to age a day. He made no effort to preserve her image, it was a phenomenon of perception that the Sarah he saw was the Sarah he had loved: dark-eyed, dark-haired, and dark in the grotto. Had she lived, she would be nearly sixty now, yet Herman was sure her skin would be smooth and her hair still black, with those copper highlights in the sun.

"Were you thinking of the baby?" Lizzie says, retrieving her hand, to tighten the shawl at her neck.

"I was, in fact. She is a miraculous find. I was also thinking that we have been side by side forever, you and I. It's why you can read my mind."

Not entirely, of course. Eleanor had been in his thoughts, but from there he had gone on to a rag of a recollection of Sarah. Though it may be a chance nexus, whereby he has Lizzie in his grasp and others on his mind, Herman does incur a moral pinch, some subtle affront to Lizzie in the simultaneity—and more especially now, as Sarah herself gives way to an image of the pretty brown-haired widow, Mrs. Stevenson. Perhaps the notion of youthful hands?

"Thirty-five years, it's true," says Lizzie. "Imagine that."

"Imagine howling!" Herman bursts out, inexplicably, to his wife; as a foxhole, for himself. Lizzie looks quizzical. Up to now, Herman has been unusually balanced, and straightforward.

"Shakespeare," he explains. *"Measure for Measure."*

"Yes?"

"You said, 'Imagine that' and it gave rise to the quotation."

Lizzie smiles and shrugs her shoulders. She is amazed, though, to have an accounting from Herman. Rare indeed, yet possible, apparently, after two weeks in New Hampshire, in a balanced and straightforward state of mind.

Not entirely straightforward, of course. And his accounting does not account for much. Why imagine howling? True that Shakespeare wrote it in a play; true that Herman's older brother Gansevoort recycled it in a memorable letter to Herman, long ago. A corpse is a man (or was one) who must now and forever lie inside the earth. If you can imagine him still a man, the Bard suggests, you can imagine him howling at this outcome.

But the meaning is less in Shakespeare than in Herman's need to obfuscate and procrastinate, for it is Sarah Morewood lying inside the earth, and it is Mrs. Stevenson he now imagines. The bottom compartment has at last slid open!

Mrs. Stevenson wants a new husband, or such is the gospel according to Crouch. Fair enough, why should she not want one? Crouch cannot always be wrong any more than can a broken clock. But now the clock moves, the earth turns, and the brief conjunction of Crouch and truth is severed. Her husband-hunting can have nothing to do with Herman. Apart from the obvious business of loose fish versus fast fish, there is the matter of rotten fish.

"She don't know," allowed Crouch. "She don't see an old salt with an old bride at home. She sees a wage-puller, with a glint in his ancient eye."

Oh doubtful, trusty Crouch. You underestimate the Stevenson perspicacity, from not having experienced firsthand the Stevenson acuity. She pretty well sees what is. Sees therefore an old man, quite taken up with children, grandchildren, and Kates enough to burn or barter. Her current task is to pass the time, and she performs it better than most, that's all.

"Ready?" says Lizzie, straining a mosquito between her thumb and forefinger, then brushing the remains away. She slaps at another one, somewhere back behind her ear. In the dark, his eyes being weak as they are, Herman never sees these insects that assail her. "Or are you still busy imagining, and howling?"

"Has Bessie retired?"

"Very early tonight. She is wisely girding up for travel."

"Yes, good. Ready."

It will be a loss if she should cease to appear. Her advent has been a gift, small and tenuous, yet with a nice flavor to it. It could help to pass our time as well. When January summarily undresses those forlorn saplings right down to their bare locust bones, when there is glare-ice on Simonson's black tarpaulins, would we not prefer seeing Mrs. Stevenson to imagining her?

Yes, is the answer.

Though plenty warm, the city days are no longer oppressive, and the evenings are pleasant. Even so, the *Sun* reports that another twenty thousand souls will leave the city on holiday this week. Perhaps it helps to cool the cobblestones, this transfer of so many human furnaces—98.6 degrees multiplied by 20,000! Will they overheat the hills and boil up the lakes?

It truly seems they have engineered this grand metropolis for the express purpose of leaving it behind. This summer's billboard remedies (Swift's Specific—Seabury's Mustard

Plaster) are deemed insufficient. The citizen must exodus. And it is less and less an exclusively summertime habit, for he will exodus by night as well: to Brooklyn, New Jersey, up the Harlem River, anywhere else. The elseness is all.

Take any given hour of the day in New York and you will find some two hundred trains rolling over a million miles of track. Soon subway trains will roll below the ground, as they do in Paris and already there are elevated trains rolling above our heads. The Sixth Avenue Special, for example: a train that sails through the air, yet has carpeted floors and soft velour seats for the comfort of your backside.

Some contend that the citizen rides because he can ride; he lives away, or goes away simply because the means to do so exist. It is also true that life in the grand metropolis is not so charming as it once was. In Maiden Lane yesterday to see about the new chairs, Herman saw a grotesque tableau of shop signs looming, overlapping, cluttered windows and crowded doorways, wagons pinched in the roadway. Down there, nothing can move anymore.

Even overhead. The prospect overhead at Broadway, Courtland, and Maiden Lane is a schoolboy's science experiment run amok. The telephone has come to join the close-hatched cobwebbery of eccentric wiring, laced and crosslaced from mansard to mansard, so that a densely woven net is cast over the city streets. A cat's cradle. Look up and you can barely see the sky.

But that's downtown. In the uptown District, traffic—and ship traffic in particular—is always slow in August. Some silks came in from the East; there was fuel oil, gold, and sulphur, and a roomful of Italian shoes. Not much. Herman has no aversion to work, but there is very little work to be done.

He leaves an empty house each morning and returns to an empty house each night. When he drinks or dines, he does it solo, apart from his workaday coffees in the District. Thus, the only faces he has been privileged to see this week are those of Barclay, Wilkinson, and Crouch. But one afternoon, a letter is dropped upon his desk. A letter!

Casual as an apple dumpling delivered by your friendly waiter. As though such dumpling-notes arrive routinely. Has Herman ever once had a piece of personal mail, here in the uptown office?

Now had this missive fallen onto Barclay's board, say, the rogues would have been on it like hungry mice. Held it one-eyed to the light, sampled a little steam on the flap, poggled away at the loosest corner. With Herman, the sachem, they are obliged to refrain, and into his pocket it goes—casual as a ferryboat billet, though inwardly he twists on the rack of curiosity. What in the world can it be? It is a note from Mrs. Stevenson, visibly, but what can Mrs. Stevenson *say*, in a note to him?

It cannot be news, for she owes him none. She owes him nothing at all. If it were news, it could only be bad news. That she is ill, and they have rushed her to the clinic in Bad Gstaad, or the sanitorium in Baden Baden. Though again, why deliver such news to him? And where is the transatlantic postmark? At least it is an early day. By three o'clock, Herman has reached his bluestone settee in Central park.

There, he weighs the envelope in his palm, peels back the diapered flap, and reads his way into a small cluster of words. Salutation, in blue ink. A sentence or two, casually inscribed, as from a friend to a friend. Then the polite closing. No more.

The note is about nothing. Deeply as Herman ransacks the text, through multiple re-readings (and the "text" is of a length to permit re-reading by the half minute), only two insignificant details emerge from it.

One is that Mrs. Stevenson is among the twenty thousand evacuees this week, having gone with her sister's family to the countryside. The other is that she has read "a certain book with such pleasure as requires me to make mention of the fact."

There is no significance in these two details; the only significance is in their insignificance. In the casual assumption of a correspondence. Herman's authorship of the pleasure-giving volume is reasonably inferred—surely it is not Lord Tennyson's verses—and that same reflexive pride arises, as when he basks involuntary in the Hoadley approbation. One ought to know better, and one does, but praise can be systemic, a germ in the blood.

Herman stands. The note has made him happy, and made him restless. His skin tingles with a sort of gladness like an itch, while a sturdy thirst has begun to crawl inside him as he tacks toward Madison Square. This note will call for further readings (in the end it will have more readings than the *Twice-Told Tales*—twice told and five times read, by Herman) and what better venue for such thorough analysis than the lee of Aiken's sky-blue awning, where the Staten Island oysters are fresh twice daily?

Two blocks along his way, however, before he can further explore the significance of the insignificance, Herman finds himself beset by moral complication. Lizzie. Surely she must be told? God know what she would make of such a communiqué, yet what is to be made of it if she is denied the opportunity? To Mrs. Stevenson, he may be somewhat akin to the wooden Indian at the Eagle Hotel: an interesting relic, antique amusement. But Mrs. Stevenson is not made of wood, Herman knows she is made of female flesh. *Revenons à nos moutons,* friend Rabelais reminds us: come back to your sheep and tend them.

Now, however, half a dozen oysters and a bolt of single malt scotch come rushing to his aid. Eureka. Perhaps there is nothing here to involve Lizzie. Perhaps this is just a small piece of his day at the District. Dockings, visits, chitchats, mail. True, there are none such visits and never no mail until today, but there could have been. Barclay gets visits, from his scarred odalisque, and McBride gets notes—sometimes hourly—from his tout at Belmont Park. Doubtful, surely, that the content of those notes and visits get back to the fireside bright, to Mrs. Barclay or Mrs. McBride. So there is precedent.

But Herman logics his way bolt by bolt. By the time another scotch goes down (anchored by six additional mollusks) he has realized the limitations of appointing Will Barclay or Jamie McBride his moral compass or precedent-setter. Their justifications have never yet been the measure of his own. One might as soon nominate Bret Harte for poet laureate, or the Tweedsmen for good citizen awards.

It needs a subtler line of reason and since devising one may take time, he elects to redouble the grog ("Debung and decant," he calls to Robert) and sit a while longer. There is no one at the house, after all, and the Irish minstrels will come out soon, with their sharp pennywhistles and comical jigs. The little beetle-browed fellow who leads the troupe is a regular Mercutio, insofar as he translates out of his quick-clipped brogue. *(Even untranslated the man is amusing, with the blackest hair and whitest smile and blueberry eyes that dart with joy—or else with relief, to be fed some beef with his naked potato, in the new world of Americay.)*

·Herman is not often so relaxed. The legions who believe him long deceased would be no less amazed than those who know him to be extant, could they see him right now: the starchy, self-styled elder, clapping hands on knees to the frilling banjo and ringing tambourine *(Whack-fo me daddy-o, there's whiskey in the jar)* and laughing like the carefree child he never was. "Robert, my good fellow," he says, "Call all hands to grog."

It is never a bad idea to step back from a difficult problem, either. If you harness the instinct for bulling your way through it, your muse may be willing to do the job for you. It is the only work she has, where you have so much else to tend to, like your taxes and your shirtfronts, and the getting of an evening meal, every evening. So out of this interlude of raucous music, Herman circles back lazily and finds a better answer waiting.

There is nothing to tell to Lizzie, because there is nothing Lizzie wants to hear. His occasional stories from the wharf have never interested or enlightened her in the past. In truth, she finds them mildly embarrassing, being mildly embarrassed to admit her husband *goes* to the wharf. And so foreign is this harmless situation (that a certain Mrs. Stevenson, currently as anonymous and invisible to Lizzie as though perched upon the newly risen moon, did undertake to converse and inscribe. . . .) that for Lizzie it would hold all the fascination of a Turkoman at his praying rug. None at all. And off to her sewing room she would go.

No more offer this tale to Lizzie than talk German philosophy with a Wall Street sharper. He don't care if Immanuel Kan or Immanuel Kant. It may be an ad hominem *sort of argument but Lizzie is the hominem here, and there's no sense pretending she ain't. The brief may be specious, and certainly it is overloaded with over-ripened metaphor, but it is cobbled from truth. It's specious yet true, topheavy yet firm of bottom*—and there's whiskey in the jar!

Herman rigs himself on stiffish legs and settles up the bill with Robert, who is on sufficient good terms to satirize a tip that is twice the daily standard: "So today's the day that rich old uncle of yours finally took high honors?"

Herman nods with mock gravity at the scurrilous charge, and starts his engine across the bricks. Soon he is moving smoothly, past the Hoffman House, past the Union League, feeling pretty well settled on the old notion of a virtuous expediency. *(Let us swear by the hair of Plotinus Plinlimmon!)*

Within the gassy shadow of the Worth Monument, his
skull is humming softly with wind and drink and minstrel
verse *(Whack-fo me daddy-o)* and it is not until he is snug in
his covers that Herman draws one last conclusion. The letter
(blue ink on a small blue sheet, bearing barely the wordage
of the Madison Avenue Church marquee, and already sub-
jected to enough analysis and moralysis to cause paralysis
or the dread erysipelas) finally yields up to him its limited
actual meaning.

*No need to parse out the grammar, or reductio the sense of such
straightlaced sentences as these, nor describe the arc of a shooting
star at 76th Street over the fifty-block radius to yon stout Hippodrome. The widow will be glimpsed again. There is a future tense
to her, or else why write?*

*Such is the significance of the insignificance, the meaning of the
mystery memorandum.* And such is the upshot of all his furious
mental gymnastics, from noon to nightshirt: that the halluci-
nate Mrs. Stevenson will be ongoing.

"Are you going?" says McBride. "Your gal is over there."

"And looking very well," adds Barclay. "Very well
indeed."

"I was going," Herman says, consulting his watch to conceal a little emotion, "so I shall go. It is time for a bumper
of the best and freshest."

"Shall I board without you, or wait?"

"Go on, Bridey. I trust you can count a few Canadian furs
without me."

"Without you to watch over me, old Hawkeye, I can count
on taking a fur hat home to my Janey, and make her like me
all week in the process."

"I am my own keeper, not yours, Bridey. Thank
Krishna."

"You're too far gone, Bridey. That's what he means."

"Bridey is on his own recognizance, Young Crouch. That is all I meant to mean."

"He's trying to shame you now, Bridey."

"Good luck with that. Like trying to tame a fullgrown wolf."

"Tame a wolf?" says Herman. "It has been done. But with a nervous-making rate of recidivism. I shall return, me hearties."

"Not elope with her, you mean?"

"Leave him be," says Crouch. "He's on his own incognizance, ain't he? Let him be his own bee-keeper, if he so sorely wants to."

No doubt, Herman muses, McBride will take a second hat for Janey's sister, to make her like him too—and to make the final counting easier. The wonder is that anyone counts anything in the District. Meanwhile, the drizzle has cleared away, the muddy lot is baking out like a pie. Down the embankment, the spreading sunlight marks each crease in the river.

Look here, though—have those rogues been up to mischief? The widow is here, all right, but so is a grinning young dandy in a pinstriped suit. Sandbagged!

Taking his cup and saucer off the shopboard, Herman shifts his resolve (and his gaze) to steer wide of Mrs. Stevenson, or aims to, until he sees her beckoning. Sees her companion rising from his seat. The wavyhaired gasconade is easing backward toward the lane, a grin still playing on his lips, no longer in his eyes. Herman is being motioned into the freshly vacated chair as a ready replacement.

"Musical chairs today?" he manages to say.

Some country sun has toasted her face. Her light eyes sparkle as she leans forward, merry and conspiratorial. "That fellow was a complete stranger, and a very persistent one. To make him leave, I told him you were my fiancé."

"I warned you, Mrs. Stevenson."

"Too young to trust, you mean? I certainly did not *trust* him."

"You had a holiday."

"With Jack and Margaret, yes. I am glad you got my note."

"And the weather was good. You look the picture of health."

"Oh, I look 'twice as lovely as Miss Lily Langtry.'"

"A truthful boast."

"No boast at all. I am only quoting the fellow you so kindly chased away."

"You seem a practiced hand at weeding out the wrong sort of gent."

"I have had a little practice at home. My brother-in-law Jack brings a steady stream of suitors to our table. Hoping, of course, to marry me off. Every bachelor he meets is obliged to come and praise me over dinner."

"I see," says Herman.

"But I am here to praise you, as it happens. To praise your literary genius."

"Oh, my genius," he laughs. "All of England agrees."

"Forgive me," she says. "It is of course presumptous of me to judge—"

"No, no, it is very kind of you, in fact."

She is stopped by the simplicity of his response. Surprised to hear something unbetwisted from his lips, something uncharged. The slant of her head seems less a characteristic mannerism, in this instance, than an attempt to view him from a different angle.

"I wondered so many things as I read your book. I have so many questions—"

"Alas, though, my chains and shackles rattle. In order to secure my soup, I must rush back and tally up some beaver hats."

"They are fortunate in having a genius to make the tally."

"And they tell me that *I* am fortunate, to have their four dollars a day. But look here, you had better line up another play-act fiancé, to ward off my colleague Will Barclay. We are on the shuttle system today and that is he, approaching."

"Forewarned is forearmed."

"Oh, I don't think you will need to *shoot* him."

Barclay is flatly astonished at the sight of Herman so lively, and of the widow laughing at his last remark as prettily as a woman can laugh. He has not the glimmer of a suspicion that he, the debonair Will Barclay, might have served as the butt of their joke.

"They pay you well enough, do they?"

Herman snorts out a bitter, merry sound. The bribe overture (all too familiar, none too subtle) is no temptation to him. He is tempted, though, to bypass the precious metals man. If they send downtown for him, they will be left standing for two hours in the windowless seizure room.

"They drown us in cash, Captain," says Herman, who has in fact gone seventeen years without a nickel raise in his wage. "They load us down until our purses burst, and all our banks run low of vaultage."

Not passionate for justice, particularly, merely hacking away at his assignments, Herman is delighted to glimpse the boil on Crouch's proboscis, as that substantial organ looms up over his chair to filter forth the crowing proclamation, "We have got the evidence on you now, old sailor man, and it's blackmail your ancient arse it is!"

"He means that your friend is yonder," interpolates McBride, who has come back with a trace of foam from O'Reilly's fine stout lingering in his moustache.

"Ah," says Herman, playfully. "My niece is here for a visit."

"Righto, doggo—your long lost niece from Greece. See if that one washes at home, with the bee-keeper's keeper."

The *Moscow* is gone from drydock, leaving the hoists and braces bare. Some boys, truants from school, have congregated in the basin to rummage for such pirate treasure as may have shaken from the ship's pockets this past fortnight. Dirty boys, in frayed shirts. But they remind him, as all boys do, of his own boys; and remind him too, how little he recalls of their boyhoods.

They were together more than a decade at Arrowhead—Malcolm fourteen and Stanwix twelve when they left the farm for good—yet somehow they were not together. There was his work always, and the press for cash. Then there was his lack of work, a time when whole weeks ended without having ever begun, when years that had barely happened to him were simply gone from his life. Increasingly, it became a blur.

And there was something in both of them that shied from him. At times they seemed to go in hiding. Herman was never angry with them, never cold or ungenerous. But perhaps he was not the opposite, either. Not loving, warm, and generous, though he always meant to be.

He did not bring his best energies to bear. He left the children to Lizzie, believing it only right and proper, until he turned around one day to discover he had no *access* to them. They were sealed off from him. Soon they had their own ideas, and rarely asked for his.

Those years did drain away so quickly. Was there anything he could have said or done to alter the course? To this day, Herman has no answer.

He can only hope they had their fun. That outside their progenitor's gaze, they cavorted freely, like these smudged lads down in the drydock, roaming like alleycats in the sun. He could hope it more easily had he not known himself as a boy—and had Mackey not put such a terrible end. *Oh not from memory lightly flung!*

"Today," says Mrs. Stevenson, "you do seem solemn."

But there were other times. There was that golden morning, on the blinding frozen snow, when Mackey had all the fun in the world. When they both did, together. Herman with his arm in a sling (the brandy flask stuffed tight inside an open fold) and Mackey at the reins! Maybe he should have gone along for the ride more often—let Mackey be the one in charge. There could have been more golden moments, holy melodies in earthly harmonies, for surely there were not enough. . . .

"Are you feeling low?" she says, trying him again.

"I will raise in a moment, Mrs. Stevenson. Forgive me, I fell to brooding on the past. I trust that you are well, and living in the present?"

Why trust it, though? The horrors of a devastated family lie but a hill or two behind her. No shadow comes across her trim bow, however; no visible lapse in her cheerful demeanor. Yesterday this woman with the slim, lovely neck had leaned to him in conspiratorial jest and said, "I told him you were my fiancé." She could have stunned him no less had she swiped him across the nose with an umbrella.

"Yes, very well, thank you. We have another fine day."

"One minute ago, Mrs. Stevenson, I saw a happy sight which, oddly enough, made a deep unhappy memory. But it is passing." (*Presto! Vanish / Whither bound? / Flit and whither / From our hearth.*)

"Perhaps my questions can distract you. You recall I am duly licensed to question you?"

"No interrogatories needed, madame. Your ancient fiancé is up and running."

"Really, there is only one question. The book strikes me dumb, it is so much to take in. But this man"—and here she waves the book in air, to represent 'this man'—"Where has this man been?"

"At Fenton's Best and Freshest, as you know."

"To think I was a young child when the book appeared."

"I was a child myself at the time. But there is a process which occurs, a long slow descent, whereby vibrant youth goes shrinking into brittle age."

"Shall I remind you how youthful you seem?"

"Seeming is one thing, being another. *Esse quam videre.*"

The widow drops her gaze to the book, as she turns it in her hands. Opens and closes it. "Your wife—" she begins, head still down.

"We must not speak of her."

"Forgive me. She is unwell?"

"Why think that?"

"I don't know why," she shrugs. "Not speak of her?"

"She is well enough."

This widow has a genius of her own, for making a man talk about himself. In general, there is no easier trick—for most women, with most men. But it is far from easy with Herman. She flatters (calls an old man young) and she tilts her head; she smiles attractively and she entertains. These are not crimes. Nevertheless, Herman is pretty sure the time has come to get back to base and greet the precious metals man. He fishes for his watch.

"Duty calls," she says.

Herman nods resignedly; duty does call. "I am government property. My freedoms are brief."

"But I have had no answer to my question. It seems there are subjects where you prefer to be brief."

"If it is books we speak of, I have been called everything except brief."

"Books, yes—though at the moment, we were speaking of your refusal to speak of them."

"All possible regrets," Herman grins. "I would stay on another four years in office, had I but the latitude."

"Is that true? Because to have this talk with you is like trying to sew a coat while being granted only six new stitches each day."

"Ah, but which is the task, Mrs. Stevenson, and which the interruptus? If an honest day's work be reckoned my coat to sew, well then I am stitching all morning and all afternoon. Stitching until my metacarps and phalanges cry out."

"My sympathies, for your weeping phalanges. But do tell me if your goal is to avoid me."

"I am sometimes slow to formulate a goal, Mrs. Stevenson, and I often never do. But I can tell you what is not a goal. I may be dutiful and I may be solemn, but I will solemnly and dutifully assure you I look forward to gamming on in the mysteries with you. I'll come clean, tomorrow."

"Will you? Or will we sew another six stitches before duty calls again?"

"As a young man, I stumbled around. Teaching, sailoring, drifting. I have, by way of securing my soup, set ten-pins in a Honolulu bowling alley and swept the dark staircases of an insane asylum. I sailored five years, yet no one ever asks me why don't you sailor no more."

"I will ask."

"Point is, I took a crack at writing up a few adventures and it made a hit. Who knows why? So many atoms batting in the air."

"You need not be so modest."

"It was a job, you see. They hired me on to write up some more and when I ran low of facts I made up a few fictions— or mixed them together, because that's how you do it. I did it ten years, until they took the job back. They fired me."

"And that accounts for the decades of silence?"

"Sometimes the weed exiles the flower."

"Can you try to be a little direct? I do wish to understand."

"I had to find some other job, or go without soup."

"That is a sort of answer. An answer devised to silence those who probe this mystery."

"You would be amazed how few have probed it. Americay has stood pretty comfortable with my change of employment."

"And you? Have you been comfortable with it?"

"You wave that book at me as if it were holy writ, instead of a forgotten fiction."

"To simply drop it, though—"

"Remember, it dropped me. That's different."

"You must have been angry."

"Humor and humility do not derive ensemble; they are unrelated in the etymologue. *Umor* for one and *humilitas,* I believe, for the other. But they make a nice mix of *human* qualities."

"And you, sir, are a slippery eel."

Not so much today. He came with good intentions. Now, however, it is time to be herded down to the Copenhagen's steeved sub-chambers.

Mrs. Stevenson makes no protest. Today she is quiet, and quietly stands to face him. Quietly offers her ungloved hand.

Herman takes it. And as surely as if he had been heaved from the yardarm into the freezing waves off Greenland, Herman is inside the shock of the physical—her eyes so close to his, her cool palm. He is dizzy from it. Mere hands! But perhaps they complete an electrical circuit to the heart or brain.

Forever carrying his dignity like a banner, Herman can seem oblivious to the sexual passions. The more generous of his colleagues would place him beyond temptation, by dint of accumulated years. At home, he is bundled clear of sensuality by his overt roles: husband, father, citizen. True, men of his age may be seen with their dancehall girls or showgirls (or worse) but men of his *class* will not. He is neither high enough, nor low enough, to qualify.

A stern family visage behind him, a fixed disinclination to outward display, the accumulated weight of habit: one plays the role of oneself. But Herman has never been dead to the carnal side of life. He has always preferred to be laughing at Panurge and the lady of Paris than pondering Hegelian synthesis. And though he has forgotten much of Aristotle, he has never forgot the flashing horseback beauty of Mrs. Bell, in Taloo, though she flashed no longer than a shooting star.

Resigned. That would be his own word for the treaty he has put his name to. It is not a question of age or station, but of resignation. Not every man can be Panurge, or Doctor Longo.

"The last honest man," says Mrs. Stevenson, so near to him he learns the sweet flavor of her breath. He is still within her gentle handclasp, attempting to reassert control. Herman is pretty good at that, but then he is very infrequently dizzy.

It has only been a second, though, a fraction of a reflex on time's continuum. Has she even noticed? Did she see him go on full alert, or read his mind as it scrambled for distance—intellectualizing, poeticizing? It does not occur to Herman that Mrs. Stevenson might have experienced her own corresponding version of the dizzying shock—and in truth she has not.

"Punctual," he says, almost fully recovered. His grin is shaky (surely transparent at such close range) and his palm is too warm—or is hers too cold? "The last punctual man. Honest is a trickier business."

Herman has managed these last few weeks with Cook to do the breakfast, and light suppers in the neighborhood, at Aiken's or at Muschenheim's Arena. One night he stopped at the Hoffmann House, to focus his lens on its inadvertent floorshow of poseurs and swells, and the notorious Bouguereau nude.

All such night life ceases, now that the girls are home. They travelled from Jefferson to Overlook, and then to Beacon Hill; now they are back. Summer is done, routine restored at East 26th Street. Cook will expect all hands at seven o'clock sharp, every night to dine.

Herman is accustomed to this transition, and to parting with his freedom at a turn of the calendar page. It is worth it to have the girls safe home. Some freedom remains, of course, in the hours that are strictly his, and some hours will be reclaimed from a laziness that accompanies freedom. So much vital work has gone neglected, in favor of wanderlust and punch. Time now to bring in the hay.

Herman is ready for this work. He can see that Lizzie is exhausted from her two-month vacation, or more from the long trip home with Bessie in tow. Laboring daily in the cistern of the city has left Herman much fresher, ironically, but then true leisure never rests in an hotel accommodation. On his own recognizance, unencumbered, Herman has been at a sort of leisure. Moreover, the monochromy of solitude has been greatly colored by the advent of Mrs. Stevenson.

It is unfair, he understands, to notice upon Lizzie's return what is only inevitable, namely that every sentence they exchange has been exchanged before, whereas each brief chapter with Cora Stevenson brings some topical surprise. More cruel contrast: the widow's lively conversation is to Lizzie's familiar drone as her satin handclasp is to Lizzie's moist, almost soggy grip.

So much the worse, morally speaking, that this friendship remains a secret. A secret from Lizzie and, presumably, a secret from the widow's sister and brother-in-law, that champion herder of stray bachelors. It is dangerous to presume, however. For all he knows, Mrs. Stevenson goes home to her supper and recounts verbatim her latest chitchat with "the old gent from Customs." He doubts it, but can imagine it easily enough.

In any case, it has no relevance. Tonight, he is Herman the maid and nursemaid, and he takes a certain pleasure in being useful. He ferries the teapot upstairs to his weary ladies, he winds the clocks, draws the drapes. Domestically, he is fulfilled.

Ordinarily now, one hour after supper, he would be at his desk, except that he has fallen out of the habit. Instead he reads ephemera, then strolls out to the gate with his pipe.

Down the block beneath the Putnam House awning, some women are laughing falsely (at a distance, the sound is so distinct from genuine laughter) and the men gesture as broadly as stage actors. In full fig, the lot of them, on a Sunday night.

A soft moan breaks in on his reverie—a child in distress? Instinctively, he looks up toward Bessie's window, then turning back he sees the cat. A stray tabby, with gaslight dodging off his marble eye.

The cat sits solid on his haunches, his gaze burning into Herman. *The face of the devil's messenger!* Then he moans again, for his milk and crackers.

Last week their visits fell in place like clockwork. Herman felt at ease and in control, until the electric charge on Friday.

Some emotions came loose around that voltage. Herman is a man who values his safety, and knows wherein it resides. The shock of arousal was not quite welcome, and less so for Lizzie's arrival on Saturday afternoon. Sunday was not an easy day.

A tangled web, to be sure, yet dominated in every final analysis, by the visceral memory of that touch. (So much for analysis!) Of course, Mrs. Stevenson, sitting at Fenton's on Monday, is ignorant of his distress. That there are complications in his life she certainly assumes, and it is true that she has begun to know him a little, to ferret out his heavily armored emotions. For the most part, though, she accepts the veneer: that he is experienced and wise, he is the one in charge.

"I am glad to see you," she says, direct as ever, and this time the shock of her touch is a little insulated. Perhaps he has relived it so many times that it is almost familiar. It is pleasing—a distinctly physical pleasure—yet not at all alarming.

"And I you. I was hoping for your company, as I do now every day. Though it does not seem quite right."

"I hope it does not seem wrong. To me it has come to seem like fate. In a small way, of course. Or do you not believe in fate?"

"I wonder what to believe when fate comes from two sides at once."

"You are beyond me again."

"Perhaps it is still just fate—even from three sides at once. As weather is still weather, even though cold is added to the wind, and then some snow mixed in."

"Must our fate be so stormy?" she smiles. "A few quiet moments over a coffee?"

"Remember, fate and fatal do derive from the same Latin root. Let us examine the case a little. Tell me what exactly brought you here, to this fatal place, the Best and Freshest?"

"I may have said that Andrew, my late husband, was with the Custom House? Not here—downtown, in Debenture. That connection played a part. And my sister's house is very close by."

"This is a gritty little backwater, though."

"I have a taste for it, to be honest. The coffee house sets out some chairs, and I like to watch the river from here. Do you live nearby?"

"If fifty blocks is near," he says. "But I like the distance, come to that. I like the exercise."

"You do not walk it?"

"When I can't get them to bring me in a sedan chair, I do. To and fro upon the earth. It also soothes the brain."

"But as to fate, your being here from fifty blocks away seems stranger than does my being here. Did you request a distant station?"

"I didn't ask them and they didn't ask me. It was work here or stay you home. But I don't mind it, as I say. I liked it for a decade at the Gansevoort, and I like it here."

"Easily pleased, is Mr. M."

"If you ain't pleased easily, Mrs. Stevenson, you won't be pleased at all. But your late husband—"

Herman hesitates, but she does not: "Three years ago, of consumption. Our son, who was two, died later that same year, of a rheumatic fever."

He feels the sting of a punishment, these two sharp darts to pierce his impropriety. To lose them both, husband and child! And Herman knows what horrors are couched in that casual phrase, 'of consumption.' *Sarah dying, leaf by leaf. . . .*

"My deepest sympathy," he says, utterly helpless, of course.

"Understood," says Mrs. Stevenson, touching him a second time. Brushing the back of his hand lightly, as it lies upon the table. The most marginal contact possible—and why not, if they are friends? "I am afraid that a trail of death attends me. I am surprised my dear sister lets me in her door, though her children have survived the curse to date."

"Her children are blessed to have you in their home. Your spirit humbles me, Mrs. Stevenson."

"We do what we must," she says. "It doesn't make us heroes or heroines."

"I also lost a child—No, no, this was fifteen years ago," he says, waving off her sympathy—"and I was not heroic, or philosophic. I was crushed by it. Or a part of me was crushed, the rest of me severely forewarned."

"It is true," she says, her eyes almost imperceptibly wet. "A part is crushed forever." Then she breathes once and summons up a smile. "I think, though, that you were forewarned at a much earlier age."

"You are waving that book at me again, aren't you?"

Can they really be lighthearted? Can they truly be enjoying this exchange of painful revelations? But they are, for it is not the revelations that are painful.

"It is a heavy book to wave," she concedes, "but then waving it does seem to make you smile."

"Don't you know, madame, that according to a very great philosopher, we smile to deceive?"

Not for the moment deceived or derailed by his folderol, nor even mildly confused between facial expression and literary expression, the widow bends herself into a sitdown, shadow version of a curtsey that she manages to render with a dancer's line, a satirist's timing.

Herman has decided, again, that Lizzie must be told. Her knowledge of the friendship will purify it. But how exactly shall he phrase the telling? A nice young widow has taken to visiting the coffee stand—We have lately entertained a pleasant widow—A woman, whose late husband had been with the Custom House—

A few feeble stabs at an opening only serve to underline, again, that Mrs. Stevenson is a curiosity not easily brought home. The facts are not so damaging, merely awkward. The truth is not such hard sauce, but Herman can see that a softened fumbling version of it, seasoned for the dinner table, will resemble the weak wine you buy at a coach-stop, where the juice of a few grapes is mingled with a gallon from the landlord's rain-barrel.

Failing of reportage, Monday and again today, Herman substitutes a box of sweets from Henry Maillard's. Lizzie, who loves to gaze in Maillard's window, is bound to love his chocolate ducks much better than any sentence she might be fed about the widow Stevenson. She may bemoan the wasteful expense, but she will surely succumb to the duck, the turtle, and the nutty bunny.

Is it insane to purchase this box for a dollar? Not if you want to eat it, Herman concludes. Admittedly, it is an uncharacteristic gesture, but it ought not be one. There ought to have been chocolate amphibians and flower bouquets through all these tightwad years. Besides, these candies will make some sense to Lizzie, where Adam and Eve do not. She has come such a distance from the apple in Paradise that she scarcely allows such motives exist in the world, much less govern it.

Decades have passed since she felt a ripple secondhand, sensed a hot wind blowing by her door, and had sufficient instinct to take her stand. Such polite jealousy! But Sarah took very hard to heart what Lizzie only half believed, half stated, and soon enough dismissed, as an atheist debating the birthplace of God may not choose to remain for closing arguments.

Lizzie hits all her marks after supper—a worried reluctance, a weakness for sweets—and Bessie matches her turtle for turtle. Peace in the valley.

But no such inner peace. He begins his tense and restless night with the Lizzie conundrum, and the difference between morality and chocolate. Then, gradually, Cora's voice begins sifting in and taking over. Before long, he finds himself wearily poring back over their conversations, like a lawyer going over depositions.

Or like a writer. For he rewrites lines he has underexpressed, erases lines he never should have expressed at all, imagines lines he may need another time. A juvenile response, he tasks himself, but perhaps at bottom a human one. *Soon or late, if faded e'en, one's sex asserts itself.* But the

192 THE HANDSOME SAILOR

strip of sky above his drapes will go from purple to gray to white while Herman lies awake, responding.

Would that he were as juvenile as his responses, for at his age a lost night's sleep translates to a loss of thirty years in the mirror. There in the morning light he sees an octogenarian or worse, a *corpus delecti*. His skin is lined and gray, and the icy water only serves to make it grayer.

Herman hardly welcomes the "exercise" this morning, as he drags himself uptown. In leaden silence, he foregoes the general horseplay at work. Weary and anxious as he is, he has encountered yet another worry. Yesterday Cora Stevenson opened up her heart to him and let him glimpse the pain inside. All he could offer in kind was ego. No help, no real sympathy—only some whining about his own pain. Surely upon reflection, she must have marvelled at his selfishness.

Moving toward the coffee stand under a frown so deep he begins to feel it, Herman is pregnant with apology, fully gestated and in dire need of birthing out this new concern. At least she is there; she has not felt a need to shun him. But when he sees her, still standing in bonnet and coat, he starts flinging apologies at her before he even flings hello.

Mrs. Stevenson is taken aback. Wonderfully wide-eyed under that bonnet, lips parted slightly in surprise. She is urged to forgive him.

"I do," she nods agreeably. "But for what?"

"I was thoughtless. Yesterday you spoke of the very deepest personal grief, and I could speak only about myself."

"You did no such thing."

"To have raced on past such tragic matters—"

"We raced past them together, I think. And probably for the best."

Herman can only shake his head, his conscience by now an unmanageable welter, a hive of confusion.

"I forgive all," she says, with playful hauteur. "And easily enough, as there is nothing to forgive."

"I believe you," he says.

"If you did not *believe* me, then there would be something to forgive."

"But there is nothing?"

"Well, there is always your schedule. Your pocket watch. I do not forgive your pocket watch."

She is laughing at him and in a way, he realizes, this brief exchange contains, or expresses, their whole connection. It is free and easy, and meets all putative difficulty with good nature and laughter. And it enlivens him. Already he has begun to inhabit himself anew.

"So you will forgive everything except my need to eat," he says.

"Your soup, yes. But I have had a thought on this problem."

"The problem of my soup?"

"The problem of your watch. Say that a man leaves his work at three o'clock, or four, and imagine, around that hour, a sky still full of light. Several hours' worth of light—"

"You cannot have such liberty."

"I understand that you may not have it. But I do."

"The social liberty, though. To be seen in your own neighborhood with a gentleman—"

"Loosely defined," she grins, audaciously.

"Very loosely," Herman can agree. Her insouciance is mighty good medicine. For the moment, he has forgotten his stinging eyes, his aching bones. Having effortlessly dismissed his shame, Mrs. Stevenson has likewise vaporized the crippling symptoms of fatigue. She is a one-woman cure-all.

"This is not the Fifties, you know. It is the Eighties. And we are in New York, after all."

"Where everything goes, madame?"

"No. But the notion that one cannot walk out with a friend? Maybe in Ohio—"

"You have been to Ohio?"

"Something of a phrase, Mr. M. You do not agree that attitudes have changed?"

"But what do you suppose has changed them?"

"Maybe the weight of being so wrong. It is such a widening world. You yourself have celebrated the extreme social freedoms of the cannibals."

"But they are cannibals. And now they all have syphilis, if you will pardon one line of plain speech."

"I will pardon any number, as you know. If they have it, though, surely they have it from the white man?"

"Yes. And we *are* the white man."

"Now I am lost again. Let me go back to my original point. That a woman may walk out with her father, brother, uncle—or friend. We do not wear labels, saying who is who, as we stroll along."

"My theory is that the Sixties changed it. The War, and all those young men going off to die for someone else's idea. And the ones who did not die: maimed, deranged, a few who survived 'intact' if you could call it that, coming back from the sight of arms and legs and heads in the dust and fields of home. Back to a world that wants to tell them what is right to do and what is wrong!"

Mrs. Stevenson, still absorbed in the arrangements and proprieties of a walk in the city, makes no immediate response to this barrage. She takes a sip of coffee, and tries to recall where the War between the States came into it.

"It is only a theory, mind," says Herman now, fully emerged from his aberrant lecture. "Columbus had a theory that the earth was flat."

"I am sure you have researched it well."

"Not one bit."

Already the air has gone out of him; the rush of impossible energy has left him. He is exhausted. No wonder he has prattled out such nonsense. It takes his every ounce of strength now to keep both eyes open.

Cora does not detect this, however acutely Herman experiences it. It has struck her that Herman's longspun sociology came in response to her widened invitation. Has he the freedom, or the inclination, to walk with her in the afternoon? The issue disappeared immediately into the swirling winds of war.

She does not restate the question, having no doubt he heard her, and no doubt therefore that he is sidestepping the issue. And however unlikely their meetings may have been from the start, here is their first truly awkward moment. Neither has a remark to offer, nor any sort of fluid closing.

Wearily, Herman bows—his old standby—and while bowing kisses her hand, largely because of its near convergence with his face. Mrs. Stevenson smiles, and curtseys. It is sufficient. Not a comfortable leavetaking, yet surely the next best thing: a leavetaking.

If sleep is an idea, then it is Herman's only idea, all he can think of. But he starts out walking south and the walking shuffles up his blood a little, as does the sport of dodging Blue Birds on the avenue.

Inside the gate of Central Park, no longer at risk of death by omnibus, he faces the new risk of a hundred hurtling carriages, and of flashing hooves in general. Heads up! This is the rule for the Eighties—or perhaps it is all a plot to keep him awake.

Even on the placid surface of the lake, there is traffic. The gondolas, pinched in by swarms of weaving launches, and a crazy man, swimming round in his woolen suit. *Exhibit A, for Lizzie. There is your madman—or maybe not, if the fellow is harmless, and enjoys a swim.*

Herman makes it safely to the Zoo, and takes an empty bench by the bear cage. There is the fence, he muses (as he has mused here before), and on one side sits he, on the other side sits the bear. If you woke of a sudden in the midst of a dream, who'd be fenced in and who fenced out?

He ponders this nonsense at half past four with a tallish tot of grog at the tavern. Abruptly, inexplicably, his mirth expands: a small explosion, half laugh and half shout, which brings the waiter running. "I would like to have seconds," says Herman, "if there is any more left in the kitchen."

Cora wonders if we are as free as she is. She has noon and four, so we must have them too. As a generality, it cannot go; as a specificity, it fairly could. At home before the stroke of six I have been a rare unwelcome apparition, jolting Lizzie from her snoozes, ghosting her from private roosts. Emergency! she all but cried, last time I lumbered in that early.

She views a three-mile foot-journey as tantamount to crossing Kalahari Desert. Lizzie cannot measure such miles, except by times of arrival. So in a sense it is possible. The hours do exist, the aforementioned patch of time floats out across the open sea of afternoon, as it has for all these years. Four o'clock, five o'clock, six—all confirmed, scientifically. They are hours that have belonged less to Lizzie or Bessie than to Aiken, or the muse. To me, really.

What is the point, though, and what next, after such rapidly expanding precedent? Cora may have her Sunday mornings free, but Sunday mornings we do not have. Or do we? It is the case, as often as not, that I roam the Fort George grounds, or the North River palisades on a Sunday. Who expects to see me down at All Souls' Church, where the aptly named Dr. Bellows wheezes out his windy truths? I have sat through it, yes, but with famous infrequency.

Hardly sharp enough for solving thorny problems (merely hoping he can get through supper without snoring), Herman pushes himself down Broadway toward home. As he passes Henry Maillard's window, however, he sighs at his most recent solution. For here is a stopper on these afternoons and

Sundays—Henry Maillard's price list! If the trend of restitution continues or expands, the cost in chocolate ducks and drakes will bankrupt him for good.

"Herman, it's six." And shrilling round, the inscrutable haglets flew.

Herman sleeps flat on his back, the one posture from which he can rise unimpaired by sciatica and rheumatizz. Besides, it reminds him of his nights in a narrow shipboard hammock, nights whose comfort and joy have multiplied tenfold since the time of their joyless cramped occurrence. (Imagine placing a rain-whipped rag-tired sailor, roughly two feet wide at the shoulder, in a foot-and-a-half wide fly-trap for his precious rest!)

From this position—the pose, he has noted, of the corpus in the coffin, lacking only the well-placed coppers—Herman gazes up at the flaking paint and water stains that serve for constellations, the semaphor of stars. Right now he sees Orion, and three clear stars in the belt of Orion, the Golden Yardarm of yore.

"Herman, ten after!" The hungry seas they hound the hull.

This gazing up and lying fallow has its uses. It has fermented many a line or phrase to scribble down now, at the traditional second call, standing barefoot in his nightshirt. Catch 'em before you lose 'em, that's the idea, though they may well come to nothing.

Even literally they may, because Herman's scrawl is quite Egyptian. Not a soul could hope to read it; he is lucky when he can read half of it, himself. Still, it's legal tender, cash in the piggybank, accumulating interest—metaphorically, of course. *The sharks they dog the haglets' flight.*

At the washstand, he thinks of Lizzie, and how her returning will return him to his routine. It is routine that yields the work, and the work compounds itself, as mentioned. Thus the role of order in a life, this tidy algebra of productivity. Herman could never be content without production, though he has also learned the value of fallow, and of rolling with the roll-and-pitch of the planet, whether fallow or in yield.

Straight to the kitchen now, where Mattie submits to his scrutiny of the coffee grounds. Herman has always loved the smell of breakfast, spattered fat and brewing coffee; he would eat in the kitchen if he could. The dining room always smells of must—and of Lizzie, if truth be told, which is not a bad smell, merely other than the smell of breakfast.

"Yes," she says, to his pleasant greeting. "I am feeling settled. Everything is just wrongfooted at first."

"And Bessie?"

"A slight fever. The price of travel, I'm afraid."

"And taken by degrees—99 to Fire Island, 101 to Beacon Hill. Maybe another degree would get her on the Venice tour, poor girl. Why don't I take up her tray."

"Cook can do it."

"I would like to, though."

"Why, that's nice. She is not in the best spirits, so you want to keep it brief. And there is the whole schedule of the day to consider. You won't dawdle getting home."

"Of course not," he says.

Clearly, Lizzie has made some announcement regarding the evening plans. What are those plans? *Why* won't he dawdle?

Luck is with him in Bessie's room. She offers a sleepy thanks through the door and goes back to dozing. And luck stays with him downstairs at the dining table. Buttered toast closes over the void in information and when the toast has cleared, Lizzie brandishes a clue.

"Most likely they will catch the three o'clock boat."

"I imagine so," says Herman, happy to have the answer, and the happiest possible answer at that. Tom, and his Kate. Herman has not seen his brother since the middle of July. In fact, he was ready to send Tom a letter, pending such minor chores as composing the note, enclosing the note, and posting the note—which, combined, will rarely take him more than a month or two.

Easier to get the lad here and feed him, than to start the search for envelopes. A nice bout of Havana blunts and French brandy will do him good. Tom likes a taste of the city when it grows too snug at his Snug Harbor outpost, or when he finds himself trapped between yet another spoiled inmate and another ambitious committeeman.

"We beat out fiery lives in our own littered stalls," he suddenly quotes, over the last of the toast. Lizzie goes on reading the news. "Travelling as a mill-horse travels."

"Pardon?" she says, glancing up from the papers. "A mill-horse?"

"I was just thinking of Tom."

"Oh yes. It will be nice to see them."

Both of us, Tom and I, snug in our sunken boats. Each one travelling as a mill-horse travels (which is to say not at all, and to nowhere!) while other hands are pulled like tides to east-and-western edges. Well, for an hour or two tonight we shall be pulled, east to the East River or west to the North. We shall pretend Manhatto is vast, a metaphor-continent, and we'll smoke away the doldrums and crawl the Rialto taverns.

Rain—or is it hail?—rings against the iron wheels, batters wooden signs and plate-glass panes. A drumhead band of varied drummings.

Herman pays his way uptown today, arriving fairly dry. He lays the office coal and hangs his coat on the hook above the fender. He lights a pipe and remembers Cora Stevenson—remembers kissing the back of her hand. What was that nonsense? And what will happen next with her? Today, in all likelihood, nothing. Not in weather this foul. Nonetheless, with the rain softening a little by mid-morning, he sets

sail for the coffee stand. Even in this mess, he is glad to be
back outside.

Everything seems to rise in the rain; rubble-stone and trash
emerge as though by science, they come boiling up to the
muddy surface of the lumberyard, and the rats are out ca-
vorting. One heavy plank, soaked dark, has been set to span
the largest puddle. Walking the plank, Herman waves his
thanks to the Negro who runs the flatbed at Simonson's.
("Carry Me Back To Old Virginny," the fellow is often
whistling, though he is not whistling today.)

Herman sees that Fenton's chairs are back in the weeds,
underneath a tarpaulin. He tries to peer inside and at first sees
only himself, faintly mirrored in the sidelight glass. Then,
pressing closer, he sees Mrs. Stevenson waiting indoors.

"It is not such a bad day," she says. "And I had some
marketing to do."

"The rain suppresses color," Herman says, absently. He is
so surprised to see her there that in a way he does not quite
see her yet. "Just as sunlight finds all color. It will find the
Indian paintbrush in a drab field, or the jimson weed in a
ditch."

Cora is taken aback by his abstraction, his seeming imper-
sonality, but if it is rain they must discuss, then discuss it
she will. "I like the sky above the river. It is gray, but there
is a kind of beauty without color."

"No one paints a rain scene," he drags it along. "Apart
from the briskish storms-at-sea business, you never see it
done."

Enough of this, she now decides. He is almost like a different person, or a person talking to himself. She is convinced
they will need to get outdoors. Wet or dry, they will need
the open air. "The rain is letting up," she says.

"It is stopping?"

She maneuvers him through the doorway onto the unin-
habited patio, where rain splashes off the bricks. He sees that

she is laughing, that it is a joke of some kind. The rain is warm, she says. The sky is fine, even if no one comes to paint it. Cora is mocking his distance, and his spurious aesthetics. But now, at least, he sees her.

"I am not free this afternoon, Cora."

"You have decided the question?"

"No, no. Nothing decided. I learned I have an obligation. My little brother comes to dine today."

"I am relieved to hear you say so. After my carefree offer yesterday, it turned out I was engaged today too," she tells him, not truthfully. "I only wish it were with your brother."

"Tom is a good fellow to be sure, always good to see. Some say he is like my twin. Meaning, I believe, he is me without the woe thrown in."

"Why don't we go around the block?" she says. "For the exercise?" Herman looks up at the clouds and shakes his head. Not in doubt, or hesitation; in simple admiration of her taste for rain. Silently, side by side, they start a circuit of the block.

"Mine," she says, "is Mr. Minton—the newest bachelor candidate. Lord knows where Jack locates these gentlemen. I sometimes fear he advertises in the paper."

"Mrs. Stevenson, I can make no sense of this matchmaking theme. I assume that your Jack does some weeding, and ferries home only the hardy plants—candidates with an income and two good legs—or better, two incomes and one good leg! And I would expect an early success in the project, and quickly on to Chapter Next, the altar."

"So does Jack expect it. He complains I am too choosing."

"And he must be right, for the bachelor candidates can only be pleased. Unless the cookery—"

Can it really be this simple? Take him outdoors and he becomes the friendly wit again? There must be something else, something she has missed. For now, Cora must plunge on ahead with Mr. Minton, though it was months ago, and briefly, that he stood as bachelor candidate. In her haste, she grabbed him from the hat.

"The cookery is passable," she smiles.

"You do up a nice dunderfunk, do you?"

"Jack is more ready for my remarriage than I am. That is the problem."

"Three years is too short a time."

"I feel so. Having loved one husband, it seems more a matter of practicality than of romance to try and love another. Though I do feel very ready to be a mother again."

"That does not seem practical."

"Of course not. But it is different with children. To welcome further sons is no disloyalty to the first."

"Esau hated Jacob. And Cain slew Abel."

"But you have Tom to dinner. Will he be visiting with you for long?"

"Tom will be on board for two broiled chops and a salad of greens. Just about the duration of time measured by one bachelor candidate. They will take the early boat back to Staten Island."

As she strides beside him, smiling but for the moment silent, Herman understands what she has asked. Not will Tom be here for long but rather since he won't, what about the coming days? What about the freedom question?

This one is like Sarah; he has felt as much already. Not in appearance, or style, or personality. What she does have is Sarah's way of getting a man into her wagon, and getting the wagon underway. And she has that same extraordinary way of leaning forward into life, of consuming life with a prodigious will.

"A man," he tells her what she clearly knows, "is nothing but a deadhead log, which only rolls when made to roll."

"Some men, yes. Other men are avalanches, and present quite different problems."

"And which will arrive tonight—log or avalanche?"

"Mr. Minton is with Comstock and Andrews. He sells parasols in their shop on Liberty Street."

"This detail counts against him? Damages his efforts to secure the nomination?"

She blushes. To prove she can, perhaps? Never before has he seen her even faintly color. But Herman is unaware that Cora has been spooling out a complex lie. The lie is essentially true, or she would not, but the process of going on with it is what makes her squirm and blush.

"Well, it makes it unlikely he will be an avalanche. Good men are found in all walks, of course."

"It is even said that geniuses tally bales of cotton for their daily soup."

"Yes," she says, beaming at his resumed humor and at the conclusion (she hopes) of the Minton fabrication.

"I will vouch for a few. White, and Stoddard, and young Barry Gray. They gravitate wholesale to the Districts."

"And who is it gravitates to parasols?"

"I suppose we shall see. Or you shall. Perhaps I shall hear—tomorrow at half past three?"

Barclay and McBride, those near spotless public servants, have lost their way this morning. Must have stepped onto the wrong train, Crouch speculates, and ended up en route to the races at Sheepshead Bay.

Herman, left to stare down a deskload of manifests, gets to Fenton's late and does not stay there long. No familiar face in sight. She may have come and gone, she may have chosen to wed the parasol man. Cora Minton? It does scan.

Back at the office too soon, mildly deflated, shifting papers distractedly, he wonders why he is hoping against such a match. Why he hopes to hear some comedy—an indictment of the shopkeeper, not a romance.

There is nothing wrong with dry goods, to be sure, or with shops. Umbrellas? His own father and his brother

Gansevoort purveyed such things and they did so as the brilliant headstrong men of a long established family. Why, then? Herman can hardly apply for the post himself, and surely he is too wise to play the baying dog in the manger.

Well, perhaps the answer is obvious. Her company has cheered him immensely. As soon as Minton, or someone like him, fills the bill, he will be without it. This is selfish, yes, but innocent enough.

Having hurried to the meeting spot, Herman's first reward is the merry satiric sight of her, striding gracefully toward him with a yellow parasol in hand.

"I knew it," he says, though in fact he knows this parasol can only be a joke, and a pretty good one. "When you failed of noon, I thought the deal with Minton was cut and closed."

"You thought no such thing."

"I fully believed you had wed the stout young merchant underneath a great white wind-filled sail of a parasol, then went partway to Paraguay under a harvest honey-moon. Do I say congratulations?"

"He is a nice man," she says, "and so very shy that one feels for him."

"But does not marry him?"

"You are just like Jack. He wants everything defined. He wants to hear what exactly is *wrong* with Mr. Minton, or Mr. Gabrielson before him. And nothing is wrong with them. I dislike this need to dismiss entire human beings."

"Good for you."

"It's dismiss him with a word—or marry him! Why must those be the only choices?"

They have gone down First Avenue without discussing destinations. Somehow they began to walk, and somehow they continued. Now Herman stops at the realization. "Is the Park too far?"

"The Park is fine," she says.

"I started for it out of habit. Like a homing pigeon, I flew unthinking."

"The Park is fine. And don't worry about the distance, I can walk home by myself in the daylight."

She nods, content they have each been reassured. He has reassured her, she has reassured him. Herman is a creature of habits, all right. It will be a nice game to research and test those habits.

"Tell me—or did you? Has your brother Tom a Mrs. Tom?"

"Alas, he has, for there went a primo bachelor candidate, and as far from parasols as they come. Tom is a former ship's captain, now the steward of a refuge for broken-down sailors."

"You are especially fond of him, I can tell."

"Everyone likes Tom. He would be hard to dismiss with a word."

"He has no flaws?"

"He does not talk, if that's a flaw. He is twice as quiet as the quiet man. But he does love to walk. We went six miles together last night; doubled the ration on my wheels."

"Six miles seems a lot," she says.

"In a day? Pity the poor corporeal shell that gets less into his wheels than that. Besides, it gives you room to think."

Herman remembers the year he went out to work, for his uncle in Greenbush. Every Friday—quite late, after the office closed—he would walk the fourteen miles home to Lansingborough, on the strength of two cherry tarts and a pint of water. On clear nights in winter, the Hudson ice would shine like a pathway, but there were wolves, and their cries would come echoing over the frozen river. It always made him cringe. If he had not finished his food, he would eat it quickly at the first hair-raising volley from the woods, and hurry home to the darkened house, with always one candle left burning for him. Then, on Sunday afternoon, fourteen miles back to Greenbush.

"So you walk to think," she says.

"I walk to walk and I walk to think. Those are my purposes in walking. Of course, I also walk to get where I'm going. It is an old-fashioned means of transport, long forgotten, but it don't cost a penny—where the cars are six cents a section."

She offers him her arm. To Cora, it has been a gently nagging issue, as they bobbed along elbow by elbow over some twenty minutes of unshaped flight. Less of an issue to Herman (who can be oblivious to issues) and not an issue now, as he clasps her forearm firm to his ribcage. He finds that he likes it there. And he marvels that no one sees them; that in a way they do not exist. As long as he has been living back in Manhattan, strolling it acre by acre, only strangers pass him by. Ten thousand strangers every day.

He feels no fatigue. Six miles, fourteen, however many. He has not felt so vigorous in years. Pressing her forearm with his other palm, touching the muscle through soft cloth, he feels a warmth come swarming into his throat.

They stop in for a bracer on 61st Street, then march on into Central Park. There they walk again, saying little, though Mrs. Stevenson's theory will soon be proven: more can be said in an hour than in ten minutes. And less of it mere badinage—though never none, for badinage is their style. It is something they have practiced together as they might have practiced waltzing, to now waltz smoothly.

Herman is about to learn a lot that he has wished to learn, restrained only by propriety. But where is propriety now? Now that they have taken arms, and taken drink. *Not so odd her arm should charge me, yet odd I can take it so easily: heedlessly, offhandedly. That we lock together as children do: naturally, unceremoniously. (These my adverbs!) But Mrs. Stevenson removes by increments all the human strophe of hesitation. By the time she*

presents you with choice, she has already resolved all choices for
you. Inevitability is her calling card.

She is the heedless one, the natural. Just as Faywa swings back
her veil of hair and takes your arm (or worse!), so Mrs. Stevenson
swings back the veil of expectation. An island-style spirit upon a
bedrock of mainland sense. Who is she that can shrug off the double
convict status of woman and widow-woman? Yes, it is the Eighties;
it is also less than twenty years since men were held in chains.
There are millions who say that women must still be held in chains,
yet here is a girl who opts for self-manumission. She ain't in a
mood to wait for her Abigail Lincoln to come. Who is she that can
brush the world from her lap like a scrap of linsey-woolsey?

Bare fact is never sufficient. Mr. and Mrs. Darwin may
yield up baby Charles, but they do not yield up Charles
Darwin, the giant of science. Likewise with Mrs. Dostoev-
ski. A time, a place, a family—and still the sons become
themselves, as Mackey did, as Stannie has, as Herman himself did and daily does. No different with daughters. Herman
need only peer out over the Christmas goose to learn that
lesson thoroughly, for here sits busy cheery Fanny and there
sits Bessie in her gloom.

Bare facts are nevertheless welcome, and Herman gathers
them to his vest like aces in a poker game. Douglas Jackson,
Cora's father, labored all his life at the carriage factory in
Cherry Street, beginning as a wheelwright and ending up a
manager. Firmly believed in education, even for his daughters. There were two of those and one son, George, who
was trampled by a horse, at eight. ("I told you, death attends me.")

Andrew Stevenson she met in the Brick Church choir.
They married in that building; likewise was he memorialized
there, in 1879. Cora has had fair schooling, continued on her
own by means of the Lenox Library, on 70th Street. She has
also had the short course at Presbyterian Hospital, to go

for nursing once the niece and nephew, Anne and Patrick, are older.

Of course she may not do it. By then, she may have a new family of her own. She will turn thirty-three in November.

"I was thirty-three in August," Herman declares. "August of 1852."

He had done the mathematics quickly; now he does the psychology. 1852 was a dark and painful year. Sarah gone, Hawthorne gone—and Evert had turned his coat. Pierre was left alone to rot.

What is a fact? Thirty-three years old, he joked, but he gave her no glimpse of the boundless sadness of that year. Did she picture birthday cakes, and pretty wrapped gifts? Some facts he had gleaned—hospital, factory, church—but such facts, cobbled together and thickened with flour, do not yield up Cora Stevenson. They do not explicate her quick heart, or the brave humor glinting through her glance.

"I feel you have counted and weighed me," she says now, "as carefully as some ship's cargo."

"Oh much more carefully, Mrs. Stevenson. Though not at all critically."

"Well, it is your turn now. Though it is growing late."

"There is always tomorrow."

"Yes. Maybe we can gam again tomorrow."

Herman raises an eyebrow, and chuckles. It sometimes seems that he laughs at every word she says. Certainly she can make him laugh. How many in the course of his life have held that wonderful power? Very few. Fly, to begin with, Long Ghost, to be sure. Evert. Cousin Kate, to be fair. Mackey, as a little boy. It is a short list, for such a longish life.

He has let this friendship grow, but was it wise to do so? He wonders and, *mirabile dictu,* is about to confess to wondering. He takes both her hands, to tell her what is on his mind. For Herman, this is extraordinary. And though pot valor helps to make it possible, even more so does Mrs.

Stevenson herself make it possible, precisely that part of her which cannot be found in recitations of fact or pale biography.

"Propriety be damned, Cora Stevenson. It is nothing to do with propriety. But I do wonder if all our gamming has been a good thing. Or is a good thing, now."

"It is for me," she says, so simply that for now it ties the thread.

Heading home just minutes later, Herman remembers asking Long Ghost about God, sitting under a banana tree on Eimeo, no less. What about God, is there God, what form has God? And Doctor Longo answered, "No." There is much to be said for such concision; for knowing what you think.

God not real? Well, trouble is. Not that it matters when you come to cases, for clearly it goes against nature to call a halt. Human nature, that is. You weigh a mistake, and then you make it. Later on, they will lash you to the gunner's daughter and render you forty sharp licks of the tail. But oh, behind these frescoed walls of flesh, stands the closeted skeleton.

Rain again late last night, rain all day today. It seems in autumn a day will either be perfecto, brightly blowing all the trees of heaven, or else a gray Canadian wind. Still, they vote unanimously for the drizzle and drear.

"Good for you, Mrs. Stevenson. I have known only one other of your party who shared my taste for foul weather."

"My party?"

"The distaff. The party of sisters, mothers, daughters."

"Oh. In that case, the party has been misrepresented. We all loved to walk in the rain—my mother, my sister, and I. We must have done so together a hundred times."

A film of tears on her eyes. Intriguing tears, subject to a surface tension: they never squeeze free. The eyes fill and then dry, as though she can resorb the liquid, and return it to the aquifer.

A close and loving family, and here she is, both widow and orphan. Not easy. It occurs to Herman (somewhat amusingly, at age sixty-two) that he too is an orphan. But very rarely did his mother walk in the rain with her children—or in the sun. He cannot recall a single instance.

Maria would nap with them, or so she liked to phrase it. She would sleep and they would watch her sleep, if that is a napping-with. Certainly it is a well-remembered routine. Helen and Gansevoort exempted, as ever; Herman and Allan rolling their eyes while Augusta cautioned them with furrowed brow; Catherine playing shadow games and Tom, the baby, squirming, writhing, sputtering. None of them permitted to stand or speak for the duration of the nap.

With his father, it was different. Father liked to walk the teeming streets along the waterfront. Hand in hand, they would dodge about the market stalls in Burling Slip. He would stop to buy them Caribbean treats, a topknot pineapple or yellow banana (all the bright tropical fruits dangling down from shanty awnings) or buy them a sweet on Saturday mornings, from the candy butcher with the three-leg dog. Herman recalls the sensation of his father's hand more sharply than he recalls his father's face. But a shy boy does not always look into faces, and it was very long ago.

He does remember their final time, on Cortlandt Street. Remembers looking up from his father's lap, across the bright sail-filled water, as the two of them awaited the Albany boat. His father's hands stroking Herman's always unruly hair; his father's voice. "My goodness, Herman, you are too big for this old chair—you have outgrown your papa's lap."

(Were those his actual words? Herman has rehearsed them so many times that they are graven, but memory has its tricks; sometimes you remember the rememberings.)

Face lowered, blushing no doubt, yet he liked the feel of that hand in his head-feathers. Was he too big for the chair? Too old at eleven? *When Mackey was turning eleven, I was coach-bound for Cincinnati, to lecture the fine ladies—ladies who would never walk in the rain. It was snowing on the highway, the horses' backs were white, Mackey was turning eleven without me, and I did not even know it.*

"Look there. The geese do not mind flying in the rain."

Herman comes docking back from his private inner sail, and sees them, Canada geese above the crown of sycamores, flying in their classic V. Then comes a striking couple, bowling down the hillside toward them. Short people, dwarfs in fact, bandylegged as sea-dogs. Hands locked tight like newlyweds, age indeterminate yet far from insubstantial.

"Do you suppose," says Cora, "the tailor charges more for that fellow's suit, or less? There is less fabric to buy, and less stitching, but then there is the cost of specialization to consider. Or the lady's bustle. There cannot be a mould for a shape like hers."

What will Cora notice next, how many bright observations will she add, before she notices that Herman has gone mute? Answer: none. She has noticed already. No response from him on the bustle, which on closer inspection is nothing tailored, just a remarkable round rump, a backside like a hot-air balloon. No response on the tailor's invoice.

Her reflex is to join him, to go perversely mute in turn. Giving word for word, as it were. (Naturally, Cora has her pride.) But she wants to use the time they have and knows the burden of change must fall to her. "I doubt I can outlast a Dutchman," she says, lightly, "if outlasting is the game."

Herman is genuinely startled, and chastened. He comes back to life as though roused from the deep. "Forgive me, Cora. The quiet makes me quiet. Like a nice country ramble with sisters and mothers."

"Our walks were hardly quiet. We were more like a swarm of magpies. But are you quiet, Herman, or are you troubled? Tell me."

"I can see that four is just another hour on the clock. But do you not agree our situation is somehow altered by it?"

"You feel it is wrong."

"There is the lingering business of right and wrong."

"But no one would say we have yet done wrong."

"Ah. If it is a question of yet and not yet, of darksome indiscretions approaching on a time line, I would say that something has been done—as a fowl is surely broiling long before it is taken from the spit and swallowed."

"I think we had better be very serious for a moment, and try to clear the air."

Clear the air! Herman is nothing but curious. He has not the faintest idea what she will tell him next by way of clearing it. Indeed, this unpredictability has been a large part of her charm, not least because the surprises have all been pleasant. But her next remark hits him like a heavy slap.

"We have joked about my second husband—"

No way to cushion a blow you have already taken. It shocks you. Here he was, wedged in a mental fogbank, ready perhaps to speak out against their expanding liaison, and now he learns she is ready to end it.

"—and since we spoke, I have made a choice."

Truly, it is like a physical slap. His face was arranged for their usual mirth, and this blow has rearranged it. Cora sees him sag. "Herman?" she says, with that female glance of sympathy. That will never do. He had better pull himself together, fire up from his gloom through some frantic interior dance. He must give her Lazarus in the flesh, up from the grave in time for supper!

"A stick of indigestion there," he mutters, behind a cheesy smile, "but it is gone. Tell me! He must have been a thumping extraordinary candidate, to strike so sudden and deep over the plum duff."

"Herman, you have not understood me—"

"I shall have all my detectives verify his bank accounts, and my surgeons verify his strength of limb." (Bravely, this; not bad. And he rallies behind his own efforts, gaining momentum through verbage, as ever.) "None of your spindle-shanked pudding-shouldered sorts will do. He must be *good enough*."

She can only shake her head at all this, far from certain what she can manage to tell him, or *how*.

"Cora, I am a democrat. I say he is good if you find him good, all coin and countenance hereinafter be damned and deep-fried. But let us have a listening-whiskey now, in lieu of our talking-coffee. All the better to hear you with."

Cora is glad enough to delay her announcement. She had meant to pace the revelation, to bring it out peacemeal, in a soft sort of dawning. The trouble is, she started badly. *Startled* him.

But now they clatter across the earth-colored tiles of the tavern floor and sit in black iron chairs with soft red leather cushions. They concentrate on ordering. For Herman, a wee dram of single malt (Dutchman yes, but predominant Scots) and then a double dose to bolster up both sides, Scots and Dutchman, through the news-telling.

"The fire is nice," she says, trying to gather her thoughts.

The shock of a second husband for Cora ignited something less than generous in Herman. Having more or less mastered the shock, he is bent on overcoming the less-than-generous, glass by glass if necessary, until he reaches the mellow state of approving all-and-any.

"Just about right," he now declares. "Who is the lucky man, Cora? Who have you got for the job?"

"This is too confusing. I meant to say, or should have said, that I have made a decision. Not a choice. I mis-spoke."

"The decision being?"

"A decision that I simply do not want a second husband. I do not want to even think about it any more."

Cora looks—what? *Solemn*. The curve of her smile folded, hemmed, flattened to a line. Herman, who has awaited the fall of a name as one might await the fall of the guillotine blade, recovers quickly and takes her hand.

"You are sad. I could never have imagined you sad, Cora."

"I am, a little."

"It is somehow not a happy decision."

"No, Herman. But I do not blame you in the least, I promise you."

"Blame me?"

"I'm sorry. More confusion!"

Amazingly, there are tears. Fallen tears, on the back of his hand. Herman is indeed confused, though not quite helpless. Genuine affection enables him to perform a simple act or two: touch her damp cheek, murmur a word of comfort.

"You have made it impossible, don't you see, dear man? If I *could* choose a second husband, I would simply choose you. And I do feel sad, very sad about it."

"Cora, it is a glorious compliment you pay. Choose me? You would have had no competition!"

"I am not joking, Herman. Why would I not choose you? Perhaps because you are above me. But you have never acted above me. You have been protective and kind, and always such a pleasure. Why would I not choose you?"

"Dear lady, I have a wife."

"Of course."

"This is what I meant when I asked if we were being wise. Because when there is such unexpected caring on both sides, it is much more than a question of four o'clock."

"You were right, of course. It is difficult, that's all. Some things are."

"Yes."

"Last night in bed, I thought to myself, what would I feel if I knew that bigamy was legal."

"Bigamy! It is not only illegal, it is impossible."

"I was only thinking to myself. And I thought it must be interesting, too. As you know," she says, her expression a fetching mix of sadness and laughter, "I am drawn to the unusual."

"Interesting, yes. I was once interested to the hilt. And I had hold of a bigamist's history—a true account in vivid detail, that came my way as a tale to write up."

"I would like to read this story, Herman. Tonight."

"Not easily done, Cora. It was written up and written down, but in the end it was unwritten in the fire."

It was for Hawthorne to write up, truly. Agatha's tale was tailored to the man as a jacket is cut to your upper trapezius, and the more I set it and shaped it, the more I knew it was Hawthorne's tale. But Hawthorne didn't want it.

I wrestled it down that winter. It was done and delivered—and refused! They declared it to be too dark, too betwisted. Oh and so was Macbeth, *I told them, or it wouldn't be* Macbeth. *In time the fireplace claimed it; if it ain't art, by God, then let it at least be fuel!*

"You could write it now. Perhaps you could do some research," she adds with a grin.

"I write only verse now," he says, maintaining a straight face. But Cora has a handle on the script by now. She has found a lighter way to frame it. Holding his hand easily, comfortably, she lets the joke out a notch or two.

"But a man who goes from monogamy to bigamy could easily go from verse to prose."

"Or on to polygamy, with the Brigham Youngers—if he weren't already an *elder*."

"There. You see? There are places where bigamy is not only legal, it is the norm."

"Indeed. I have seen such a one firsthand in the South Pacific, where I chanced to volunteer for the boeuf bourguignon. In Nuka Hiva, every wife has two husbands."

"So it is not a joke in Nuka Hiva."

"No. But neither is eating your second cousin a joke there. It is another country, altogether."

And a lonely country, as I well know, with irony galore in the simple tally. We knew the engine, Sarah and I. We ran through snows, and hatched out plots, ratcheting up our excuses in advance. I had my name on mortgage and marriage-ban, while my soul went scurrying through the forest, to try light games of love.

"A man cannot be in two places at once. There's the rub."

"Two places at once is hard," Cora concedes, a little puckishly.

"My brother Allan and I tried that as an experiment. Tried running so fast as to be at the top and bottom of the staircase simultaneously."

"My idea was more *sequential*. First one place, and then the other. More or less the way a man will go from his house to his office."

"I comprehend sequential. But emotions are never so sequential. They are very hard to schedule."

"I am curious, Herman—and I deserve an answer, since I have been so open. I would have chosen you, but would you have even considered choosing me?"

"Dear Cora, it is an impossibility. As far from any choosing as life can take us."

"Consult your heart a little, though. Please. For example, would you be happy to learn that I had found a husband?"

"My preferences do not matter. I would prefer to be a man of leisure, in a world at peace, on a galaxy benign, of an ordered universe."

"The question is so simple," she says, ignoring his most freshly constructed wall of words. "Though I know it is hypothetic. Would you prefer to have me, or to lose me. Think about it that way. I would prefer to have you, and have said so."

"I am fully obligated elsewhere, Cora."

"You would have no obligation with me. I fear I may have overstated, by using such words as husband and bigamy. All I am saying is that your company is the company I favor having—insofar as I can have it."

"If you were to ask your sister or brother-in-law how they view such hypotheticals—"

"No, I am finished asking and arguing. You know now how I feel. That alone makes me feel a little lighter."

"Please, do not misunderstand how *I* feel, Cora."

If she has misunderstood, it is his fault. Why has he not told her one emotional truth? He tells a small portion with his eyes, but why not *say* that he is flattered, tempted, smitten. That he is lonely and treasures all their time together. And yes, that he would prefer to have her than to lose her, were the equation ever so easy.

"Don't worry, Herman, my pride is not hurt. I tend to speak my mind and now I have done so—rashly again, I know. You will have to judge our future by your own lights."

Would that his lights shone clear! Is he the man who can tally out right and wrong as confidently as he tallies up cases of Beaujolais wine?—or is he the man who understands that virtue and vice are two wan shadows of the same one nothingness? Ten minutes back, he tasted the flavor of old despair, when he thought he was talking with the future Mrs. Minton. Why does he work to secure that despair with every bland utterance that escapes his teeth?

But for a man long resolved on minding his business (and accustomed to minding it in an absolute vacuum of emotions), Herman is weighing an outsized cargo here. Her revelations are as jarring to him, as disorienting, as if he were grabbed by the sleeve and told his house was on fire.

"We must leave it be for now," says Cora.

"Yes."

"Can we make a small plan—to let the week-end pass, and Monday, but then to meet on Tuesday, at four o'clock? And try to clear the air? Maybe we can find a way to circumvent my rashness."

"Yes."

Herman does not mean yes; he means impossible. He means he has no choices any more, if he ever did, and that he is old, and long in the marriage-chains. That he is devoted, in his way, to Lizzie and to doing right, though no one lately has tested this formulation as Cora's green-eyed frown is testing it now. Her sweet breath and curving lips draw him forward instinctively, and instinct is an unfamiliar siren.

"It is dark," is all he says. "Let me take you home."

"No," she smiles, she presses him back affectionately, two palms against his lapels. "I like the dark."

"Dinner is waiting, Herman. And there is news."

"I am late."

"I knew you would be late," says Lizzie, removing his stick from the wall where he just left it leaning, and rearranging his coat on the tree. "With the rain."

"Well, I was going to be wet and I am wet—why care exactly how wet? I should have been on time."

"You should have taken the cars, and not got wet at all. But fetch the claret, before Cook comes after you with her carving knife."

A solid meal. Braised veal, stewed tomatoes, and a fresh loaf of bread still hot enough to melt the butter. Herman has plenty of appetite left over for the raisin cake, which Cook has baked in Bessie's honor. She is back at the table, after her week of lingering fevers.

Whether because she has been weakened, or because she is glad to be strengthened, or perhaps on account of the raisin cake, Bessie is very easygoing. Nothing provokes her, not even her father's tardiness. She lets the wetness story pass,

with none of her jibes about supporting the tavernkeeper's
children.

Lizzie's news is of the best sort, a note from Stanwix. That
he writes is always more news than what he writes, in part
because of when he writes. A sensitive boy who knows his
mother pretty well, Stannie never communicates until his
medical accounts can be safely framed in the past tense. I had
a bout—I suffered a visit—I lost some days. . . .

"I am feeling strong again," goes this one, for example,
"and our current delightful weather can only help." His
breezy manner is enough to skim a layer of concern off the
bedrock of Lizzie's terror. By the time she makes her sociable
relay to the Kates, the tone will have mellowed even further:
"Stannie had a bug of some sort, but he is fine now and
keeps in touch with home."

(When it comes to second removes, Herman will color it
up a bit himself, telling John Hoadley, "Stanwix is sounding
downright cheerful. It would be nice to have him on board
this year for Tom's Christmas pudding.")

Reporting directly to himself, however, upstairs after dinner, Herman is not so sanguine. Stannie is Stannie, after all.
But Herman does resolve to get an answer into the mails, to
write back before anything too bad can happen, as though
the process of correspondence plays a part in the calculus of
fate. He makes a serious commitment to a humorous letter—
a letter without a trace of the critical note, or even the wis-
domish *fatherly* note. It will only have affection in it, boiled
down and pure, forty gallons sap to make one gallon syrup.

The letter will be calm, and kind, and little else—other
than *soon*. It must be soon. Always with Stannie, Herman
feels the press of time; always a sense of reprieve. Now and
invariably, he notes that at the precise moment Stannie made
these marks in ink, he was alive and ongoing. There were
chapters yet to be writ, groping adventures yet to be lived,
in the young man's desperate scattered life.

For Herman's richest wish, in a way, is simply that this
son (about whom hangs a sadness you can see, as one sees
the air on a foggy day) outlive him. More critically, that he
outlive his mother. It is no more than every parent's wish,
except that in Stanwix' case it has become a plea, that feels
unlikely of success. Each time Stannie goes from home, or
writes back, Herman fears may be the last. One terrible question always fills his wake: will we see the boy again, alive?

He can hope it is only a case of nerves. Certainly, Mackey
has made them vulnerable. But how many times has Herman
stood on the small iron balcony at night, silent among the
chimney-pots and roof-gardens, and wondered if his son was
in fact alive? For of course he could so easily be dead—one
such night he would be dead—and they would never know
for weeks, or months.

If word came slow—death in April, no word until May—
would the gap in time help soften the shock? Is a present
truth disarmed when relegated to the past in a distant future?
A tragedy can be so long-since true that in a sense it is *no
longer true,* or is by now a different truth, as last week's
hurricane may leave behind it crippled lives and shattered
houses, yet no longer hits at one hundred miles an hour,
ripping the coat from your back as it goes.

Saturday night. Shreds of cloud, as thin as steam, file past
the half a moon. A cold damp night on the balcony, just the
sort of air to keynote a disease, according to Doctor Lizzie.
She will not step out to join him.

But free of all wifes for the moment, Herman charges his
pipe and puzzles why a man would wish for two of them.
*More happily subtract a wife than add one, no? And double the
odds whenever you crave the silent grass-growing mood about your
ears—or when all passion's spent. (Oh we'll go no more a-roving,
down to the fiddler's green.)*

You store your life in boxes, some in this one and some in that. Have I uttered three sentences of hearth or home over my long career on the wharves? Conversely, how many tales of those scalawag crews have I brought back inside the family-circle? Very few, as I have lately rationalized. Hoadley likes to ask, and Evert just loved the stuff; oh he soaked it up with glee. Excavated each rough gem of chicanery as if he planned to exposé it, muck-rake style.

A bigamist has his two repositories, so to speak: one here, one there, and never the contents to mingle. He could take two trips to church and hall, two Catskill Mountain honeymoons, and bring two litters into this lamed and catastrophied world. A Kate and Harry here, a Kate and Harry there, and never the twain. Does this entice a man, though, or does it sound more like hell-fire on a damned short faggot?

Possible, yes. Murder is possible too, so long as you do not mind your guilt, and your happy victim favors an early seat in Heaven. And so long as you don't get nabbed.

In the ashes of Agatha's tale resides your sole exception: that man whose habits are formed at sea, and who retains the foundation of a sea-faring life. Like Max the Dutchman, he may have a wife in every port, and mostly no wife at all, living on the brine. He can find a clean bundle waiting for him on both sides of the broad Atlantic, and old Jenny Brown in London town need never meet young Jenny Gray in Sheepshead Bay. There are always two sides to the moon.

The wondrous part is that Cora Stevenson sees me eligible. Glory be to her for that, for to be seen differently is to become different, sometimes. But the rules of thumb apply: never lie to a wife, and never tell her the whole truth. Who can begin to math out the exponent of complexity in telling such different half-a-truths to two of them? Who can point to his bowl of milk and declare it not shot through with poison? The case is sad, to be sure, but at least it is clear.

Time to move this meeting along—and maybe move it indoors to some warmth. What's the next order of business, though? What else can we resolve, under this chilly moon of resolution? The Stanwix letter is next, if we are up to it. Remember, it must be cut as careful and artful as any verse. It must say everything there is to say of love, while seeming to say nothing at all, beyond hail and farewell. Tis a chore that calls for more strong coffee, and another charge of roughcut barley.

My dear boy Stanwix,
We undertook today the short sea-voyage over Hudson's chopped and shining waters to Nouveau Jersey—for the purpose of lifting and weighing your pretty niece Eleanor, and trying out a rough thumb on her rose-petal cheek. She has a face and a will to make the boys cry. What Eleanor wants she wants, as is maybe the case with us all, before it gets hammered out in the cause of Civilization (which be Greek for "Do what we say and we'll stamp yr. papers").
The arguments fly back and forth. She looks like her mother, she looks like her father, she looks like her father's mother. To this old mariner's eye, she looks like you did, lad, at the same tender age, before you went and waxed your moustaches.
~~Your sister Bess stood home~~
~~Your mother is very well, and Bessie much improved by~~
All home are feeling well, and all most glad to hear that you are stronger. ~~Since you asked for advice As to the issue of seeking new work~~ As to occupations, my conclusion (from having hauled to sea and hauled to deskwork indoors) is that life in a chair is twice as debilitating as the strenuous life. It may prove to be the case that life at twenty versus life at sixty is more the crux of it—in which case a man of thirty-two (which you to our shocked amaze do speedily approach!) might want to steer a middle passage, some sort of half-and-half.
Shall we run a contest together, you and I, back and forth across the Great Plains? ~~Objective: to shape the perfect life, and then perhaps together go off and live it, whether building bridges or vagabondizing in the shade beneath them.~~ When I remember

Herman lifts his pen and leans back, closing his sore eyes. Ink on the heels of both hands; all his energy siphoned out. Tomorrow is another day, and a good one to have another go at this letter-writing.

He pours himself a sip of brandy, then shuts his eyes again. It is almost impossible for him to picture Stanwix as a grown man. Sometimes Stannie is four years old and sometimes fourteen, but he is never thirty-two—unless he is standing there.

Last week, Herman had asked Cora about her nephew, a fair-skinned lad, glimpsed one time from duelling distance. He was looking for a fact or two, just his idle curiosity at work, and Cora said, "You must meet him. It would be a treat for both of you."

Meet him for a day in Central Park, take him to the Zoo. Show him the hippopotami, with their big peg-teeth grown up like stumps from the foothills of the lower jaw. Hippos, Patrick, escaped from the Hippodrome!—where they were poorly attended, by hippocrites. Herman racing with his joke, Cora persisting in earnest: "We should plan to do it."

Could he manage that trick? Would Master Patrick stay inside his designated box? Because things become so *tangled* now, as provinces must come tangled at the boundary line. Hippo jokes and ice cream treats for Master Pat, when Stannie's portion seems so small? Everything under your roof is related, as the upstairs pipes may overflow onto the carpet downstairs—may and will, though admittedly it is a *bath*etic metaphor.

Perhaps he should lecture on this topic. On Boxes, and the failure to box or be boxed. So much of the human comedy is *contained,* as it were, in this theme. They will need to know about it, to know the whole truth, in windy Cleveland and chill Milwaukee!

★

Sunday morning. For an hour or so, Herman has leafed through Balzac's correspondence, inattentively. Turning pages.

He is fed up with his own company. How good it would be to walk down to Duyckinck's, and have a fine old-fashioned Sunday there. The day was manufactured for idling and reflection, and there was such a ripening in him on those long-ago Sundays on Clinton Street, under the sacred basement stair. Dialogues and trialogues, and maple logs for the glowing hearth.

There were later Sundays, to be sure—the two of them surviving like old club men, or dinosaurs outlasting the Mesozoic times. There was pipesmoke and punch and the sort of tall talk that could only go with Evert, could only be placed in the Duyckinck Box. No place to place it now. Sunday now is a day when you pass yourself a few times too many in the mirror.

A day for marking absences. Earlier, he had stood at Mackey's door, remembering every detail, not going in. *The guest room!* And was it last year or the year before that he drafted up four thousand words to Hawthorne, a weighty tome to that long vanished sound-post, as to him alone it could form and be framed? (Then saved on postage, for it could not be sent, or not successfully, to under the sod.)

Unless a whole new genre, letters to the dead! Why not? Attempting his letter to Stannie last night, Herman had again and again seen Mackey's face, had sighed for all the volumes he would say to Mackey. Why not say them? Draft a letter to the dead and buried; poor Mackey is in his box, no doubt.

Sunday afternoon. Herman is still upstairs, and bored, whether from without or within. Stale. *Is sleep a genre? Dreaming is. It's either sleep away these endless hours, or flee outside to sip a toddy on the Square, under the newly raw autumnal sky. Better a thumbnail of Barbados rum than another pot of this coldish Souchong tea.*

Lizzie, though. His guardian angel ranges below, guarding his health after the putative strain of a day in East Orange. She guards it by guarding his coat, in case he would put it on. Will a body at rest stay at rest, or become a body in motion?

He flattens on the narrow bed, to ruminate a while. Maybe ruminate till hunger strikes, or the dinner bell tolls. He closes his eyes. Exhausted from doing nothing, he is a little too weak to tussle it out downstairs with Lizzie.

A Sunday sort of Sunday, bad enough, but now comes a Sunday sort of *Monday* too. Or not so bad as that, yet a morning of damp air flying under the shanty roof, and an afternoon in the filthy bowels of the *Carolus*. And, by prior agreement, no chance of sighting Cora.

"This is not your sunny atoll morning," Herman says to Barclay.

"No dancing girls today, old matey."

"How about O'Reilly's," McBride suggests. "Might serve to brighten up the morning."

Herman looks askance, granting Bridey his half-a-smile.

"I'll second the motion," says Bridey's running mate Will Barclay. Then, in an altered voice, falsetto: "Make it unanimous."

"You can't vote twice."

"I didn't. That was Herman's vote I casted. Shall we go carry out policy?"

They go, and Herman stays. It is not O'Reilly's cream stout he craves, it is Cora's tilted, tented frown (which is only another kind of smile, as you can see in the eyes). *A man may not want two wifes, true enough, but he wants a glimpse of Cora Stevenson's face by Monday. The day is no damned use without it.*

Way back on Friday, this prescribed hiatus loomed a welcome prospect. A relief from impossibility. It was welcome still on Saturday, when Herman walked the strand with baby Eleanor and Fanny, and ate baked clams at Weehawken. Saturday was fine. Then Sunday got clogged. *Something always dies on the tracks of a Sunday, and here it is, still flavorish as the week begins. The hell with O'Reilly, let us all go back home and crawl in under the covers! A clear mistake that we ever crawled out, when sleep is the revolutionary genre.*

The world is nothing but a tunnel now, leading him straight to Tuesday at four. This much Cora clearly knew. She knew it in tea-leaves and tarot-cards, while the sachem had to find it out. *A wheelwright's daughter, desk clerk's wife, somebody's mother, and nobody's fool.*

Oh, time is a toothy trap, that locks your leg like iron. Step inside the trap and you cannot step back out; someone else has got the levers. Hard to believe your watch keeps time, when all it says is 9:14, 9:14. . . . and then, at best, after numberless tasks and perambulations, 9:15, 9:15.

He had doubled the grog, to fortify sleep, then tripled the grog at midnight, when sleep was exposed as a hoax. But now, four in the morning, is when the time trap really has you. "The night of time far surpasseth the day, and who knows when was the equinox."

Sir Thomas Browne, who knew a thing or two. What was that other pearl of his, on defeat and the keys to the city? Worth a candle to search it out, but quietly quietly, for Bessie wakes at the scratch of a branch on the glass. Dusty volume! No wonder the quotation's forgot, it's centuries since last we opened this tome—Like clapping erasers to open and shut its powdery gates. But here it is:

"A man may be in possession of the truth, or of a city—and yet be compelled to surrender."

He may indeed. But to whom? To whom surrender?

"I was hoping we could walk the river path today. Do you mind?"

"It's muddy, Cora, and very rough in spots."

"I have come well dressed for the outback. See my muckalucks?"

Gaily swinging up a toe to show off some sort of fishing boot, Cora is in full bloom today. Her chestnut tresses fly loose of the combs, and there is a bounceful absence of reserve at play in her bright cheeks.

"'How much more doth beauty seem beauteous/ When hung with the sweet ornament of truth,'" he says. Is this the text? Does this account for a change, the disburdening? She has never seemed plain, or even middling; always pretty. But beautiful?

"Do I take that as yes, or no?" says Cora.

Herman shakes his head in wonder, and studies her from the muckalucks to her smiling lips. Full in the middle, tapered at the cheeks to a delicate crimp, those lips are never exactly still. There is something so lively inside her that it bubbles out. Her face is not an American face nor of this century; it is a portrait pulled from Boccaccio's gallery, of a woman who wears no false reserve.

And all this abandonment aimed at him? Doubtful of his own magnetism, highly conscious of his graybeard status (and of the long long coitus-interruptus that can mark a man inside and out), Herman does not quite believe it. Perhaps her vivacity stems from Bachelor 442, whom the widely-acquainted indefatigably matchmaking *Jack* has most freshly summoned to sample the pie. There has been a hiatus, remember, so there has been time enough for Number 442 to make a loud impression; to stir up this liquid in her eye, and endow her grin with ticklish nuance.

"Your cheerfulness is startling. Surely you are the most cheerful widow on earth."

"A widow is not deceased, Herman—her husband is. Which makes a great difference."

"Irrefutably."

"There is an odd illusion, where I feel I have been sad for such a long time—yet I also feel that life goes by too quickly."

"It races like the tide," he says, if only to be in agreement. On the heels of his recent tortuous perdurable days and nights, it is nicely ironic that she should mark the speedy passage. But she is right: the days can be interminable, while the years do race away.

"I have very few illusions, really."

"Do you know the illusion I miss the most? That it matters. How I would love to believe it matters whether you do or you don't get out of your bed. Not that I don't like my breakfast, mind."

"Of course it matters," says Cora, to whom this exchange represents nothing more or less than hesitation. Herman's questions are not questions, and his answers are not answers; they are the boulders he likes to strew about him.

"To whom can it possibly matter?"

He is playing the child now. Cora sighs, and pampers the child with answers; touches the child's brow with a sweet, maternal hand.

"To yourself above all, so you may continue to eat your famous soup. To me, as I have been at pains to make clear. And to your wife, of course—"

"You must not speak of her."

"Never?"

"Please."

"But why is that? You have occasionally spoken of Andrew."

"Poor Mr. Stevenson, dear lady, is under the rolling seas, where he cannot feel the cold half-gale of our frivolous talk blow over him."

"Nor can she, if she is downtown."

"There's a notion! The streets of Manhatto as a sort of holy rolling sea, that closes over its citizens till they are lost within its limestone waters, in a vast cold soaking oblivion. You put a good question."

Whatever it was. Cora cannot recall the question in question, and she would be no less surprised to hear a response to the question, whatever it was, than to see Herman go sailing off the escarpment and fly up the river to Hell Gate. Her goal is to keep him in motion. She is not managing him, to her way of thinking; she only wants him to manage himself.

Negotiating extruded roots and half-buried stones, they dance the muddy path: now gentleman left, now side by side, now lady left, now donkey-file. Cora's playfulness is in abeyance as she concentrates on where next to put her toe. Where the pathway begins to converge with the hospital fence, they execute a wordless faceabout. This too begins with footwork, or choreography, and a formal hand in the small of her back. But Cora halts the dance figure at three-quarter turn, and searches out his eyes.

The barest trace of vapor, through her parted lips. She seems as light as air, as translucent as water, and under her gaze he seems, to himself, mighty ridiculous in all his tortured study, inward and churning. *Let go, let go.* Does she even guess there are ten thousand loud unspoken words?

She feels him letting go, a little. "You realize," she says, "that a man is expected to do the wooing. Or worse than that, to act the beast."

"A gentleman, however loosely defined, would never act the beast."

"A sailor might. Or a genius. They are expected to be irresponsible, not irresponsive."

"You have read too much George Sand."

Below them, through the rose and gamboge leafwork of late October, a barge is gliding past the island. Some neighborhood men are out in rowboats, to fish through the swill for dinner. On his last legs as a ratiocinator—but still churning weakly—Herman is trying to incorporate Lizzie. Would 'bigamy' impact Lizzie? How, exactly?

The most conspicuous impact would be providing her a cheerier husband—and soberer into the bargain, which is to say wealthier. Surely these are all benign effects, if the ends can justify the means. Can they? Perhaps they can, where they do not conflict with existing means, Lizzie-wise.

But alas, Herman has done some reading too. He has read his Voltaire, and knows that a man's ideas, so-called, are cut *ad hoc* to fit his actions; that a man's logic, so-called, is as a crab's perambulation, *backwards,* from the act to its hopeful justification. That clear thinking is naught save thinking skillfully clouded.

"Here is the key, though," he says abruptly, and aloud. "Voltaire would have laughed as he made out his case. It is not a complaint he makes, only an observation."

Herman has halted their wobbly march to emit this isolate pearl, and follows it up with a hard-won facial transition: he is birthing up a smile. Not one he would be eager to see, however; best keep this version off the official portrait.

Cora's response, Voltaire-free, is that characteristic sweet-cast frown of hers, the tent of affection pitched upon her brow. She takes his hands, and tells his laboring cheese-eating face:

"Enough Sand and Voltaire, Herman. Shall we plan some sort of partnership—or shall we try to part?"

The crux, to be sure, and very plainly stated. Somehow they have arrived at a moment when the test is both precise and final. Can Herman pass it? Or will he say, Wherein lies passage and wherein failure; which is the question and which the answer?

He will not do that, because the test is so precise and final now. He will do his best. As he managed the cramped half smile, he manages now a half caress, whereby his tentative leaning-down intersects her tender lifting-up. It could not be called a bestial act.

They meet softly, falling easy-familiar into a pleasant warmth of coats and shoulders, and his chief sensation is of lips larger and sweeter than his own, hers of a mouth somewhere inside the blanketing beard, and each of them slightly weak with relief—that it is over and that it can begin.

V

BERMUDA

(1888)

There is a stunted smile (outwardly stunted, inwardly one of purest pleasure) at the epicenter of the tangled, graying deacon's beard. (Invisible, anonymous, unencumbered: these my adjectives!) *Something perverse in it, understood, but perversity has its place and it is simply true that some pleasure comes from having fooled them.* (Ah ye roses that have passed, accounting me a weed!)

Fooled himself as well, if that can make it less perverse. There is a clarity now: if ever dead (as widely rumored) he now is resurrect; if ever griefed, aggrieved, or heavy-freighted, he now is relieved, auspiciously aflight. Oh heavenly flight, aboard this good ship *Trinidad*—though heavenly by way of Hamilton pier, heavenly on a low-skimming plane, waterborne and waterbound.

Why the sea at sixty-nine? An everyday case of come away to sweet Bermuda, where the bright lantana and rare banana rattle in trade-wind breezes? A weary retiree's late turn in the sun?

Not at all, is the answer. We have come for the coming (not to mention for the going) and for the sea itself, specific rigors of the sea, the swell and swallow, the swirl of message-bearing air. We come booming through the billows to see this water cleaved anew, and study close up the gannet and haglet, pintado and shear-water, as they flutter and squawk in that invisible cone of air above the widening flattening wake.

And he is here to complete a mood that has taken up residence inside him (message-bearing mood, well enough remembered, if long since neglected) *and make of that mood some sea-*

gone story-telling; to make a sailor's tale ring forth with the old conviction of being there. If life is a sort of game, then say he has come to cash a last handful of chips.

Considered (considered, mind you), the linear chronologic life scrolls out a lengthy registry of loss, a near exhaustive compilation. He knows it, and often feels it. To have two sons dead and the father living—ain't that loss enough right then and there? Or those little immensities that can never be mentioned, loves that lived and loves that died. Losses, yes, and also consolation, in the damned fine loss of the damnable self. That is religion in its way, to let go the self into something larger. Even adulterous it is moral, even if pagan 'tis holy, sacred vows and sacred cows notwithstanding.

The books are the least of it. Oh, lost and forgotten, to be sure, those mildewy maunderings, and their steward a 'failure.' It could be worse, old matey. Down in sunny Florida, they have got Geronimo in jail. The horseback warrior in a dusty fort; two paces west and he's spanned his continent. Truly forgotten is he. (Tamed, forgotten, and damned near rotten, in that soft and rancid light.)

Forgotten's one stop on the spectrum, the calaboose another. Death is another still, so it could be worse. We ain't dead yet, and everybody else is. Mackey and Stannie ("Each bloomed and died, an unabated boy") and brothers three (Tom, ah Tom); friends and elders, Duyckinck, Allan, Augusta, John. All truly lost, all our points of reference. Too late in life the crushing hand of poverty lifts.

Or not too late. Thus far today we are alive—definitely alive at reveille, alive for steak and eggs—and without the grace of late-lifting legacies, we would not be cruising these Atlantic swells. We would be sitting at a sleety window, with Swackhammer's badge worn over our heart and little enough enchantment residing inside. So I will call it timely.

Considered, the life has gone from bust to sod-bust, yet that is not the way I feel, or the way I am. What I feel is a highsailing electrical threat in the charcoal arch above us (and something like Yahweh in this bottomless bowl of salty water that goes rolling and rolling beneath our keelson) and what I am is plenty young in the blood of the brain, plenty eager for the work of Guert's tale—and finally primed to take it on. No accounts to render here, it's just the way she goes, me hearties; the way she blows. It's why we are the men, and they are the fish and apes.

In Saintly Augustine, the hucksters crouch behind their cameras like hunters, and shoot. Every half a block along the cobbled street, they offer to sell you your very own face. "Picture, sir"—"Grandest likeness, my good man." (Uh oh, now: beware a *likeness*.) And my fellow travelers come so enamored of their likeness that they do dearly purchase what comes to them free of charge in the stateroom mirror glass.

Of course, they want to take it home, to Peg or Alma, there is that. And it is proof we do exist, or proof we make a mark, a facial imprint, shadow-shape on paper. (This proof be proof, my good man. I blink, therefore I am.)

As to cameras, I carry my own—lens internal, lens eternal. Took it to Augustine, as I take it everywhere I go, and imprint all I see. Spanish gals with their pretty thread lace, Seminole men with fans and egret plumes for sale. The dentist's leaky boat moored in the river, the slow dig of his burring drill. Chain gang at the edge of the piney woods, turpentiners in rivers of sweat—and the one with his thumbs elongated. Hung by the thumbs all night for what? A word out of place? A step too slow?

And Geronimo. All captured on my camera eye and placed in storage there, as it used to be. The mind's alive again. You forget what it is when a fire is licking at the heels of the world; when every thread of life mingles in with every other thread, woven in the poem.

So where is the life of tears, of losses? Where has it gone, and where's our sad and bended man? Not here. Not on board el *Trinidad*. Just two days back, in sunny Bermuda, that very fellow took on a happy seizure—his second of the decade, sixth in his sixty-nine years. We keep a close track, you see, we imprint all, which is not hard to do with something so rare as six times in a lifetime.

What is a happy seizure? A seizure of happiness.

Pleasures accumulate by the hundreds: pipes and flasks, river rambles, ferry rides and mountain-toppings, lunches. All happy experiences to have. The seizure, though, is holy experience. It is as close as you get to the magic incarnate that cannot be chosen, composed, sought after (or *bought*, God knows) but must needs descend upon you. Maybe six times in a lifetime, if you are lucky.

What more can we say, by way of definitions? That you are physically seized, *invaded*, by a wide and unthought joy. That your soul is wholly dissolved into nature, so completely absorbed into the fabric of the natural world that every pain and regret must vanish. You wear the passive vacant smile of the opium man, but you never wear it too long. The seizure is rare, as noted, and it is brief. May not last out the hour. It is convincing, though; it proves the point.

More? It has to do with place. With the conjunction of place and being out-of-place, as when you find yourself in bright Bermuda among fruits and flowers, and not in cold New York, in damask-darkened rooms. So say it concerns a certain dislocation, that wakes you up, and that it concerns the sun and wind, for it is always an open-air moment of green and golden freedom.

And of solitude. That's by definition too: you go alone.

He was gazing out over the Causeway, just absorbing light, and watching the dinghies race on Harrington Sound. Dinghies so-called! These Bermuda dinghies carry more canvas than an Amagansett yacht—yards and yards, more sail than boat—and so they must be loaded low in the keel with lead to stay mast-up.

But how they fly! How the mast will flex in the shove of air, and the prow jump up to cut a path that's quickly foam on either side, twin hedges of foam and the watery blue lane between. They swoop like massive birds, like wind-wound fowl, yet sped by perfect science. Oh they do fly, and the shining brown-faced sailors laugh so loud you can hear them from Flatts to Bailey's Bay.

It lifts your hair a little. 'Tis a joy so wide and deep it will tickle your scalp like a good night's sousing, though you sit cold soberous in the sunsimmered air of paradise. So keenly attuned to the goodness in life, you forget the rank and fetid counterpoint. For now, no Claggarts walk the shores of earth.

No wonder that it don't last long! For there are Claggarts aplenty, matey, there are men who are evil as a rose is red— through and through. Men who do their wicked deeds as cattle browse the herbage. We will get on to these Claggarts soon enough. We will have thesis, antithesis, and synthesis, all laid out and pasted up. Time first to let the wind blow through us, and see what the handsome sailor sees, in his full bright fair-haired ease, his deep-accepting joy.

You must be alone, axiomatic. ("Bachelors alone can travel freely.") You may not bring along the charming Mrs. Pfister, and must shun young Grandmaison, the thousand-year-old man who so readily attaches to one's sleeve at the groaning board. Grandmaison and Wifemaison, nice people. *Good* people, with nary a trace of evil in them. God save me from these traceless people, who would move me into their moveable household; who dog me from breakfast egg to dog-watch; who come scratching at my stateroom door to offer dilute companionship when I have the best and freshest, my own!

They can formulate naught at sea but thoughts of land, and the trinkets they yearn to purchase on land, for the Grandmaison grandchildren. Thus they pass by the startling jacaranda and confide in me that ever so soon, in good and traceless Teaneck, their little forsythia will come a-bloom. Pass before the wrinkled elephant poinciana, the japonica, and the miraculous elasticus and describe for me their pretty willow, where the children skip-a-rope.

How nice. How good. How *traceless.* I always love a willow tree and I love my grandchildren better than the wood of the true cross. Grandmaison's grandchidren too, sight unseen—sign 'em up for the voyage out. Had I been one hair less practiced at the art of evasion, however, one thin strand the less elusive, this happy seizure number six would not have seized me. There I would stick, at five, though Yahweh had assigned me six.

You must meet your fate halfway is the point, for right there in the willingness is half your fate. *Quo fata ferunt,* they say on breezy Bermuda, but the wind won't lift you from your bunk unaided. The first steps you must take on your own, lest fatelessness become your fate.

Cora would not have come along, that much was a joke. It had to be, given Mister Pfister, and the little one. Still, with the good and no-ways-traceless Mrs. Pfisterson, it has been proved that nothing is impossible. My first glimpse of her in more than a year—*"Better later than never," said Cora, and each confessed to stopping by the old checkpoint more than once, in case the hand of fate was flexing. Fenton's Best & Freshest, remodeled and enlarged, sadly, to the point of charmlessness.*

But they crossed paths in Central Park; took refuge by the tavern fire. "Scandalous," she laughed, that music of female undilute, as much as the slick of her thigh, or the silk of her lower back. Were he deaf as a stump, he would be invulnerable; outside her presence, happily finito, as in the days before. The cure she worked was like Christ's cures, where the lame discard their crutches and the blind cry out, I see! I have a sort of infirmity of the back, he had started to explain. She had laughed (naturally) and said: "Come, let us see this problem."

"Scandalous being indoors, I mean. Were we ever?"

"Oh once or twice that I can recall. But today, my dear Mrs. Pfisterson, the temperature is right at the freezing point."

"Hence the Bermudas."

"No, it isn't that. Though the ancient bones do rattle."

"I hear them, Herman. They are saying, Bermuda, Bermuda. But it's the going out, you say? Because you will write your book?"

"I will write my book, yes."

"Your best-selling book."

"Hardly, Cora, as you know. It will not be a public book, for anyone's curiosity or anyone's pocket—least of all my own, as ever. It will be in my very best mode: my hand to God's eyes, as the sailors say."

"You have it firmly in mind."

"Very firm, and firming daily."

Sixty-nine years old and he could feel himself begin to blush. It still thrilled him to please her, however much he still concealed it. Cora leaned across the table and kissed him lightly. "Shall I travel with you to Bermuda? As amanuensis?"

"Yes, Cora, come. Amanuensis to the genus genius. Come, and bring the babby. Bring Mister Pfister too."

"Herman, you know we must never speak of Mr. Pfister."

What a wry devil she is! What a mountain to climb, and a pool to swim in at the peak. "You should indeed travel with, it is agreed. I will book the passage for two or more."

"Herman—"

"She retreats! And so quickly, now that the ring is on the other finger."

"You've caught me out," she laughed, but blushed a little too. (Her turn.) "I'll go straight home to pack my bags."

"Sir? Excuse me, sir."

"Hello, sailor. You are excused."

"I wanted to say we have a storm approaching, sir—"

"Gardy-loo! So you have said it, and now we are free to let it approach."

"Yes, sir. What I mean, sir, is that the wind is strong— very strong—and you will wish to be safe below."

"Strange to say, I prefer to be unsafe for the present. Up in the crow's nest, preferably. But the wind is yet an hour off."

"Less than that, sir, Captain assures us. Exactly when is always hard to say—"

"Ain't that the beauty, too. What if your rabid tornado came in like Pullman cars: 4:10, 5:10, 6:45. What if your hurricane blew on shore at the toot of the noon whistle—and came to rest in the trees, by agreement, at six o'clock sharp?"

"You'll step below with me, sir?"

"Absolutely, sailor. In a minute. I'll finish my cigar up here, if you can kindly grant me the minute."

Sky portentous, no argument there. Thunderheads in the sleeve of that charcoal cloak, and a restless agitation inside the air that makes its molecules sing up storm. *It* knows what to do, and when to do it. We never under-rate the wind—not us—but why not first enjoy the hour? For here is nothing less than life in microcosm, compressed and emblematic: we move from early calm and health into the fogbank of later troubles. Let us enjoy the calm while it lasts, and enjoy the troubles too, where possible.

Calm and storm, day and night. The old dichotomies are still instructive. Clichés to be sure, of circularity or linearity, but trot one out and be instructed.

Say we travel out by coach, in daylight. A pleasure journey, no need to rush and no call for worry. We have ample time to admire the small red farmstead with its shapely wooden gate, hanging between two crooked granite columns; its freshly cut fields, outlined in neatly piled stone. Or perhaps that tavern is worth a stop. The heavy door is thrown open and sunlight makes an inviting path across the maple floorboards.

Oh yes, the road is sunny, dry, and clear, and all these roadside scenes delight us. All the charming checkpoints reinforce our smiling expectation that we will arrive on time (or late, who cares!) and be well fed at our friendly destination.

But let us make this same journey by night, and perhaps in a downpouring rain. We may have lost our way—easily, for all the farms are dark—but how can we be certain? Stretches of uncut forest make us come to doubt the very direction; markers that have become invisible (no sun, no moon, no stars) make us doubt the map.

We squint in anxious quest of clues, but now the sky explodes in thunder, one carriage wheel begins to wobble ominously in the thickening mud. And we pray for nothing so much as that it be. . . . *daytime.* Oh that the daylight would return, and the road be sunny, dry, and clear.

Why go so far afield, however, when we have a case right here at hand? Today has not been sunny, but dry and clear it was; the water clear enough to count the stripes on thick-lipped grouper gliding past us. It is scarcely five minutes since that bosun spoke his piece, and already the flags are ripping, the water is churning blackish green. Between the wind in the cordage and the wash of the sea, you could slide a man overboard and never hear the splash, nor see him bob away, spinning down toward sunken weeds.

Do we leave him in the weeds, though? Why these oozy weeds, when our handsome Billy Budd might travel clear to China before he met an ocean weed? He would be eaten, digested, and belched afar before he found that fathomless bottom, that's a given. But so too is poetic license. Say our weeds are dreamed weeds—that's fair, ain't it? Like the weeds and reeds in that Floridian bye-canal. We saw them once, then dreamed them twice.

That was the day we checked into Flagler's famous hostelry; same day we sent the first box home. Such a bright and lazy place, that Saintly Augustine. Crumbling. I liked that. A crumbling city suits me pretty well. Creamy cracking cockle-shell, bedecked with flowers: orange blossoms, garish bougainvillea, plumbago of the patriot strain—red, white, and blue. I liked the blank stare of the sun on those creamy southern walls.

And Flagler's gilded cage, the Ponce de Leon, no less. That restless little business man has purchased outright some corners of the world, and transplanted them in Florida. The towers of old Madrid are there, loggias of Rome, stained-glass pillaged from a French cathedral. Tis as much a fantasyland as a traveler's accommodation, this Hotel de Henry Flagler, and you won't come by your terrapin stew for 35¢ at the table-d'hôte there!

In I strolled, straight into the lens of the maître d'hôtel. 'Shabby genteel' would be the category in his inside handbook, as we meet upon carpet lush as Berkshire's summer lawns. Squash my cigar in a crock-tubbed palm (*nota bene* the high steward's wary glance: More shabby than genteel, it doth remark) and have a lordly look around.

Oh to have Mrs. Pfister at my side right then, for the fun we could wring from a place like that. Cora has some Bernhardt in her—maybe more Bernhardt than Bernhardt herself, I can say, from having seen them both in costume. She would dive right in on any good hoax, as she did at Muschenheim's, the afternoon we ordered up walrus steaks, and played the indignant aristocrats when politely informed they had "run out of that particular item." A safe bet they had!

May I be of assistance, sir—Yes thank you, garçon, I have come in search of my old friend Flagler. Owner of this handsome little establishment.—Mr. Flagler, sir? I could ask Mr. Murchison to inquire.—Murchison? Don't know him. Henry's not about?—I cannot say, sir.—Look, garçon, just tell him that Pillow is here. He'll show himself soon enough if you say the name. Gideon J. Pillow. Flags and I were at school together.—Of course, sir. A coffee while you wait?

Sprawling now, sultanically, in the thickly cushioned wickerwork. Thank you, garçon, a coffee would be nice (and the flying-fish fillet with conch fritters, *tout compris*). Off he goes toward the interior, and off goes I toward the door. Got out pretty quick for a genteel elder.

Failure of nerve there. Why not carry through in style, and let old "Flags" do the heavy sweating? Let him step from the shadows of a potted palm and gain eternal bafflement. Flags, with his inn the size of Cincinnati. Pillow, er, Pillow— oh *Gideon,* of course, my dear boy, my good man, blather blather.

Not five minutes' stroll from that opulent ersatz palace with all its well-heeled guests, stands the calabozo, with just one guest inside, not exactly wealthy. Old Ned. Very glum is Ned, in his irons. A tall dark lanky fellow, sans teeth, but with worrisome red gums. He brightens when you come, and raises a kindly face. Bunking in for the night, following a good carouse?

But then go another block or two and you come to the market-place for slaves. The stalls still standing. An open-air market for human souls, where Old Ned's mammy was spun and shown: feel this sturdy thigh! behold these child-bearing hips! Oh what a fine and moral nation.

Did they step up and proudly say, "I like that one, Charles, oh let us have that one." They did. And not a hundred years ago, but more like twenty-five. It was not just Ned's mammy, then, it was Ned himself and all his kith and kin— on sale, to be owned—as thread lace and egret feathers are sold and owned.

And now they are "free," poor souls. Cheerfully handed wages that scarce can buy an orange, much less a dinner roast; crowded into shanties of houses, with open ditches fore and aft. And lo, hitched up to the bicycle-taxi (*Afromo-*

bile, so nicely styled) as if to beg the very question of human versus beast of burden. I saw the same grotesquerie a half century back, in Honolulu: the deacon's wife in her clean white linen, conveyed by the oldster in shoddy-rag, a man assigned to a donkey's life. Gee! Haw! Whoa, boy!

In sweet Bermuda, they all salute. You go past the Negro and the Negro salutes. Does he also salute his brother Negro, or is it for palefaces only, this reliable hello? When did this saluting start? What does this saluting mean? "Far down the depth of thousand years . . ."

(And traceless Madame Grandmaison comes murmuring into my collar, "They look as noble as statues." Oh easily, madame, if not moreso.)

"*Sir? Sir!*"

"Greetings, bosun. How is our famous dark cloud coming on?"

"Coming on fast. Captain was sure you'd want to be safely below by now."

"If I were safe. But safety is no such knowable, is it, bosun?"

"Mist is filling, you see the rain in the glass. The word is buckets, sir—bucketing down and blowing sixty. That is to say, the wind—"

"Understood, lad. I know the wind a bit."

"Good, sir. You'll come along?"

"One moment more and I am ready. It is hard to believe, I suppose, but I am enjoying myself here. They bill this as a pleasure cruise? Given the difficulty of locating pleasure at my advancing age, why not take it where found, eh?"

"Well, yes. But then the Captain—"

"Understood, understood. All assurances given. I am on my merry way below, in the moment to which we have alluded."

Enjoyment to be had below as well, after all—the hold is luxury writ large. You could stow away for a year in the belly of el *Trinidad* and live like good King Perceforest. This tub is no close cousin to the boats of old: merchantmen, men-of-war, or God-forsaken whaling ships. None of your great gray heaves of salt-pork and seabiscuit, no shot-soup or bullock broth in *Trinidad*'s cellars. This one is a grand hotel afloat, a Flagler's built above the brine, with more than a mossy barrel of pisco to distract the surly sailor from scratching his fleas.

There is a regular South Street meat-locker down there, as nicely chilled as Bermuda's toasted, with a team of oxen hung on hooks behind the door. Numberless point-toed porkers straining the chains at half a ton each, and fowl sufficient—pigeons, partridge, grouse, and turkey—for Grant's victory night in '68. A full-bore abattoir under the plush of the salon carpet!

And the proprietary shepherd of this diverse and dangling flock, proud butcher with his berry-red hands. He found no humor in our Gee and Haw to his skinned and docile oxen, and shooed us out. (Then shooed us again as we peered inside the door next door, where there's barrels of beer, cases of French champagne, plus scotch and bourbon, and slivovitz into the bargain.)

Well and good, but we did not sign on for the eating and drinking. We will eat and drink our share, fear not; we will order up a porker at dawn, and wash him down all day. But this next chapter, this wild hour to come, is why we signed our X and what we plan to savor. This sailing galing frailing air, this stormy world up top that roils all the water, races past the bowsprit, and goes lakelike o'er the decks. 29 dollars' worth of it I bought of Captain Beetlebrow, and 29 dollars' worth I shall have.

You go upstairs to write your poem (Ain't that the line?) and you go to sea to tell your tale. Why is that? The answer is in the word, prosaic. Prose can lack the life. You must put the life into the prose, so you must have the life within you, stockpiled. Simple Simon met a pie-man. You will never see or grasp the wind from your window, yet know it by the path it clears; by snapping canvas and shaking mast.

Take the island of Bermuda. A speck upon the ocean, smaller than Count Tolstoy's estate. You could call it bland as a sugarless pudding, with its crisp white coats, cool salutes, and careful garden crops. The highest hill is barely past two hundred feet. In Berkshire, I had me a tree that high! Viewed from a fan-back easy chair, this place is only here on earth so the onions at Burling Slip can boast a return address.

But come out of your chair for a closer gaze, and you may find some things to wonder at. Nothing's bland when you stay awake. Here is a country made of skeletons and shells, a wind-built world behind the barrier reef, with a red shell-fed soil that hosts the brightest seed; hybiscus, nasturtium, and oleander. Your lanes and alleys made of shell; your houses. They row a two-man saw right through the cheek of the quarry, they slice it like a cake—except it is not cake, or rock, or lumber, it is skeletons and shells, basked and baked and ossified, then sheared away in sheets or blocks to make your bedroom wall. Bland?

Is this sea bland? Lavender paletted in with a pale transparent turquoise, all the shallow shawling sea. That lumbering turtle with legs like thick old lilac, or this omnipresent coughing bird? Ca-how ca-how, goes he, *ca-how* like a rifle shot, singing in the jungle. And the skink, a quick and slithery lizard, who keeps appearing at a second blink. Ca-how indeed, and ca-why? Leave us not omit this blandless iridescent *skink*.

Pastel stairs, screw palms, pepper trees. The network maze of old St. George: Silk Alley, Salt Alley, Shinbone Alley, Sally's Alley. And Nea's Alley, the least of bland, named for the married lady who cavorted with a poetaster lodging next door—"and shied the fractions through life's shutter, to try the universal sin!"

One woman, one man: a simple enough recipe for something so thickly tangled as sin. The human integral, re-integrated. Simple, maybe, but never *bland.*

The finest piece of architecture on the island is a ruin. A *recent* ruin, strange to say. There it stands, the Unfinished Church as it is called with accuracy, and like the Unfinished Symphony, good enough to keep regardless. It was finished unfinished, with that lovely lancet-archway framing off the sky, that limestone stairway winding toward the sun. How fit it is *as is,* for individual worship, and how manifestly unfit for the worshipful herd to cough up nickels for the bishop.

"Sir. Are you awake, sir?"

Looky here, a pair of them this time around. They know what they are up against in Gideon J. Pillow. And isn't this the Captain's right-hand man, his peach-cheeked, rosewater sailor and youthful Fairhair of the Forecastle? They are sending in the first string now.

"Wide awake, I assure you. Come, gentlemen. Come worship with me in my roofless unfinished plein-air church."

"Thank you. But the time has come for all passengers to be under a roof."

And Fairhair consults his watch, as though that tidy tool can tell a tidy truth. Is it 2:23? Well then, time to clear the decks, reckons out our young Professor Fairhair. A handsome enough lad, so far as features go, but hardly the Handsome Sailor. Bred and schooled and neatly combed, he is more a type than an archetype. Slumming, in all likelihood—as some of the very best have slummed!

"So we shall test this vessel of yours, Professor, if the storm is worth one half the prognosis. I do not hear the death-watch beetle ticking in the wood"—*inclines his head and feigns to listen*—"for 'tis steely cold and solid. But will she float is a separate matter."

"Why don't we step out of the wind, to debate the ship's engineering. Allow us to treat you to cake and coffee in the grand salon. It will soon be very dangerous—"

"The iron hull give way? The iron sides not hold the sea?"

"Dangerous to you, sir, here on top."

"Ah, danger to my person. Washed off the boards and into the drink. I trust you carry good insurance?"

Perverse, admittedly. Credit where credit is due, however: Fairhair cracks a smile on the insurance. The lad could be a damned sight worse than that.

The mate has got him now, albeit very gently, by the elbow. He is taken aback by the sinew there, the latent force. This old blusterer is no ordinary trade-winds cruiser. But come he must and come he will, down to the dining room, where no one is eating cake at the moment. All retired, and gladly so, to the lace-lined berths, whether in anguished prayer or queasiness, for there is an epidemic of mal-de-mer from stem to stern this morning. A dozen seaworthy crewmen as well, ralphing into the tanks, yet here stands this rock-hard codger like Lear in the tempest, hallooing the devil. Very likely in his cups.

And down the winding brass they go, the King's officer (by way of Mallory Steamship) and one upright barbarian, impressed into the Mallory navy. My corporeal housing impounded, my skeleton and shell. I'll come along, no fear. Impressed to be impressed—like fairhaired Billy, and on the virtual eve of creation. I'll make some art of such *impressions,* and of all the King's ironic bargains.

What's this, though? Let me squint a little harder on my captor's placket, where his name's inscribed. Is he Fairhair for a fact, form-fit to our fiction? Too much to ask. Farquahr's the name—a near hit there.

"I fear, Professor Farquahr, that you judge me not quite right in the head."

"Heavens, no. I confess I thought you might have taken a little drink, to brace yourself for the bad weather."

"A little? Why I was suckled at a puncheon, lad, and have had a *lot* to drink, for the weather without and the weather

within. Why take a little if the wind is up and there's gallons
in the aft hold?"

Farquahr stands behind him, silent. Holding the chair. He is a
gentle man and patient, for his years.

"You should see it all, Professor. There's enough to drown
a herd of moose."

Nods, politely. He wants us seated, so we shall sit. Seated
in this empty room, seated square in the middle of the ocean.
The glassware rack above the bar is playing a nervous tinkle;
the chandelier has widened out its pendulum swing. The
wind is up, all right, and our captor is turning waiter! A
man of his word, he wants to bring us a bumper of hot.
We could play Bartleby here (very easily and pleasingly) but
Farquahr is a likable lad. A green shoot to be sure—you
could sell him a quart of Chinook olives—but likable.

"I appreciate your cooperation, sir. I do understand you
were content up on the quarterdeck. By the same token, you
do understand—even as a gentleman quite confident at sea,
or more especially for that—the position we take."

"Delicately put, mate, and you may be sure that I do. Just
so long as your colleague yonder will grant a speck of sherry.
Have you noticed how it is always when you come inside
that you finally feel the outdoors chill?"

"Not hot coffee?"

"Not yet, thank you. Sherry, I think."

Farquahr has the bedside manner. He must be the shipboard specialist in phrenologics—and in semaphor too, or
semaphor's second cousin, for here he sends a high sign to
Willie at the taps. Some nouveau language of the sea, as
meaningless to me as the secret guarded handclasp of Moose
and Mason, but look how it results in sherry.

Grog at sea, coffee in port, that's my rule of thumbs,
unelongated. Did anything in life ever taste better than that
pot of java on Sweeny's table, the first of October in '39? I
can call it up on my palate right now. No better greeting in

the port of home than a breakfast at Sweeny's: a plate of the famous buckwheat cakes in thickest maple syrup, and a silver pot of the strongest coffee. There I sat in my sunny window, the boy who went to sea, the so-called man who came back home, with a few loose dollars in his pocket.

Very few, in fact! Still, what a feeling it was to regain the land, to stand again in the port of New York, ranging the Battery with some grist in my grist-mill. Home and away, more of our formidable phenomenon of opposites. Land and landlessness, if ye like a hint of overarching Bulkingtonian significance; anchor and adrift, if ye take it straight, sans the hint of the dust from the crust of a concept.

But who knows which was the bitterest pill back then, at twenty, between the forced voyage out and the home-coming to less than a home? So much the less that we were soon enough launched out again, and not by way of Sweeny's cakes and scones. By way of new Bedford, on a morning to freeze the beard of Sweeny's bride: oh Lord, that day was damp and cold, and lonely to the chalk of the bone. Gone, yet who knows where. Scheduled back, yet who knows when. Or *If.*

A far cry from that sort of voyaging to the soft Bermuda sort, where everything is knowable. Bingo bango breakfast-time. In goes forty ton of coal (the downdraft from Funnel Number Two will dye you black as an African baby) and you flog the sea at twenty knots, notwithstanding all the winds of heaven. Back then you set your sails from top to bottom, fore to aft, a chorus of canvas duck, and if the wind's up you fly, if the wind drops you flog the sea at zero.

Never mind turning for home, either, until you have killed and carved and cured the devil, somewhere out in the vast Pacific. Next October or the following March, 'tis all the same to Captain Pease. No sign of your shipboard humidor, or your lofty dinner salon with mural art and carved oak cornice. Electrical lights? We had the stink of the blubber-lights, and the stench of every sailor from stem to sternum.

"There you go, sir. Best to keep a hand on the glass."

"Or siphon it safely down. I thank you."

"Did you say you were a seaman yourself?"

"You said it, Professor. I only heard you say it."

"Perhaps I saw it on the passenger list?"

"And believed what you saw?"

That stops the stripling. It never furrowed his collegiate brow to doubt the written word. Had I scribbled down "The Prince of Prussia, age two," he would be telling his wide-eyed fiancée how he entertained the young crown-prince, and glimpsed firsthand the future of Europe.

Merchant seaman, age 37. Isn't that what we put down? Could Farquahr have so little notion of thirty-seven? Is he orphaned, disuncled, and blind into the bargain? Or is he the humorist here? For remember the lovely grin he gave us, in lieu of insurance bond. Perhaps I think I am humoring my keeper, while my keeper humors me.

"It is untrue, I take it."

"Not strictly true, Professor, no. Do I look to be thirty-seven, by your educated eye-ball?"

"I know that people shade their ages. And certainly you seem at home on the water."

"As do you, Professor. Tell me what brought you to the sea-going life?"

"My uncle," he shrugs.

And blushes. Suddenly the lad is twice as human: young, open, no longer disuncled! His white sea suit, sailor-boy bright, has loosened a notch at the collar.

"My uncle is a Mallory shareholder. He wanted very much for me to spend a year at this, before I went for law school."

"Law school. And here you are impressed, into your uncle's private navy."

"I didn't resist much—and I haven't been sorry. There are days I can hardly imagine sitting still in a classroom again. I know we are only a pleasure cruiser, but it does open one's eyes to a view of the wider world."

"It's wide, all right—though you may discover it repeats itself. They sell you an alligator tooth in Saintly Augustine, and they sell you a pencil by the shrine of Christ in Holy Jerusalem. Still, I find it wide."

"Even at the ripe age of thirty-seven."

"Yes, Professor, still. A ship, as they say, was my Harvard and my Yale. They do say that, don't they?"

"They may, sir. I was at Columbia."

The boy is better than all right. He's bendable, in the better sense. Sent to ply an old fool with coffee-beans, he bends to fetch me wine—then sits with me to pass the time. He makes his choices on his own, and on the fly.

"You'll make a good one, Farquahr. Attorney, that is."

"Not a good sailor?"

But now our salon tilts isosceles, caught in the path of a celestial wheeze. The famous storm is coming on in fragments and our mate did finally blanch when the room went sideways. Now he is grinning meekly.

"Oh that too, no doubt. Not that you can handle a marline-spike, or set a dead-eye. But you'll do fine at whatever you try. My guess is you'll want a sound profession: name on the door, dollar in the vault. It's the Eighties, you know."

"Mother's concern—about the year at sea—is with the company one keeps. She would be greatly relieved to meet the likes of you, sir."

"There is the question of company. You find some awful mangy mutts on shipboard, and a few rare souls as well. But the company you keep, constant and forever, is your own good company. Whether you sail on the water, or walk on land."

"Or walk on water, I suppose."

Truly, this Farquahr is full of beans. He's a wakeful one, with the juice of New York humor in him. They taught him how to field a blowhard.

"I have walked on water, Farquahr."

"Certainly, sir, as I have done the same. Whenever the ponds and rivers freeze."

"Not bad on riddles! Do you recall when the harbor froze, from the Battery to Brooklyn in '71? The Grand Street ferry locked in ice?"

"I was four years old in '71."

"Tell me this, friend. Are you assigned to baby-sit me? Because I will gladly swear my word to stay right here—"

"But then you'll break your word."

"Eagerly. But I will sign a paper first, to indemnify you in the matter."

"I think the storm is exciting too, you know. We get very little weather, normally. It's a calm route, and a calm place, Bermuda."

"Bland, would you say?"

"No. Just not so dramatically beautiful as—oh, one reads of places like Tahiti, in the South Seas."

Oh and we are close, very close, to revealing that one also *writes* of places like Tahiti—writes, perhaps, the very lines a bright romantic lad might read. Naked maidens rushing through the blue waves; sheer escarpments, waterfalls, and hidden valleys verdant thrice-times-Eden.

"Lovely in its way, Bermuda?"

"Very lovely, sir—and nothing in the least unlovely. But why do I get the feeling that you are managing me?"

"Do you?"

"Yes."

"But then, what if I have the concurrent and diametrical sensation that you are managing *me*? Very pleasantly, I hasten to add."

"Really, I'm not. No one actually said what to do, once you came down the hatch."

"Excellent. Then I can go back up."

"Theoretically, I suppose you could. Logically, though, it would seem outside the scope."

The lawyer in him. Look now, though: through the thickly muntinned lattice of the dome, night-time looms at noon. All these fancy curtains cannot hide the mangling green-black waves, the wilding gray-black gale. This precious room is just a witty package, another box. Inside is luxury and ease; outside, the manitou rages.

Lizzie.

Why Lizzie, now? (Or better, why not?—after forty-plus years.) But what makes her jump up onto the train of my thought?

The theme of boxes, maybe. I sent her a box from Hamilton town—or so they called it, that whipped-up book-rack thing. Brackets, joined by boards, in fiddlewood. The other box, from Augustine, was a finger-jointed cypress gem, even *sans* the alligator teeth. (*Lizzie dear, They like to include inside these a tiny alligator with a row of tiny teeth and a skin of tiny pickle-warts. I liked the box for itself, empty, and hope you do the same.*)

Empty boxes and empty bottles, these my offerings. Blownglass amber, tailor-made for Lizzie's fever-few—an empty bottle has its uses, too. More generally, though, a bottle will want its contents, be they whisky, sherry, or the healing waters of Green Cove Spring. Now that was the gift I wanted to send to myself, the elixir. The promise of a cure for damned St. Anthony's Fire. But send it they would not.

They post Madeira wine and Moscow vodka, not to mention the parfum of Paris by way of leviathan's regal feces. They probably ship those little alligators packed ten-tight in fancy jars, priced as the latest delicacy on a shelf in Kreilkamp's grocery. Why not a gallon or two of the healing water? Three thousand gallons flow up from the earth each minute, and they cannot spare a few drops to anoint us against the demon erysipelas?

"Oh no, sir, it is entirely an immersion process. Like a baptism you might say. They drop you bodily into the pool, and leave you to soak for quite some hours." Swim in the stuff? I'll immerse my phalanges, you pilgarlic—I'll soak and pickle my palms, you rapscallion, till the devil be baptised right out of me. But no—*Oh* no.

It wasn't the boxes, though, it was the storm itself. It was knowing this selfsame storm has visited Lizzie and home, before it came hurrying to visit with myself and my young attorney. Waist-high drifts on Broadway, horses trapped, poles toppled into the snow-locked yards. Imagine the fury of this wind in New York, when it wanted so badly to come all the way *here*.

Who is there to help? Have they food enough, are the water systems working? Perhaps they go about their normal business, and all is well again—but then what is their normal business? What is Lizzie doing, right this very minute? If I were good enough, loving enough, I would know the answer. Is she sitting in the parlor with her cup of tea? Bessie too, with her cup, and little Fanny with a picture book in her lap, if they brought her in before the storm?

What about her face, though? Is it possible she is happy? I used to think it was. I would imagine her brighter and gayer, the instant I was out the door. Cousin Kate would tell of good times they two had shared, and Fanny had done the same. "Mother laughed so hard I was afraid she would drop little Fanny in the pond!" A laughing grandmother, charming friend, cozy sister-in-law? I used to think it possible, before I came upon her at the Fire Island restaurant.

A terrible portrait that one was, of Rembrandt strength and Biblical woe. I felt responsible for that face, for her face and her fate. (*Quo Herman ferunt*. After four decades, can it be otherwise?) And I have meant to be better, since that day. Not merely better, to be good enough. To be loving.

It was the sequence that brought it home, no doubt. Cora that morning on Broadway, sheer chance, and Lizzie in the afternoon. Like John L. Sullivan's one-two punch. True, it was once a daily sequence, the one-two punch, but for that reason precisely, it could go unnoticed. Quotidian; *prosaic.* I did not see Lizzie because I could not afford to see her; could not wish to clarify the obvious. You drink the wine of the country in which you travel.

Lizzie knew nothing, and yet travelling over the bricks toward her (the neatly tented linen, a vase of yellow roses, her large hands so perfectly still) I felt a shock of guilt go through me, sharp as a bayonet. Somehow I had never seen it; how it all was one, could not be walled off, winnowed out, measured into boxes. Mackey, Stannie, Bessie . . . and Lizzie. And I could not dodge the blame. If your best is never good enough, consider how wide of the mark is your worst.

One person can destroy another, surely, but can one person save another? What portion of your own portrait is etched by the mate you choose? Had I died at Antietam in '62, would Lizzie be happier now? And what if she had died? People do die before their time. Mackey and Stannie, each bloomed and died. Sarah.

Lizzie did not die, of course; happily she didn't. There were no clear meadows sighted. Maybe it could have been different through death or fate, and maybe not—but never by mandate. You take what you get. And you will never know the machine as the machine knows you.

Sometimes you stretch your chains a little, and find some room in the world. Even the human links at that Floridian chain gang can find a crack of sunlight: earthly chains, celestial song. But nothing comes free. When you find some room, you are closing other rooms behind you. No fresh meadows. You are in the machine till it has finished with you, one jolly way or another.

I had not laid an eye on Cora since before her marriage. Standing there by Sloane's bay window (awaiting Mister Pfister?) she was a sight to glorify the God who made her. And we fell in step as easy as ever. That was the problem, of course: we liked one another. She was young and lovely and I was not, but we were drawn.

"Don't you need to stay put here?"

"I would rather walk and talk with you."

And tells me, to my astonishment, that when we parted ways, she had not entirely *meant it*. "Or, I was not sure what I meant. You were so firm in my affections."

"In with the late Mr. Stevenson, and the ongoing Mister Pfister! Yet you looked so horrible solemn, my dear sweet lady, when you delivered yourself of the awful edict. I was sure you meant it firmly as religion."

"You never over-ruled me. Never once. On principle, no doubt."

"Cora."

"And you never made the pace. You always made me the immoralist."

You can "mean it" and still be free to lapse. Sarah meant it—like iron—and would have lapsed that day in Hancock. Be ye ever vigilant! Likewise you can *not* mean it and hold fast regardless, because mean it or not (whatever it is!) we are leafs in the wind and we come to earth by twists and fiddles, face up or down.

Suppose she had put it to a vote at Sloane's? I never mentioned Stanwix to her, then or after. We are crushed to dust in diverse ways. But Stanwix made it easy on me. His dying made it a necessity, and a sort of relief. And it is always a relief to be returned to the status of honest man, bundled back to a simpler life of peace and productivity.

That's on the one hand. On the other hand, Cora. The
wry uplifted shining eyes, the well-remembered rest-of-it.
Peace soon becomes a sort of death, and productivity a joke.
(Produce what? And why?) True that we are never safe. That
as the pilot-fish to the maldive-shark, we lurk forever in the
port of serrated teeth. But it would seem that the moment
has passed.

I cannot bring back Stannie. And perhaps I cannot bring
back Lizzie, either: no illusions there. But what higher use
is there for me, after forty-plus years, than to suffer at her
side? To weed the path to old affection, within the very welds
of death.

*"Sir, you are pale. Perhaps you would like to try your berth,
during the very worst of it."*

"Ah, garçon. I shall try the wahoo chowder today, and
sample the broiled amberjack."

"Very good, then," Farquahr bows, bemused. He is still
in the joke, good fellow!

"Sincerely, Farquahr, I am all right. I was only lost in
thought. Thinking of my wife, back home."

"She was wise to stay home, as it turns out."

"She doesn't care for travel, in the wide world sense. Travels only to get a destination."

"You don't mind going alone?"

"Oh, I like it."

"We rarely see folks on their own. This boat is like Noah's
Ark—everyone paired off, two by two, up and down the
gangways."

"Something of nature in it, I expect. What has four legs
and two backs, as the riddler says. But you go as you are
sent, and sometimes I am sent alone. I don't mind it."

"Well, you'll have some tales to tell back home."

"I surely will!" *says—or shouts—this unpredictable elder, with
a smile far broader than such a casual remark would seem to warrant. Unpredictable is the word for him. The man comes in and*

out of focus by the minute, first sharper than a math professor, then gone off in the clouds. And now he is shouting again, "Sing with me, a verse or two of 'Audacity and Tavern Wine'!"

One tale to tell, in fact, and surely I will tell it. Guert's tale, refashioned to fit the Handsome Sailor. This Bermudas pleasure boat and that misbegot historic war-ship are voyaging out in tandem, unbeknownst to all. Didymous ships, yet with little in common beyond such trivial ties as overarching dark-sea stars, wind-shove clouds across the Golden Yardarm, and the ancient scrivener hisself. Thus we have narrowed it down, a lifetime funneled into one last business that remains to be writ.

Or two. Guert's tale, and my own Last Will & Testicle. That too must needs inscribing, for Lizzie is like a weeping willow. She will bend and sag (and weep!) but there she will be when I am gone. She will outlast me, I'll wager all the cockle-shell in Featherbed Alley, and she must eat and sleep in her comforts.

Willie over there is a cool customer, calmly stowing all his glassware. The famous lights go flickering above him (the swaying chandelier rattles its chains) and all the chairs, so freshly set atop their tables, must be settled back down, four-square on the carpet. And it's not so easily done, with the ship lurching drunkenly. A whole room set upon one ear, then slapped right back the other way.

And now comes Captain Beetlebrow himself, in person. Slides his brow through the portal and slides it out of sight, like a snake poking up from his rock-pile wall. A pair of petty officers too, trooping past us. Signs of life, suddenly, in the hollow echoing salon, where we three (I, my young attorney, and Willie-of-the-Taps) have so comfortably presided. There is a restlessness inside the hive.

The majority remains in hiding. We are bucking on sixteen-foot seas, or so—battered by winds of sixty-five. Twenty thousand ton of pig iron and cold-rolled steel reduced to a balsa-wood toy! How fare ye, master Grandmaison? (And Wifemaison, one inch away.) How fare ye, stolid Wilsons and jolly Swans, stiff in your berths as alligators in a pickle-jar?

"We have been married forty-two years."

"Remarkable," says Farquahr loudly, above the rising gale.

"Is it so remarkable?"

"I think so, yes. for a man of thirty-seven to be forty-two years betrothed? Some Chinese system of historical dating, I suppose?'

"Wholly occidental, I assure ye."

Rain beats down on the dome with all the bombast of an army of horseback, while we sit in our chairs like jolly prisoners-of-war, brought up from the brig for inquisition. Willie has poured us out a full carafe, and offers it to my attorney.

"I could never swallow the stuff," he says.

"Let us help him, Willie. Us can swallow."

The lull is over. The room jumps abruptly, and unseats the seated, landing us like primitive dancers at the hula-hula ground: hands forward, legs apart, in a posture of ready springfulness. Here is a ship the size of a three-storey factory building, a gravid mass the length of a city block, and she wobbles like a home-made rowboat in the sidewash of leviathan.

The gale is up and roaring now. Hailstones smack the hull like distant axes felling trees, and glass comes blowing through the room, hefty fragments from a porthole. And just when the whole proposal seems marginal at best, the force of the storm redoubles. A wave as broad as Lake Surprise pivots the ship ninety degrees, and the famous lights go dark. A dozen screams resound from the cabin bellies. The lights flicker briefly, then go out for good.

Snuffardo! And the darkness seems to thicken, hard rain flying willy-nilly, as the ship is brewed into the yeast of the gale. Where is my attorney, though?

"Professor! Now this is not bland, Professor!"

"Hold on. Hold tight."

"Nor is it safe! I say it's safer up on deck."

"Sir, really, no." (His serioso mask.)

"Come on, you Columbine, we need a breath of air. Come up to my Harvard and my Yale, you'll see."

Farquahr shakes his head in amazement at this man's incurable passion for the top—and at his own complicity, for here he goes, flying up the spiral after him. They squeeze the cold wet brass like climbers on a belay-line, as foaming water rushes past them. Chased and chaser, they haul up hand over hand to the hurricane deck, where the torrent comes at them full roar. Waves loom up like crumbling mountains.

"Hang on!" he cries, but the safety gate twists loose of a gusset and flaps free. Collapsing waves race over the boards knee-deep and smash against the glass partitions. "Come back while you can," Farquahr implores him.

John Farquahr sees the end. Blown and shoved over the side, into the roiling darkness, down to a fathomless lung-crushing death. No more days of grace and beauty. And this will happen soon—it is happening now. (So this is death, he thinks, this is my death. . . .)

Flood Rock, last year, sown deep with dynamite. They shook the bed of the river and blew its waters to the sky in spires, and all the rooftop watchers cheered.

The little bald Floridian, on his stool in the hotel plaza, playing the same refrain over and over, day and night, as though he were a music-box. "When I first said I loved only you, Maggie—and you said you loved only me." (But why did I think of Sarah then, and of her goose-bumps in the cold?) You go to supper, you go to bed, and there he is next morning with his wheezing accordion: "And you said you loved only me."

That tribe of wild turkeys, birds as big as labradors, floating up in Sarah's elm. Perched like buzzards, twenty on a limb, as the yellow leaves fluttered and sailed.

"Can you hear me?"

Farquahr is yelling at the top of his lungs, but the passenger seems not to hear. Wading toward him, Farquahr feels trapped. The certainty of his own death has receded slightly—after all, it has yet to happen—but a new certainty looms. If he loses this man overboard now, it will haunt his nights forever. It will change his life, and he knows it.

Mackey, soaked to the bones. Racing through black puddles toward me, hair slicked to his head in a driving rain, eight years old. Mackey on his bed. Each bloomed and died an unabated boy.

Lizzie on the restaurant terrace, softly weeping. . .

"Can you not hear me, sir?"

We will get back. Back to the Blue Posts for Havana cigars, back to Sweeny's for a stack of cakes, back to the little girls. My sweet Eleanor must hear her *Landseer Dogs,* and little Fanny must have more swan-boat pirates off the Barbary coast-line of Central Park. And I must regain the desk-front, midst figs and brandy and burley smoke. I'll prose it out there, soon enough. Presently, though, this here—*this*—is just about right.

But where is my attorney? Washed back down the hatch? He is missing the very best of it, and I liked him being with me. An excellent lad, and a fine attorney.

"Yes!" he is saying. "Just about right!" he is saying—or so Farquahr, however incredulous, is hearing. Perhaps the man is a lunatic after all, some kind of holy fool.

The funnels groan and sway. One dark gust blows the old man back against the deck-house, where plate glass breaks with a whoosh and crankle. The water, sliding underfoot, upends him. He is driven to his hands and knees. Beard and coat soaked and matted together, eyes tight against the lash of the gale, he is clearly laughing. Shakes a fist and laughs. "This has gone too far, this research!"

Here we go, boys, swept to Heaven on a magic carpet, bound for that high snug harbor, and a sweet reunion with dear Tom. "We hereby renominate and duly rename this good ship *Ariel.*"

Fists tight upon the taff-rail, back on his feet between gusts—but there is no between no more, the monsoon comes powering through, to loosen all his newfound stances. Hanging on, his legs are flying up and twisted, like a gymnast flying round his pommel-horse.

Gymnastics be damned, that last one nearly took us away. Back to our knobby knees for safety—hold on tight and the boat must hold—these businesses not negotiable. All else is negotiable; survival is a necessary, for how can a dead man birth up a book?

*Crawling toward the open hatch, he travels a body length or two before the speeding wash strands him at a bulwark, dazed. No more images from the past assail him there, only the terrible force of the storm, and a litany moving through his mind—*one damn injun, two damn injuns—*and now a deafening explosion, the boom of Heaven's cannonade, and jagged lightning out over the water. Pinned and blinded—* three damn injuns!—*he finally looks to be afraid.*

Aware.

(Fathoms down, fathoms down, and roll me over fair.)

Just one day out from sunshine and plumbago, and each thought may be our last. But no. As though heralded by that final world-wide thunderclap, the air is radically becalmed and softened; the wind is merely flowing warm. Everything has sea-changed. Mine eyes can open, and the sky is opening too, breaking into shards of blue. The waves have sunk below the stripe.

Here's young Farquahr back, and several others, faces bobbing under caps. Has all this been a minute, or an hour? The crisis is past—our little storm is visible now, boiling off toward the east. We can see it go and we can stand. Shivering like a wet kitten, soaked clear through to the pancreas, but standing on all twos again.

"Now we are ready to order up breakfast! Buckwheat cakes in a stack, with syrup. Bring us a bumper and bring it quick, old Sweeny, we're bound up the river to home."

Were there but a fore-topmast in sight, I'd surely clamber up it—climb to the crow's nest and crow, what else?—but all we get on this iron-ic ship *Ariel* are those skimpy poles to fly light pennants. Light and duly gone are they, stripped like leafs from Berkshire's trees.

Farquahr has him by the arm at last, and tries to meet his eyes. The eyes look glazed, and distant—truly, a little wild—and gusts of laughter come blowing off him. Mad for sure, alas, and understandably, perhaps. Temporarily, it can be hoped.

But now he breaks free and scrabbles onto the deck-house roof. "All hands skylark!" *he cried, in the grip of a new and extraordinary lucidity, a rush of absolute clarity.* A seizure! In this softened, darkly luminous wind—a seventh seizure, scant days on the heels of number six. Incredibly, for none of the usual elements abide: no sun, no peace, no solitude. Here is a whole new sort of happy seizure, green and gray, wetter than water, under the mate's approaching gaze.

He embraces the mate, in gratitude and affection long-deferred, then whoops again, a cowboy sound, and races toward the bow calling Land ho, Land ho!—though no land is in sight, and though it will be another day before the good ship Ariel *can sail into the Narrows, between the forts and facing shores, and bring this orphan home.*

Historical Note:

In March of 1888, Herman Melville sailed to Bermuda. That summer he wrote his will and, in the fall, composed a draft of BILLY BUDD, his first novel in over thirty years.

It would be another thirty years after Melville's death before the manuscript was discovered and published.